CROWN'S JEWEL

Cynthia D. Toliver

CROWN'S JEWEL

A Novel

Cynthia D. Toliver

iUniverse, Inc.
New York Lincoln Shanghai

CROWN'S JEWEL

iUniverse books may be ordered through booksellers or by contacting:

iUniverse
2021 Pine Lake Road, Suite 100
Lincoln, NE 68512
www.iuniverse.com
1-800-Authors (1-800-288-4677)

Because of the dynamic nature of the Internet, any Web addresses or links contained in this book may have changed since publication and may no longer be valid.

Certain characters in this work are historical figures, and certain events portrayed did take place. However, this is a work of fiction. All of the other characters, names, and events as well as all places, incidents, organizations, and dialogue in this novel are either the products of the author's imagination or are used fictitiously.

ISBN: 978-0-595-48335-8 (pbk)
ISBN: 978-0-595-60425-8 (ebk)

Printed in the United States of America

To Jehovah, Father, the giver of all gifts

Ecclesiastes 11:1-6

CHAPTER 1

▼

The Southern Express slowed only long enough for Crown McGee to hop off without breaking a leg. With his lone bag in one hand and the other hand holding a floppy, wide-brimmed hat to his head, Crown jumped, landing in soft mud that splattered over his new Sears overalls and leather boots. The blowing rain slashed at him sideways. Lowering his head against the cold rain, he followed the echoing ring of metal hitting metal. The livery was just ten paces from the siding, but by the time Crown got there, he was already drenched and chilled. He stepped inside where a cloud of steam promised a bit of warmth. A tall, burly man with skin the color and grain of sand stopped his hammering to eye Crown with unabashed curiosity.

Crown lowered his head, using the cold as his excuse and his hat and coat for cover.

"I need a wagon and team. I got cash."

"When?" the smithy asked turning back to the hub he had been hammering.

"Now."

"Can't stop what I'm doin'. Promised the widow Martin I'd have her surrey by noon. Don't s'pect she'll be doin' much drivin' on a day like t'day, but a promise is a promise."

"I need that team today."

"What's your hurry? It's been raining nigh on three days. These roads around here just pure mud after a good rain. You might be obliged to wait it out in town."

"I got my own place just ten or twelve miles from here. I reckon to spend the night there."

Crown hesitated, then used a phrase he'd heard a man use at the depot in Beaumont to get a ticket on an already overbooked train.

"I'll make it worth your while."

"Your own place, heh? Round here? And you say you got cash?"

The man sounded skeptical. Crown pulled his right hand out of his pocket and without looking up unfolded his palm to reveal a plain leather pouch.

Eyeing the pouch, the smithy stepped toward Crown. "Name's Cooper, Coop for short. Didn't catch yours."

Crown grunted, stepped back into the shadows thrown by the eaves of the livery and thrust out his hand.

Coop stopped short, apparently reading Crown's signal to keep his distance. Coop took the pouch and emptied it into his open palm. He counted out what he needed and returned the rest to the pouch, leaving Crown with the impression that Coop was a man that could be trusted. When he was done, Coop handed the pouch back.

"Anythin' else?"

"I'm gonna need tools I guess, supplies, that sort of thing."

"You'll find just about anythin' you need at the general store."

"That's where I'll be then. You can bring the team there. I'll load up and be on my way."

"I'd stay the night here if I were you. Rain might ease up; give the roads a chance to dry."

Crown shook his head and hunched lower.

Coop shrugged. "Suit yourself. Take me about an hour to get that setup for you. Amos Miles over at the general store, two doors down on the right. He'll take care of you real good."

Crown had already turned his back on Coop, but he nodded just the same. He scanned the two blocks that made up the town, then headed out into the rain. In 1923 the town was so small no one had even bothered to give it a name. A Colored town, it existed only for McGee Farms and benefited the tenants and the dozen or so smaller farms that dotted what had been Jebediah McGee's own corner of Colwin County in East Texas. There were only a dozen or so houses, a general store, a livery, a bank, a railway siding, and a one room church and school with a steeple up above and a school bell in the yard.

The town was closed up against the rain, but the doors to the general store were open. Mr. Miles was behind the counter. He jumped when Crown walked through the doors, though he'd been staring right at them, like he was expecting a customer any moment. He was dark all over, at least the parts Crown could see.

His hands and face and bald pate were the color of Crown's knees and just as ashy.

Crown stood in the door of the mercantile suddenly overwhelmed by the assortment of goods from plain to frilly to fine. On the right were barrels of fresh fruit, a table lined with vegetables in season and a shelf with jars of homemade preserves side-by-side with canned peaches. From the rafters hung jerky and two sides of ham, one smoked and the other salted. To the left, Crown spied hammers, nails, brooms, hoes and shovels, and an axe and sickle. One rack of unmentionables lined the back wall along with two racks of plain dresses, most of which resembled colored gunnysacks. Just behind the women's garments stood a shelf of overalls and cotton shirts for men. On the wall above hung two hats for show amidst a dozen or more hats for working beneath the East Texas sun.

Mr. Miles eased from behind the counter. "Lookin' for somethin' in particular?"

"A bit of everything."

Crown pulled his left hand out of his pocket. In it he held a list he'd started the day Sister Abigail had told him Jebediah McGee had died and there wasn't any way that Crown could stay at the convent with no one to pay his room and board.

Crown wished he'd had the courage to ask Sister if all his years of scraping and hauling behind chickens and cows and nuns wasn't worth two meals a day and a room in back of the stables. Instead he had begged and pleaded to no avail. Sister Abigail had helped him pack his few belongings and bought him a ticket to Boone in Colwin County. She said that Crown wasn't to expect much, but that Father had written a Judge Bishop and the Judge had agreed to consider Crown's case whatever that meant. That there was a brother Jackson that Crown had never seen, and maybe if Jackson McGee were generous and Crown were humble then maybe Jackson would see that Crown was taken care of.

As it turned out Jebediah didn't see fit to leave Jackson anything either, and Jackson McGee didn't even show up for the reading of Jebediah's will. Judge Bishop took a liking to Crown to the chagrin of Jebediah's lawyer, and now in a nameless Colored town, Crown was standing with a list full of necessities for a home he never thought he'd see.

Mr. Miles had gently extracted the list from Crown's hand and was perusing it with eagerness when Crown looked up from his musing. Mr. Miles flinched ever so slightly, but did not look away.

"How you gonna be payin'?"

Crown pocketed his left hand and extracted his right. Mr. Miles took the small leather pouch, weighing it from one palm to the next. "I think I can handle this. Yes, suh. I think I can."

Mr. Miles took only a moment to size Crown up, then began to rattle on about Coop, Coop's wife Nettie and their six kids, Deacon Bibee who ruled the church/school, and the widow Martin whose old man used to own a good portion of land north of town till he fell sick and died and the widow had to sell out to old Jebediah McGee. Amos Miles was friendly enough though and did not require that Crown either listen or answer, which suited Crown just fine.

In an hour Coop delivered the rig as promised. With a twinkle in his eye, he introduced the team, a stubborn old stallion named "More" and a spirited young mare called "Less".

Coop stroked Less as he eyed More. "A little gentle coaxing is all she needs. But More won't answer to nothing but a little Less. So let her lead and he'll follow."

Coop turned his attention back to Crown. "You sure you won't spend the night? Nettie and the kids would love the company."

Crown looked at Coop square on then, but there was barely a glint of surprise in a face that still smiled welcome. Crown answered the only way he could, swinging one load and then another into the back of the wagon. With Coop's help, Crown was loaded and ready to go in half an hour. He nodded a polite goodbye to Coop as Mr. Miles watched from the comfort of his doorway.

Ignoring Coop's warning and his own good judgment, Crown headed out into that three-day rain with his wagon loaded with supplies. He hadn't relished going back to a town where he had never before been welcomed, so he'd bought more than enough to last through the soggy fall and well into winter, what winter there was in the low lying marsh of Southeast Texas. But to his surprise, Coop and Mr. Miles had offered him warmth and respect if not friendship. Crown shook his head in confusion. "Get up there, Less," he urged over the pelting rain.

For the next ten miles Crown saw nothing but the outline of trees to his right and fogged over rice fields to his left. When it wasn't pouring down raining, water rose off the fields like steam from a pot of boiling soup, giving Crown the sense that Jebediah McGee was cooking and stirring beneath the land he surely never meant for Crown.

The rice fields ended abruptly, with only a narrow road between the fields and the quarters. Beyond the quarters, the woods took up again, forming a dense canopy that shrouded the road in darkness. Crown pulled to a stop before the last row of paintless, clapboard houses, still two miles from his new home. The map was drenched and useless. Dusk had settled under a quarter moon. Crown knew one thing about this loathsome county, if he continued, he could get lost. From the nearest house, a light beckoned, but Crown was wary. Not many would welcome the likes of him.

But then what choice did they have? Crown need only show them the papers. They would have to be hospitable, if only begrudgingly.

Crown left the road decidedly, turning the team toward the houses. The horses struggled through thick mud. Crown heard a sickening, sucking sound. The front end of the wagon lurched then stopped. The horses neighed loudly, straining against the harness, but they were going nowhere.

Crown eased down from the wagon. His boots sank into deep mud. He cursed. Using the wagon then the harness for support, he felt his way slowly toward the team. When he found Less's bit, he grabbed hold, clicking his tongue and pulling the horses behind him. Less followed obediently, but More balked and neighed. The wagon sunk deeper in the murk and mire. Crown swore.

"Cursed animal. You're more burden than useful."

Exasperated and angry with himself for being so impulsive, Crown dropped the reins and trudged on, pulling his boots from one mud hole to the next. Near the house, he stopped at the sounds of a woman moaning and children wailing. He decided to go on until he spotted her, a frail, beautiful child with auburn hair and gold, freckled skin, standing on the rickety porch.

Instinctively, Crown raised his hand to cover the harelip. He lifted his head and stared at her, his face warmed by the glow of her lantern.

The child, undaunted, did not look away. "My mama needs help, Mister. She's havin' a baby."

The girl took a step closer. Crown took a step back and shuffled, unsettled.

"I don't know anything about birthing. I'm just looking to get out of the rain."

"It's dry and warm by the fire," she bade him. "You can come in if'n you'll help. We got rice and cornbread and molasses, but not much else. My pap's out with the rest of 'em, drinkin' moonshine and spittin' and cussin' I guess. Ain't nobody else."

The girl stepped to the end of the porch and reached for him. Crown shuddered. He had never been touched before, at least not kindly. She was young and warm. Too young. But something stirred deep inside him, something that made his cheeks burn with shame.

Crown wanted to turn around, but couldn't. He let her lead him into the house. Inside, he squinted, adjusting to the dim light of a lone lantern and a waning fire.

Crown surveyed his surroundings with a wary sweep. What struck him first was the gaggle of snotty, wailing children. They peered at him, huddled as they were in one small corner with their dirty feet and missing teeth and hand-me-down clothing.

Looking down, Crown took in the rest from the corners of his eyes. It was a single cramped room that smelled of too many people in too small a space. The odors mixed and swirled so Crown couldn't distinguish soiled diapers, from human sweat, from day old rice. But there was one odor familiar and distinct, bringing back memories of Sister Abigail and the bloodied rags bundled and tied for the curious boy told only to burn them.

Heady, Crown exhaled then inhaled quick and shallow. Needing a way out, he stammered. "That fire's about played out. You got any wood?"

"There's plenty scraps out back. I'd send Troy or Earnest, but then I'd have to ask you to tend to these younguns. I s'pect you'd rather fetch wood, but it'll have ta keep till we tend to Mama."

In the corner on a bed of old straw, a woman moaned, low, long, desolate like a sick cow. The mass of children wailed in reply.

"Hush now, ya'll," the girl hissed. An eerie quiet fell over the room, leaving only the baleful moans of the woman.

Crown hesitated. The girl looked at him reassuringly and offered her hand. His own hand rose to take hers, an act so new and foreign, he could only stare at his hand in hers.

"Mama, this here fella's go'n' help us. It's go'n' be all right, Mama."

Crown stared at the woman spread naked and gap-legged before him. He'd never seen a woman like that. She was slimy and bloody and stretched so it pained him to look at her. He looked away, but the girl jerked him to attention.

"Listen, I done this b'fore. I just need you to keep her spread and still, that's all."

The girl squatted, pulling Crown down with her, bracing her back against his chest, drawing his arms around her and placing his broad hands against the woman's ashen knees. With her hands shadowing his, the girl pressed firmly, till Crown could feel the woman's bones against his palms.

"Hold her still now."

Crown did as the girl directed. Awed, he watched her lean over and reach between her mother's legs to grab the bloody crown.

"Come on, Mama. Push. It's almost out, Mama. Come on now."

After all that pushing and tugging and pulling, the baby shot out of his mama and into his sister's skilled hands. True to her word, the girl caught him. She whacked him soundly, and the infant gasped, his face contorted, his legs kicking and swollen purple balls swinging. She swaddled him in the hem of her dress while Crown surveyed her thin legs.

"You have a boy, Mama. Whut you go'n' name this'n?"

The woman didn't answer. She was unnaturally thin, like her daughter, with dark, sunken eyes that looked like she hadn't slept or eaten in days. Still there was a hint that she also might be pretty, if she were cleaned up and not so worn.

"She all right?" Crown asked though he was more concerned for the girl than for her mother.

"She's fine. Just tired, that's all."

With the baby cradled in one arm, the girl wiped a tendril of wet hair from her face. Crown was suddenly aware of her pungently sweet smell and his proximity to her. He leaned back, giving the girl room.

"You are pretty good at this."

"Look around. I've had lots of practice."

"You birth all these brats?"

Crown said it without thinking, but the girl took no offense. She smiled at Crown and answered with candor.

"All 'cept my brothers, Troy and Earnest. Jewel was my first. I dropped her. I ain't dropped another, and Jewel ain't been right since. I'd give my right arm to have that day back."

Crown looked at the only other girl in the room. She had wailed the loudest and longest. She looked at him and smiled, wiping a long stream of snot from her nose. He almost laughed, but as always he just grunted. He turned back to the sprite of a girl who had him tied all up in knots.

She smiled at him. "Give me a minute to git this'n settled, and I'll tend to you."

Crown stood, hesitated and offered her a stiff hand. She accepted, popping up spryly, even with a newborn cradled in one arm.

Suddenly chilled by the damp clothes that clung to his skin, Crown idled to the fire. He watched the girl and waited. She grabbed a towel and wiped the baby clean as she could, then rested him next to his sleeping mother. The woman's breasts sagged and flopped over like they were as tired as she was. The girl took one milk-laden breast in her hands and offered it to the baby, holding it there until he found the nipple and sucked.

Crown should have turned away, but he could not. While he watched, the odd one ambled toward him, grinning from ear to ear. She reached for his hand. He drew back, but she just kept reaching and grinning.

"Git away from him, Jewel," the girl chastised gently. "Can't you see he ain't to be bothered? Go on to bed now. Sing us a little ditty like you always do. Mama'll like that."

Jewel did as she was ordered, though she was a head taller and ten pounds heavier than her sister was. Crown relaxed.

"Whut they call you?" the girl asked.

"Huh."

"That ain't much of a name." The girl laughed at her own joke. "My name's Carrie. Whut's yourn?"

"Crown. Crown McGee."

"McGee? You any kin to old man McGee?"

"I'm his son," Crown admitted without a hint of pride.

"His son? Didn't know he had a son other than that no good Jackson."

"Well, now you know," Crown retorted, suddenly defensive. He'd never been more than Jebediah McGee's shame. Imperfect, unloved, he'd been abandoned in an orphanage in the next state just so no one would know Jebediah was a spineless bastard with weak seed. Denied even in death, Crown was beholden to Judge Bishop for what should have been his naturally. Crown scowled, consciously masking hurt with anger.

"You don't have to git so riled. I'm just askin'. Makin' conversation. Besides, all that frownin' ain't good for nothin' but wrinkles."

Carrie smiled, soothing the feathers she'd managed to ruffle, till Crown felt sorry he had any feathers at all.

"I didn't mean."

"Ne'er mind. We're Giddin's by the by. Just about everyone on this here farm is kin to us one way or another. Giddin's, Johnsons, Robertsons, we all one clan. Heberts and Provosts, well they be another, though the line's been blurred by birth and marriage. That's my Mama, Mae. Pap'll be in come sunup, I reckon. Over there's Troy and Earnest and Jewel. The rest you can just call little Giddin's."

Self-conscious, Crown looked down, watching the way his toes turned inward like they had a will all their own. It was more than he could take in at one time. More than he'd known in his nineteen years, and it was all his. The people, the land, the girl.

"Well, come on. That fire ain't go'n' light up all by itself. You git that wood now, and I'll git you some suppa."

Carrie handed Crown the lantern. He stepped outside, where the rain had dwindled to a fine drizzle. Chilled, he huddled and pulled up his collar to cover his neck. He found the pile of wood under a shed out back, stumbling over a board before he saw it. With arms outstretched, he braced against the pile to break his fall. The wet pile collapsed beneath his weight. His hands drew splinters from the few dry logs that were untouched by the rain. By the time Crown headed back with his arms loaded, his palms were smarting.

Inside he dropped the wood in front of the fire. He had not picked well. He had not picked at all, just grabbed the first thing he'd found. "Most of it's wet." Crown shuddered involuntarily, drawing Carrie's sympathy.

"Just let it lie, then. I reckon we'll make it through the night. Grab that chair and pull it over to the fire. You, sit now."

Crown obeyed. He didn't want to know what happened when Carrie Giddings didn't get her way.

Carrie handed him a bowl filled with a lot of hot water, a few beans for flavor and a spoonful of rice. Crown ate it more for it's warmth than for anything else.

When he finished, Carrie was waiting, summoned only by the clack of his spoon against the empty bowl. She took the bowl from him, noticing his hands for the first time.

"You got splinters."

Crown drew back his hands, and felt the blood rush to his cheeks. "It's nothing."

"Still, I'll git me a needle and pull 'em for you. Jewel, come git this bowl. You kids, git on ta bed now. You got church in the mornin'."

Crown watched the children stretch out where they had sat, all bundled under the same quilt. Carrie stood on tiptoe and stretched to reach a tattered tomato-red pincushion. She extracted a needle, and with her bare foot edged an ember out of the fire. She squatted and held the needle to the ember until the tip blackened. Then she turned and sat cross-legged in front of Crown, took one of his big hands in her small one and probed with the needle.

Crown flinched, and she laughed.

"A big, healthy boy like you ain't afeared of the needle are you?"

She finished with one hand and started on the other before Crown could think of an apt reply. He fell asleep in the chair with his hand in hers and her image planted in his dreams.

CHAPTER 2

▼

Crown stretched his neck. He'd slept worse, but the damp evening, rain-soaked clothes and stiff chair had him aching in places he'd forgotten he had. Sunlight peeked through the thatched roof and rough hewn slats. He watched the dust dance a bit, then surveyed the sparse room. In addition to the corner pallet there was a table with just the one chair and a crate that held the lantern. He wondered where they all ate.

Across the room, Carrie tended the fire. On the cot, Mae Giddings had come to life, and a sallow baby gently sucked her breast. The rest of Mae's mottled crew of children lay asleep, sprawled in a tangled heap beneath that matted quilt.

Mae smiled at Crown. "Come here, let me git a look at you."

Crown bristled, then realized Mae meant no harm. He sidled over to the bed, his head down, his hands forced to his sides. He couldn't hide forever. He might as well let her see and be done with it.

Mae sat up bracing on one arm, taking care not to rustle her sleeping baby. "Jebediah's boy. Coffee, no cream. Just like yo' daddy."

"Huh?"

"Them eyes. Wake you right up, them eyes will. Just like yo' daddy's."

"I ain't nothing like him."

"Can't tell by lookin'. But looks don't make the man. If it did, yo' daddy would'a been a mite better than he turned out ta be."

Mae stroked Crown's lip, considered a while, then smiled. "Don't you worry none. I don't remember much, but I got me a mouthful from Carrie. You already proved more man than Jebediah."

Crown shuffled and turned to watch Carrie bent over the fire. Desire and shame bundled inside him as she turned to look back at him.

"I gotta take a leak," Crown announced stupidly, unnerved by Carrie's sudden smile and slender young body, the first hint of breasts budding through her thin sack of a dress.

Crown stamped outside and relieved himself, then trudged to the wagon. More looked tired as though he had been struggling all night to rid himself of mud. Less was wide-eyed and very still. She whinnied as Crown approached. He rubbed her snout to calm her. "Settle down there," he said to both of them. More snorted, seemingly unimpressed with Crown's gesture of comfort. Crown would have to free the horses before the mud caked beneath the rising sun, but first he'd tend to Carrie Giddings.

Crown made his way to the back of the wagon and shuffled through the packages until he found the one he wanted. He wondered where the men folk were. If they didn't come back soon, he'd have his hands full freeing the team and wagon.

What kind of man would leave a woman near birth with a house full of children? But Carrie had warmth in her voice when she'd spoken of her papa, a warmth Crown had never felt for Jebediah McGee.

Fearful that Carrie was just an apparition and all that would be left was the woman and the now sleeping children, Crown tucked the package under his arm and hurried back to the house. He ran his tongue over the roof of his mouth and back down again. He longed for a swig of coffee to cut the bite of yesterday's supper. Instead he settled for the rust-colored water that he drew from the well and splashed liberally over his face and neck. Still, there was nothing to help the sticky dampness that wore on him like an extra suit of clothes.

He stood on the porch for a while surveying the landscape, his landscape. It stretched for the next ten miles, row after row of rice fields and one room clapboard houses. Crown pictured the farm at harvest—bronzed, shirtless men wading through the marsh-like fields swinging their sickles to the rhythm of some toothless old-timer. Come noon, the women would emerge, bearing dippers of water, jars of cold coffee, and rags wrapped around molasses & cornbread lunches. Heads covered, they would fan their dark sweaty necks and breasts that sagged beneath sack-like featureless dresses. For a while they'd chat, catching up on the latest gossip, and swearing, "By Lord, it's hotta than the day b'fo'." Just off the fields, a passel of children in ragged overalls would enjoy their last days of play, too old to be underfoot, too young to work the fields or thresh the needle-like grains of rice.

The door creaked behind him, ending his musings. Crown turned to see Carrie smiling at him, her hands on her slippery hips.

"Whut you got there?"

"Thought you could use it, with the younguns and all."

It was Carrie's turn to be defensive. She spit a wad that arced past Crown's face to land with a slimy plop in the mud below.

"We don't need yo' charity."

"It ain't charity. I'm hungry, and I don't want no molasses and cornbread."

Carrie laughed and took the package from Crown's outstretched hand. She peeled back the paper and hefted the package to her small, slightly upturned nose.

"Ummh, coffee, oats, and bacon. I could whip us up a helluva batch of cracklin's. Wouldn't that make Mama smile?"

She reached for Crown again, just like she had the night before. "Well, come on in. Whut you standin' out here fo', anyway?"

Crown steadied his eyes on the rice fields stretched low and wide as far as he could see. "I'd rather sit and look a spell, being as I ain't never seen the place. When you reckon the men folk will be back?"

"Hard ta say. It's Sunday you know. But don't you worry. They'll be back before sunup tomorrie."

Carrie paused for a minute before talking to Crown's back. "When I holler breakfast, you best come runnin'. Them younguns ain't likely to care that you're Crown McGee."

Crown grunted, but inside he smiled. God, he liked that girl. He had never liked anyone that way before.

Crown was still on the porch when a little Giddings tugged at the loop on Crown's overalls and stared up at him with hungry unapologetic eyes.

"Carrie said come on now."

The boy tugged again on the loop for emphasis. Crown followed him into the house and took the chair by the fire. The children ate where they had slept. Mae Giddings sat up now, her youngest child asleep beside her. Carrie bustled about filling plates with oats and cracklings; Crown's first, then Mae's, then the rest of Mae's stair-stepped brood. Having served everyone else, Carrie eyed what was left. She looked at Mae, and Mae nodded.

"Pap ain't here, and oats ain't no damned good warmed over."

Carrie emptied the pot of oats into her bowl and sat down on the floor with her legs folded under her. Two of Mae's babies crawled up on Carrie's knees to eat from the same dish.

"David Lee, ain't it yo' turn to say the grace?"

David Lee nodded and bowed his head. "God bless this food and him that brung it." A chorus of amens echoed through the group.

They ate noisily, smacking and chattering and laughing for the sheer joy of it. Even at Montagne Parish, Crown had preferred to take his meals alone, and Sister Abigail had indulged him that one luxury. Now he found all the noise unnerving. He handed his bowl of oats to David Lee, who took a spoonful and passed it around to his siblings.

With their bellies full and round, Troy and Earnest brought in water from the well and offered everyone a ladle of water to wash down the oats.

Carrie drank, then wiped her mouth with the back of her hand. "You boys git washed up now. Lenetta be here with the wagon b'fo' long. Jewel and me go'n' stay with Mama and the babies."

The boys stacked their bowls on the table and filed out of the house oldest to youngest. The screen door never set until the last boy had left. Then it clattered noisily, giving rise to another of Mae Giddings' smiles.

"David Lee, how many times I tell you not to let that door knock."

"Sorry, Mama." David Lee yelled back as he jumped off the porch. Outside the confines of the cramped house, the boys played leapfrog while they waited their turn at the well. Their laughter filtered in filling the small room.

Carrie took a small white bundle from the stone mantle over the fireplace. She unfolded it revealing a tarnished comb and brush. She sat on the floor and motioned to Jewel. Though her eyes flooded with fresh tears, Jewel took a seat obediently on the floor between Carrie's legs. Carrie brushed, and Jewel whined softly.

"Hush up now, Jewel," Carrie soothed. "Mama, we got anythin' for Deacon Bibee."

"Naw, if I'd been thinkin', we might'a spared him a few of those cracklin's. But he can't miss what he never knowed he had." Mae chuckled. "Naw, I reckon fillin' his pews with Giddin's on Sunday mornin' ought ta be enough."

"You a church fella, Mr. McGee?"

Crown grunted and shook his head. His church was the small black Bible Father Georges had given him on his thirteenth birthday. He had no trouble talking to God on his own terms, irreverent as that could sometimes be. Sister Abigail would have boxed his ears, and Father Georges would have taken the cane to his behind if they'd known. And he'd already seen more people than he cared to see at one time in the Giddings's one room house. Not that they'd been bad. They'd been nicer than most.

Crown stood and stretched, reluctant to leave. "Naw, I best get on home."

"Don't you make yo'self a stranger. Now that you seen more of me than any man but Sam, I reckon you're family as well as boss."

Crown looked away, this time more ashamed at Mae's candor than at the harelip that marred his looks.

"Mama, I think you made him blush," Carrie joked.

Crown smiled then, the first time he'd smiled to his recollection. It felt odd the way his lips curled up on top of themselves. He left taking care not to let the door knock on his way out.

The boys piled onto the porch as Crown stepped off. Crown looked back. Troy opened the door wide and all eight beady-haired, straw-colored boys streamed inside. The door clattered shut behind the youngest and Mae yelled, "David Lee."

Crown wished Carrie were on the porch, waving him back but she was tucked away in the house. He couldn't seem to get enough of her, but he'd had enough of her odd sister Jewel touching him and singing, "This Old Man" in his ear.

Annoyed, Crown dismissed the Giddings and concentrated on the mired wagon. He scoured the yard until he found a solid branch of oak, broken from a tree by lightning, to use as a lever to free the wagon. Behind the house, he rummaged some boards from the wood heap. The boards were damp but strong enough to serve his purpose. He carried the wood back to the wagon, gently coaxing the nervous team as he wedged the boards in front of the wheels. Crown was kneeling with his hand deep in muck, trying to persuade More to lift his hoof, when he heard a snicker from behind. Crown whirled to face a half-dozen men still giddy with the swagger of moonshine.

"Boy, he's the ugliest cuss I eva' seen," jeered a short squat young man with little cause to call another man ugly.

"Whar you hail from, boy?" asked another through the taunting sounds of their laughter.

Crown drew back as a hand slapped at his shoulder. He lowered his head and returned to his task, perturbed.

"Give you a hand, boy," an older man offered apologetically.

"Not from the likes of you." Crown was angry and almost crying. He never cried, at least not before and not since he'd left the security of Sister Abigail and Montagne Parish. Damn that Carrie Giddings for making him feel like he was almost human.

A tall thin, wiry man stepped forward. The others crowded in.

"Well then, you best git done and be on yo' way. We don't cotton to strangers."

Trembling with anger, his lip crawling up over clenched teeth, Crown squared his shoulders and stood up to face them. With a narrow waist and strong hips that tapered to long sinewy legs, Crown stood a head above the average man. He was done shuffling among men with his head bent. He stood tall forcing his hands to his sides.

"Well you best cotton to this stranger or look for another place to live. Name's Crown McGee, and I reckon I'm yall's new boss. You just take a cotton to that."

"Aw, Sam," the older man complained. "Why'd you have to go and git him all riled? We didn't mean no harm, boy."

"You might as well get used to it. It's Mister McGee to the lot of you." Crown sneered scornfully. "Fact is there ain't no sense in me getting all down and muddy when I got you fools to do it for me. The lot of you can free the horses and this here wagon yourselves. When you're done, you'll find me at that cabin over there having a cup of coffee with Miss Carrie."

Sam bristled, but four pairs of hands reached to hold him in check.

"Sam." Crown let the name linger. "So you're the ornery cuss that run off and left a woman near birth alone with that passel of brats. If it weren't for them, I'd run you off this place right now. You have a boy by the way. Finish this here wagon, and you'd be obliged to go see him."

Crown turned away, satisfied with himself and the introduction he'd made. He was sure he'd made an enemy of Sam Giddings, but it didn't matter. Crown made up his mind in that lightning of an instant. He intended to have Sam's daughter Carrie just like he had his father's fortune. He'd bide his time, till she was ripe enough to satisfy the warmth she'd spread through him like fire. He'd bide his time till she was ripe for the taking.

CHAPTER 3

▼

Crown tramped back to the house, stopping at the well to wash away the mud and quell his anger. He turned as the door creaked open and Carrie peered out at him.

"I thought I heard water runnin'. Everythin' alright?"

"Wagon's stuck in the mud is all. Men folks are back," he added matter-of-factly. "I left them to tend to it."

"Pap with them?"

Crown nodded, trying hard to hide his disgust.

"Well come on in. Keep us company till they're done."

Crown followed Carrie inside and returned to his seat by the fire. While Mae cooed and cuddled the new baby and Carrie bustled about cleaning the meager cabin, Jewel took to studying Crown. At times she was so close Crown could smell her breath, still sweet with the smell of oats. Question piled upon question, answered only by the shuffling of Crown's body on the lone chair and Mae's and Carrie's gentle admonitions.

By the time Sam Giddings stomped into the house caked with mud and wearing his pride and anger from his wrinkled brow to his clenched fists to his feet planted firmly apart, Crown was glad to get on his way again. Crown rose to his feet. His mouth twitched in anger, he stood with his legs apart and his hands clenched at his sides, answering Sam's silent challenge.

"Sam, what's got into you," Mae chastised. "We got company. That any way to greet a man that brung your son into this world?"

Crown's ears burned as Mae lit into Sam for staying out the night and half again another day and for being rude to a man that had only brought them kindness. All the while, apparently too angry for words, Sam glared at Crown.

"I'll walk you out." Slicing through the tension, Carrie grabbed Crown by the arm and ushered him outside. "What happened 'tween you and Pap?"

Crown shrugged. He was more used to being treated the way of Sam Giddings than the way of Carrie or Mae, so he told himself they were just caught in the moment and the next time he saw them, things would be back to normal. Carrie and Mae would ridicule him or fear him or pity him just like all the rest.

Carrie followed him out to the wagon, her hand still tucked firmly in his arm. "You ain't go'n' try to take this rig down that road," she ordered more than asked. She pointed the way, her hand moving to the small of his back.

"Your home's just two miles or so down where the road ends. You'll come to a cemetery, and the house is in a clearing just to the other side. I'd go with you, but I best git back. Pap's got Mama so riled she's subject to upset the new baby and Jewel. We'll be by to check on you once Mama's back on her feet."

Still unnerved, Crown wasn't sure he'd welcome Carrie's visit. He let the moment pass without reply, and Carrie turned back to the house. Crown took her advice to leave the wagon and set off on foot. Despite the sunlight, the trees draped the road in darkness. He'd have to be careful, but Carrie had assured him if he kept to the road and didn't make any turnoffs, he'd wind up right where he intended. In fact the road was called Cemetery Road because it dead-ended into the McGee Cemetery.

Carrie had promised to see that the wagon and goods were delivered. Crown didn't know why, but he believed her. Besides he'd been foolhardy once and wound up stuck in that one room shanty. But then maybe he'd have never met Carrie Giddings. God knew no other woman could abide looking at him, much less touching him, except Jewel and that didn't count since the girl was obviously daft. He shook his head, more to chase off the mosquitoes already swarming than to shake off his thoughts of Carrie. He found that he liked thinking about her. It was the closest thing to joy he'd ever known.

Well fed from the long summer, stirred by the first hint of cold, the mosquitoes were as big as dragonflies. They bit right through the two layers of clothes Crown wore. He'd been too ashamed to accept Carrie's offer to dry his clothes so he'd kept them on, shivering half the night. Now the cool October air pierced through the dampness, biting his skin along with the mosquitoes.

The sun, barely discernible through the dense canopy of trees, brought little warmth. Crown was wet and cold and miserable but he trudged on. At least at the end of that road he'd be all alone on a place of his own, the first he'd ever had.

About the time Crown had gone as far as he thought he could, the road ended suddenly, and Crown found himself surrounded by woods on three sides. In front of him, just six feet wide was a high arched gate with towering wrought iron bars tinged green with algae and draped in Spanish moss. The gate was locked. He'd have to climb over the fence or break the lock. He wished he'd had the sense to grab a few tools from the wagon.

He peered through the bars and the sight drew the breath right out of him. The cemetery was muddy and dark. A mere spackling of sunlight glinted through the trees revealing rows and rows of headstones—square ones, crosses, arches, angels, Madonnas—some tall and thin, some squat and thick, some flat like the ground they lay on—as far as he could see. Funny, he thought, how Colored folk would spend more on a piece of concrete to mark their dead bones than they'd spend on a roof to cover their living flesh. Old women were the worst, scraping by just so they'd have the horse and wagon, the fancy casket, the preacher and the band trailing behind. The plaintive sounds of mourners, the plodding hooves of horses had called Crown many times to his window at Montagne Parish. It felt hauntingly familiar, giving Crown a painful sense of home.

Shaking off the melancholy memories, he surveyed the cemetery again. A black and gray granite headstone with gold lining its borders stopped him cold. Atop the ornate headstone sat a vase, its fire extinguished. It had to be Jebediah's grave. Jebediah had most likely picked out the headstone himself well before his time.

Crown scaled the gate. An assortment of spiders and lizards scurried out of his way. At the top he sprang over and jumped down in one fluid motion. He clambered over the soggy graves disregarding hapless others buried there. The dead would never matter to him except that they would keep his ledgers full and the Colored folks of Colwin County beholden to him.

Crown reached the gravesite and stared down at it. Up close, the headstone appeared more pretentious than imposing. The mound of dirt covering Jebediah oozed sideways into soft mud. Crown wondered who'd dug the hole. He wondered who'd been there when they lowered his father into the ground.

Crown cursed and spat. He noticed then the grave beside Jebediah's. With its staid simplicity, the ivory cross marking the gravesite reminded Crown of his mother. She had visited Crown twice yearly and each time she had seemed more fragile. The hint of red ocher on her cheeks and lips had been inadequate to mask her natural pallor. With prim clothes covering her thin arms and neck, a laced handkerchief frequently raised to her lips, she had always appeared to be teetering on the verge of death. That she had suddenly disappeared altogether from his life had not come as a surprise. He had not grieved then.

Crown leaned closer to read the brief inscription.

Elvina McGee
1884–1920
Beloved wife of Jebediah, mother of Jackson

Crown moaned, bent over his mother's grave and vomited. His fury grew. Though his gut cramped and his head pounded, he struggled to stand upright. He intended to see Jebediah reburied in the manner such a coward deserved, if he had to claw Jebediah out of the mud himself.

In the distance, before the woods began, Crown could see a large barn and a house, alone and majestic from where he stood. Ignoring the radiating pain in his legs, his feverishly aching head, the burning fatigue in his eyes, Crown set out for his new home in search of a sledge hammer. Anger, old and deep drove every step.

As he neared the house, he could see the once fine structure was now in disrepair. The moist air had long ago stripped its paint. The eaves sagged, old rains stained the dingy windows, and the raised porch slanted as if it too wanted to sink into the muddy ground below.

Crown turned instead to the barn. After all, Jebediah was waiting. The house would still be there come dark, when Crown had finished what he had to do. He could imagine the inside of the house was in no better shape than the outside. It was probably filled with cobwebs and dust. God knew he'd slept worse. Why just last night, he'd bedded in the Giddings ramshackle cabin with that pack of snot-nosed brats.

CHAPTER 4

▼

The deed done, Crown didn't bother to admire his work. Covered in mud and welts, feverish and aching, he crawled back to the house. He was sure he'd never get the mud off of him, but he didn't care. It was his mud. Without bothering to wash, he fell into the bed downstairs with the musty covers. He peered deliriously at the half-rotten lace curtains hanging in shreds at the window until he drifted to sleep. He thought he was dreaming the morning he spied Carrie Giddings and her dumb sister Jewel at the foot of his bed.

The smell of oatmeal, coffee and cracklings woke him three days later. The scents brought back warm memories and a longing so deep it hurt. His hands stole beneath the covers where he had stiffened with the mere thought of Carrie. Believing he was alone in the house, he rubbed until the burning turned inward and he erupted, soiling his bedclothes.

"Whut you doin', Crown?" Carrie asked. "Ain't you too old to be playin' with yo'self thataway? I swear you're just like Troy."

Startled and embarrassed, Crown moaned and turned his face to the wall. He realized then he hadn't been dreaming after all. The scents and visions had indeed been real.

"Never you mind bein' ashamed," Carrie assured. "Mama says it's just nat'ral. Says we all do it. I used to do it myself 'fore I got all growed up. I guess it takes you boys a bit longer. Gran says it makes your skin pop out. Smooth and pretty as yours is either she's a liar or she's dead wrong. Tain't never known Gran to be neitha."

His blanket clutched under his chin, Crown lay there, unable to look at her. He wished she'd stop talking. The more she talked the more embarrassed he got.

His blood rushed, just like he hadn't rubbed half the skin off himself already trying to release the hold she had on him. He found himself wishing she'd draw back those covers and climb in with him.

Instead, she touched his forehead gently. "Fever's gone. Think you can handle some breakfast?"

He grunted and pulled the covers over his head.

"Suit yo'self. Me and Jewel need to git back and help Mama if you're sure ya'll be all right. Mama's takin' this last one a little harder than the rest. Answer me, Crown McGee. Well are you all right er ain't you?"

Crown didn't want her to go. He didn't want her to stay. He didn't know if he could wait till she was really all growed up. But he had things to do and he couldn't afford to lie there sweating and thinking about her.

"I'm fine. I got things to do that's all," he grumbled.

"Looks like you already done aplenty," Carrie retorted. "Guess I don't need to ask if you cared much for your pap. Not that anyone else around here did eitha, but he was your flesh and blood. Seems like you owed him a little respect for that."

Crown glared at her. Carrie glared right back.

"You don't have to like whut I say, Crown McGee. You don't have to listen eitha if you don't have a mind to. But you can't stop me from the sayin'."

"By the by," Carrie continued. "Troy and Earnest always made a little extry helpin' your old man dig the graves and tend the yard. They're out thar right now tendin' the mess you made."

"What you waiting on, girl? Didn't you say you had to go?"

"You don't have to ask me twice, and you're obliged for the nursin' and the washin' and the prayin' and the singin' me and Jewel's done over you for the past three days. Don't bother sayin' thanks neitha. We'd do the same for a dawg. Come on out a thar Jewel. We's leavin'."

Crown couldn't help but think about what Carrie had said. He hoped she'd been the one doing the washing and not her dumb old sister Jewel. He could almost feel Carrie's hands bathing him all warm and gentle. Maybe he hadn't been dreaming after all.

CHAPTER 5

▼

For three weeks Crown was almost too busy burying the dead and avoiding the curious to think about Carrie Giddings. It seemed like folks in Colwin County took to dying all of a sudden just so they could be buried by Crown McGee. Friends and relatives stopped grieving long enough to gossip and agree it was shameful the way Crown had pulverized his daddy's headstone and moved old Jebediah to an unmarked grave. Troy and Earnest had done a good job covering up Crown's mess. Crown didn't bother to correct folks when they trekked across his land just to view the rumored site, fifty yards south of where he'd actually planted Jebediah.

The fever that had rocked Crown for three days was spreading through Colwin County. Crown would have been completely swamped if it weren't for Troy and Earnest. The way word traveled in the county, Crown didn't even have to fetch them. They simply showed up at burying time.

Finally the burials eased up, and Crown had time to tend to the house. The plans had been among the papers Crown inherited. With little else to occupy his time, he had studied them on the train and committed the details to memory. Two stories, eight rooms and an attic, the house was more than one man needed with two bedrooms below and two above, a dining room and parlor, a study and a kitchen and pantry as big as Sam Giddings' one room shanty. The house had everything but an indoor bath. The outhouse stood out of place fifty paces off the kitchen.

With a lantern and a set of keys Jebediah's lawyer had handed him unceremoniously, Crown set out after breakfast one morning to explore the house. It was furnished sparsely downstairs, with only a hint of the fine pieces that once adorned its rooms. What was left was worn, lackluster and tattered but sufficient to Crown.

In the library, Crown found a treasury of books. He picked up a heavy atlas from the shelf. Thumbing the pages, he sent silverfish scurrying. He made a note to revisit the library later to examine each of its dusty volumes. He crossed the room and unlocked the desk and the safe beneath. Finding nothing of value, he proceeded up the stairs.

The second floor had two rooms, one on each side of a narrow hallway. At the end of the hallway, a trapdoor led to the attic. Curious, Crown tried the bedrooms first. Crown turned the door knobs, first to one room, then the other, but both of the doors were locked. Crown tried each key on the heavy metal ring until he found one that fit.

He opened the door to the room on the right. Heavy curtains covered the window and made the room dark. Crown raised the lantern and stepped inside. A lacquer game table and fraternity rug centered the room. Walking toward the table, Crown struck his knee against heavy wood. He rubbed his knee and cursed, swinging the lantern to inspect the cause of his injury. The bed was seven feet long with four massive posts. In rich cherry wood, detailed carvings of jungle animals decorated the bed, the matching trunk and armoire. Across the room, the deep closet was empty of clothes, except for a black and gold letter sweater and a camel coat. The shelves were lined with a dusty set of encyclopedias and an assortment of sporting awards.

Painfully aware that he'd found his brother's bedroom, Crown backed out of the room and closed the door. Envious and shaken, he crossed the hall to the second room, turned the key in the lock and swung the door open. Light streamed in through sheer curtains and illuminated a nursery, staler and mustier than the rest of the house.

Taken aback by what he saw, Crown relocked both doors and returned to the first floor. He imagined the attic held boxes and boxes of items used and outgrown and otherwise discarded, but he had lost his curiosity. What lay upstairs could for the time remain a mystery, stowed in the upper reaches inhabited now by spiders and rats and squirrels. He removed the key from the ring and stored it in the safe with no intention to use it again.

The sorry state of the house, its darkness, dust and mildew, overwhelmed Crown as much as its size. He spent as little time as possible indoors, coming inside long enough to sup and to sleep. He felt more comfortable outdoors doing what he knew, a little carpentry, white-washing and handy-work.

In a week, Crown had done just about all he could to the house without going back to town for paint and lumber, a new door, window panes, hinges and nails. He decided he'd stop by the farm on his way into town, and if he were lucky, he'd have another run-in with Carrie. He was beginning to enjoy their feisty discussions, although she did most of the talking. Still he liked her spunk among other things. Trouble was she always came as a pair. That Jewel seemed to tag along wherever Carrie went.

They'd come by once to bring Crown some quilts that Carrie's grandmother had made and to wash Crown's musty linens. Before she left, Carrie had offered to sew Crown some curtains if he supplied the material, so he added that to his list as well. Of course he'd have to ask her to hang them, since he didn't know about such delicate things. And she'd need a chair for such high windows. He could almost see himself holding her by the waist as she balanced precariously on her tiptoes in that paper-thin dress.

Images of Jewel intruded, and though Crown tried to concentrate on the road ahead, he could not shake her last tune from his head. Jewel had been as annoying as ever with her infernal singing and twiddling with anything she could grab hold of. She'd taken a particular interest in Crown's books, and he knew for a fact that she couldn't read a lick.

Books used to be about the only thing Crown ever cared about, and he'd been silently joyed when he found the sizeable though dusty library in Jebediah's study, his study now. Crown guessed he'd gotten something worthwhile from the old man besides the land and the money. Jebediah must have loved reading as much as Crown. And they seemed to like the same kinds of books, on war and history and politics and finance, not the mindless fiction that most common folks called writing.

Crown added a couple of books on rice farming and some generic books on farming to the collection. He'd read the books over and over till the pages had lost their crispness. He had been reading about techniques for growing other crops in alternate plots in alternate years, to keep the ground fertile. His farm's sandy soil was saturated with water and generally unsuitable for anything other than rice, but if Crown could find the right crop and the profits were good, he knew he'd try it.

Yet with all his reading and all his intentions there was a reason Crown had delayed a trip to the farm. The funerals and the house repairs were convenient distractions. The truth was, he was scared. His knowledge of farming was limited to the nuns' ample gardens, which he had plowed, seeded, weeded and picked for the last ten years. From what he'd read, rice was nothing like peas, greens, tomatoes, onions or potatoes. Rice needed water, lots of water, and the tender seedlings needed care before planting just like babies needed care before they could crawl.

Crown slowed near the Giddings' house, but the place looked deserted, so he decided to drive on. All the fields were deserted too, but then it was November. With harvest over, there wasn't much to be done in the fields this time of year.

Another seven miles down the road Crown came upon the granary. Unlike the fields, it was bustling with activity. Crown turned down a narrow dirt road that ambled through several silos to a larger square building with McGee Farms sprawled across its front in fading black letters. Sam Giddings and another man were talking heatedly outside. Crown pulled to a stop, jumped down from the wagon, and walked right up to the two men.

Slight and wiry, Sam Giddings had the same stance he'd taken the last time Crown saw him, and he didn't seem too happy to see Crown. He looked like a spring that had been wound too tight.

Crown nodded and spoke.

"Giddings."

"McGee."

A head taller and fifty pounds heavier than Sam, the other man started smiling and reached out a pudgy hand to Crown. Crown didn't take it, but he nodded his hello.

"Karl Johnson, your general manager. It's good to meet Jebediah's other so …"

Karl Johnson's voice trailed off as he realized he'd just made a huge mistake, but he regained his composure quickly. He moved closer and squeezed Crown's shoulder with the same hand Crown had refused.

Unnerved, Crown grunted and frowned. Crown could see that Karl Johnson was a true politician, but he'd need more than charm to impress Crown. Johnson would need to know how to run a rice farm. Crown stepped back, reestablishing his space.

With a toothy smile that seemed false and real all at the same time, Karl Johnson continued.

"Giddings and I were just having a little disagreement. I want to plant the fields a little early. It's warm yet, and the winters here are generally mild. We could get a head start, and with a little luck, we'd have a crop to market ahead of everyone else."

Uncertain of the merits of Johnson's argument, Crown turned reluctantly to Sam Giddings.

"I never was much for luck. What you have to say about this, Giddings?"

"Johnson's forgittin' that cool spell we had last month," Sam added. He loosened his stance a bit, apparently still wary. He continued, looking Crown dead in the eye as he talked.

"I ain't seen the day yet when a man could count on luck or the weather, except that it'll be what it'll be and that's likely to be what you don't want when you don't need it."

As much as Crown wanted to dislike Sam Giddings, he had to admire his directness. Karl Johnson had tried, but he had this skittish look to him, like he couldn't quite settle his eyes on Crown's face.

Karl Johnson's forehead was beaded with sweat, and his cheeks were puffed like a squirrel gathering nuts, but his words were deceptively calm. Sam Giddings on the other hand was spitting obscenities amidst loud accusations of stupidity.

Crown listened to both men battle back and forth but realized no matter what they thought, it was his decision to make. Karl Johnson's idea was enticing—to be first, best and a little richer for it. But it was not without risk. Torrential rains, a late freeze, the threat of bugs and disease were all too real. Crown was used to having nothing, but he didn't want to fail at this. If he waited he'd have a decent year. If he didn't, it could be boom or bust, and he couldn't afford the latter. Having heard enough and certain of his decision, Crown finally stopped the argument with a grunt.

"I like your idea, Johnson."

Karl Johnson smiled prematurely.

"But I can't afford that risk my first time out. We'll do the usual. I do have some other ideas I'd like to talk to you about. We could talk while you show me the place."

"Certainly. Would you like to start with the granary, then take a ride out to the fields?"

"That sounds fine, Johnson."

"McGee." Sam grumbled through gritted teeth.

Crown turned to face Sam Giddings. Crown had accepted Sam's idea while disagreeing with his philosophy. The gesture wasn't lost on Sam. Sam shuffled, his hands clenching, his yellow neck pulsing red.

"Giddings," Crown answered calmly in return, dismissing Sam. Crown's face was expressionless. Inside though, he smiled. He had managed to bring Sam Giddings down a notch, just by showing his approval of Karl Johnson.

Crown followed a beaming Karl Johnson inside the granary. They wound their way through the workers, tools and machinery until they were outside again. Before them stood three large silos. Crown had read of horrible accidents in silos, men falling in and suffocating, explosions and fires costing grain as well as lives. Gigantic and silent, they hardly seemed the menaces he had read about.

"I'd like to see the fields, Johnson."

They turned back toward the granary. They were met at the door by a gaunt White man with thinning hair and salt and pepper stubble. Five grimy, stringy boys filed out behind him. "Go on, git," he ordered, and they fanned out to play a game of tag amongst the silos.

"Go on Micah, scoot," the man urged, but the youngest stayed behind, hanging onto the loop of his father's overalls.

Karl Johnson offered the usual smile, but the man looked past him and starred offensively at Crown.

"You the new owner?"

"I am." Uncertain of the man's intent, Crown kept walking. The man followed, with Johnson right behind.

"Johnson tell you about our arrangement?"

Karl Johnson, guffawed, still smiling. He tried unsuccessfully to position his body between the man and Crown.

Crown stopped and turned. "Arrangement?"

A wry smile crept across the man's face. "I supply your stores with shine. You supply me with grain, at a reduced price of course."

"Shine?"

"Hooch, boy. Rotgut. Liquor. Shine."

Crown remembered his first introduction to Sam Giddings. He'd been 'full of shine' by Carrie's admission. Startled, Crown looked to Karl Johnson for answers.

"That right, Johnson?"

"This here's Nate Comeaux, Mr. McGee. He's the best moonshiner in these parts."

"Why should I pay you to keep my workers liquored up," Crown pressed Nate Comeaux.

"'Cause the shine's the only thing they work for. 'Cause it takes their minds off their misery and keeps them beholdin' to you."

"I see. Well, I'll consider the matter, and let you know my decision." Dismissing Nate Comeaux with a perfunctory nod, Crown started walking again.

Trying hard to keep up with the youngster in tow, Nate followed Crown across the granary. Crown noticed the boy was stooped. He thought ironically how a poor, hardened moonshiner was more considerate to his crippled offspring than Jebediah had ever been to Crown. Crown stepped outside and headed toward the wagon, contemplating Nate Comeaux's revelation.

"Well, don't consider too long," Nate yelled from the doorway. "You ain't the only rice farmer in these parts you know."

Crown climbed aboard the wagon and handed the reins to Karl Johnson. Johnson climbed in and accepted the reins, hastening the horses into a steady trot and leaving an enraged Nate Comeaux behind.

When they were out of earshot, Crown turned to Karl Johnson. Beads of sweat again dotted Johnson's forehead.

"Anything else I need to know?"

Johnson cleared his throat. "There have been deals made here or there. Not a one unnecessary. It's the way of it around here. Some things are paid outright others are bartered. You expect to be changing things?"

"I'll change what needs changing. I'll keep what don't. Just you mind the decision is mine. I won't abide secrets. We understood?"

Johnson nodded, and urged the team to a faster pace. Crown sat back and tried to observe as much as he could, noting he had a lot to learn about McGee Farms. He fired questions faster than Karl Johnson could reply, and Crown made a mental note of each unanswered question.

By the time they turned down the last levee, the sun was high in the sky. The fog of the morning had given way to a clear day. Crown had counted eight fields, four on each side of a manmade culvert, now nearly dry. During the growing season, the ends would be dammed up with logs to retain water. Off-season though the culvert opened up into an endless sea of marsh, that also belonged to Crown. Karl Johnson explained that all the land had begun that way. It had been cleared, drained and backfilled with sand from a pit on the south end of Boone, then leveled with three feet of native gumbo clays. The soil was well suited to the rice, holding the grain and just the right amount of water until the rice was ripe and ready, then releasing the grain with ease and allowing the water to drain back to the marshes.

Dismissing an invitation to lunch, Crown dropped Johnson off at the granary and headed back through the tenants' quarters. He hoped for a glimpse of Carrie, but there was no sign of her. Instead Mae waved him to a stop from her front porch. There were four babies clinging to her various parts. The youngest suckled greedily at Mae's breast while she swatted at the next one, who being only recently displaced, was trying to reclaim one of Mae's nipples.

Mae grinned at Crown, so at home with her own body, she didn't even bother to cover her breasts. Crown looked down to keep from gawking. It unnerved him that there was still more of Mae to see than he'd seen already. He wondered if all women eventually turned into sagging, shameless creatures like Mae.

"What you pondering so, sweetie? I been wonderin' when you'd git 'round to see us."

Crown wanted to ask where Carrie was, but he was afraid Mae would ask him why he wanted to know or worse yet, laugh at him for daring to call on Carrie.

"You alone?" he managed to ask, ignoring the babies around her.

"Alone?" Mae laughed, loud but pleasant like Carrie. Crown was reminded again of the similarity between mother and daughter, and it scared him.

"I ain't been alone since me and Sam got hitched. Before I got big that first time, Sam never left me alone. Since then I always had me one or more of these younguns underfoot. I think I might like to be alone though. Just one minute. Just me and my thoughts. Yes, suh. I'd 'bout kill for a minute with nothin' and no one but me."

Mae laughed again, and Crown nodded knowing perhaps too well the peace and comfort of solitude. A barrier from the loneliness that had once threatened to suffocate him, it was the one thing that kept him safe. He had walled himself in so completely that he had forgotten what it felt like to need someone until Sister Abigail had led him outside the gates of Montagne Parish. Then he had come to McGee Farms and met Carrie Giddings and learned again what it was to want for affection and acceptance and something else, something new and unspeakable.

"You headed to home?" Mae asked.

"No. Town."

"You pick up a few things for me? I'll send the girls by for them on Sunday."

Crown looked up then and nodded perhaps a bit too eagerly. Mae rattled off a few meager wants, then sheepishly asked Crown to put them on account.

"Account?"

Mae smiled. "You best git Johnson to show you the books. I s'pect most tenants here got accounts at the farm sto', but now and then, I like to git me somethin' from town."

Once again Crown was puzzled. Didn't he pay his workers well enough and put roofs over their heads? Why shouldn't they pay outright for the things they bought? Crown wasn't sure he liked this business of accounts any more than he liked paying Nate Comeaux for shine, but he didn't want to fight with Mae. He did understand though that Mae had a need and so did he.

"I don't know about accounts, but I could use someone to help clean the place. I'll pay a dollar for Carrie and a half dollar for Jewel, if they'll give the place a good cleaning. Far as I'm concerned, you send them up and this account is set-tled."

Mae smiled. "Well, I reckon that's some deal. Yep, I'll send the girls up with Troy and Earnest on Sunday. Best not tell Carrie I bartered for her, though. By the by, them boys been doing a good job for ye?"

"Yes, ma'am. They're good workers."

"That I reckon is one thing they got from their pa. He'll work hard for ye too, Crown, and he knows rice as good as he knows me. He's been round it one way or t'other, most all his life."

Crown grunted, finding it hard to acknowledge out loud what he already knew to be true. There was much he needed to learn that wasn't in his books and no one better to learn it from than Sam Giddings.

It was already midafternoon. By the time Crown returned it would be dark, and he'd have to pick his way back home. He wished he hadn't spent so much time with Karl Johnson. He'd seen the land, but had learned little more than he already knew from the books he'd read. Anxious to be on his way, Crown flicked the reins to signal Less. More eased into a slow trot behind her.

"Don't you make a stranger, you hear," Mae called after him.

Crown turned on to Cemetery Road. With nothing to keep him company except his thoughts of Carrie, he settled into the ride.

CHAPTER 6

▼

Crown listened for Carrie above the drone of rain and the occasional clap of thunder. The storm was getting closer, and he wondered if they'd show. It had been over a month since he'd seen her. Were it not for Mae, he'd have little hope of seeing Carrie on a day like today. The bag of miscellaneous goods Mae had been so intent on still sat undisturbed on the kitchen table. More to impress Carrie than out of any affection for the others, Crown had thrown in a few extras, peppermints for Jewel, licorice for the little ones and toilet water for Mae and Carrie.

Troy and Earnest had been coming regular on Sunday afternoons, the one day of rest they had on the farm. Mae had promised that they would bring Carrie and Jewel along the next time they came. Crown had taken a bath, washed his hair, and put on the best duds he had.

He combed his hair, which tended to curl when it was wet, then rubbed his hands over his mustache and beard. Even as a youth, he had been hairy. His legs, arms and chest still bore evidence to that. He had allowed his facial hairs to grow soon after he arrived in Boone. At Montagne Parish the children had been used to his odd looks, and Sister Abigail had insisted that he be clean shaven, but in Boone he had been the subject of stares, taunts and cruel jokes. He found the mustache and beard made it easier to walk amongst the townspeople without drawing undue attention to his deformity.

When Crown was as satisfied as he could be with his appearance, he sat in the study reading and pretending he didn't have a care in the world with everyone else to do his bidding. But now it was raining with the threat of a storm, and Crown wasn't sure they'd be coming.

The old clock chimed, and he looked at his watch out of habit. Then someone slipped wet hands over his eyes. He tensed then relaxed.

"Crown I swear if I'd been up to no good you'd a been a goner. Whut you readin' got you so tied up you can't tell who's comin' or goin'?"

Crown put the book down, conscious that he hadn't been reading.

"Don't you knock?"

"What I'm go'n' knock for? Didn't you ask us to come?"

"You bring Jewel along?"

"Wasn't it you asked for me and Jewel? Wasn't it you told Mama you wanted us to come give the house a good cleanin'? By the by, we do the same work for the same wage. Jewel works just as hard as me and maybe harder. 'Cause when she's singing, time just flies, and she don't seem to know she's working at all. You pay a dollar for both. Take it or leave it."

"Fine. Troy and Earnest with you?"

"How else you think we come? They reckoned they'd best do some weedin' while the ground was soft. Now if you're through takin' roll, whar you want us to start?"

"In the parlor, I guess. And I don't want Jewel in this room."

"Suit yourself. But the cleanin' goes betta with two. Anythin' else?"

"No, just mind you keep an eye on her."

"When you go'n' learn she's harmless?"

"I don't aim to argue with you today, Carrie."

"Then don't."

She turned and left before he could answer. He felt warm inside though just knowing she was there. He picked up the almanac and began to read in earnest.

An hour later the house shook with thunder. Outside the gabled windows, the day was dark, pierced only by sporadic lightning. Crown could see Troy and Earnest running toward the barn as the wind whipped water around their legs. The trees shuddered and bent. The house groaned. Crown laid the book aside and rose to check on Carrie.

He found her kneeling on the kitchen floor. She was scrubbing intently, while Jewel cowered in a corner, mindful of the storm.

"Ya'll alright in here?"

Carrie looked up at him and pushed the hair from her face with the back of her hand.

"Storm's kickin' up somethin' awful ain't it? Troy and Earnest said we'd have to ride it out here. They got some chores they can do in the barn. With no whar to go, me and Jewel ought have no trouble gittin' done."

"Don't look like Jewel's much of a help."

"Jewel never did like storms. I find 'em peaceful though. Good for workin' indoors."

Carrie sat back on her haunches. "You hungry? A hot bowl of soup sounds good don't it?"

"I reckon. I got some potatoes, wild onions, and a bit of beef."

Carrie's eyes glistened. "Beef?"

"Payment for old Widow Duncan's funeral. They slaughtered that old cow of hers. Gave me a side of beef. Wasn't much to her. Might be a bit tough. But it'll do."

"I'm bout done here. I'll git that soup started in a minute."

"I'll cut a bit of that beef for you."

Crown retrieved a package from the ice chest and unwrapped it on the kitchen counter. He took his time selecting the choicest cut of a poor slab of meat. He carved a thin slice, just enough to flavor the soup. He slapped the slice of meat against the counter a time or two to ease the toughness then left it steeping in a pot of water for Carrie.

He was about to return the rest of the meat to the chest. Then reminded of Carrie's enthusiasm, he cut the slab in half. Beneath the counter, he found cheesecloth, string and fresh paper to wrap the two slabs. When he was done, he put the meat back in the chest, reminding himself to add a slab of the meat to Mae's bag before the girls left.

Satisfied, he returned to his study, but he couldn't concentrate, at least, not on the weather or farming or rice. In a few minutes he heard the chop, chop of a dull knife. Before long, Carrie was calling him to supper.

"Don't mind if I take Troy and Earnest a bit of this soup do you?"

She had stretched it, and Crown could see there was more than enough for the lot of them. He nodded, then reconsidered.

"You going out in this storm?"

"How else they go'n' git it?"

"I'll take it." Crown rose gruffly, aware he'd look like a wet hen and smell worse when he got back. But he hoped Carrie would be more grateful for the kindness and less concerned about the way he looked.

By the time Crown got back, Carrie and Jewel were nearly done. He was annoyed that Carrie hadn't bothered to wait, but he said nothing.

Carrie rose when he entered. "I kept the pot hot for you. Jewel and me, we just about done. We'll be gittin' back to our chores, but I thank you for the suppa. I'll clean this mess when I'm done."

Crown nodded. He'd hoped for a bit of her company, but the storm showed no sign of easing, and he half expected they'd have to spend the night. He'd have plenty of time with her when the chores were done. Restless, he ate hurriedly then cleaned the kitchen, anxious that nothing else occupy Carrie's time.

It was a while before she appeared again, looking worn and frazzled. "Ooooo this is a heap a place to clean. You best git someone regular, else it'll end up just the way it started."

"Job's yours if you want it." Crown answered hurriedly.

"Once a week ought to do. That suit you?"

Crown grunted, having no words for what he felt about the chance to see Carrie regularly.

"I'll take that for a yes. We'll come up on Sundays with Troy and Earnest same as today. By the by, you got a key for the rooms upstairs?"

"No," Crown lied.

Well we go'n' turn in. You got a place for us?"

"Suppose so."

Crown hadn't thought where they'd sleep. He hadn't thought of sleeping at all. "You can take the room across from mine."

"That'll do nice, thanks. The boys'll do fine in the barn I s'pect. You git some rest too now you hear. That storm's liable to be rockin' through the night. You best sleep while you can."

Disappointed, Crown retired too. He lay awake, naked to the waist, the hairs on his chest prickling. He lay there getting accustomed to the idea of Carrie coming regularly. He was drifting to that quiet state just before sleep, when he heard her. He turned to see her standing in his doorway all lit up in the lightning.

"Crown, you sleep?"

"No. You?"

"Was. Jewel couldn't sleep. I just got her back to bed, but now I'm all coiled up like a spring inside."

Paralyzed, he lay there, afraid she'd come nearer. Afraid she wouldn't.

"Want to talk?"

"Talk. What you got to talk about, Crown?"

"Ain't got nothing to talk about. You the one can't sleep."

"You're an ornery cuss, sunup or sundown."

The earth shook. Across the hall Jewel whimpered.

"I best git back to Jewel."

Come back when she's settled, Crown wanted to say, but he didn't. Instead he lay there listening to the storm pass. He lay there while morning broke, and

Carrie slipped quietly out of the house leaving only her bare footprints on the dew-covered grass. He awoke to the certainty that the house was empty, and he was alone again with that nagging desire and the realization that the slab of beef he'd cut just for Carrie was still in his ice chest.

CHAPTER 7

▼

It had been a bountiful harvest, even better than the year before, and Crown was proud. He had a feel for the land, and with each success, his confidence had grown. With two years of studying and hard work, the farm was prospering. What Crown couldn't find in books and journals, he had gathered in the grain market in Boone, shuffling around the White owners like any laborer, inconspicuous and ignored.

Other than the John Deere tractors that he bought to replace the teams of oxen used for plowing, Crown hadn't made many changes in those first two years. He'd been content to study the land and the rice and the manual techniques Jebediah had employed ten years past due. With the money from this harvest though, Crown had already ordered one thresher and set aside monies for another.

He'd put just as much of his heart and labor into restoring the manor. What he couldn't do with sweat and paint and nails, Carrie had done with far less.

Carrie and Jewel would come up before dawn, finishing just in time to freshen up before their cousin Lenetta would pull up to the house in a rickety wagon already full of Giddings. They would head for church leaving Crown with the sounds of their raucous laughter and the scent of pine oil and lemons still clinging to the house.

Crown admired the way Carrie had haggled with him for even wages for Jewel. And he had to admit Jewel was a hard worker most days. Crown had gotten a bargain with the two of them. There was nothing Jewel wouldn't do at Carrie's bidding. Together they had turned the drab house into something Crown could almost call home.

Salvaging what she could, Carrie washed the lace curtains until Crown was afraid what remained would fall apart. Crown had fetched and emptied buckets of water before Carrie was satisfied. She stitched tie backs by hand with remnants she'd instructed Crown to buy at the mercantile. She had beaten the throw rug and hung it in the sun to bleach it clean again. Together, Carrie and Jewel had stripped the floors and oiled them till they shone.

Crown looked over the house once more before dimming the hall lantern. Like Jebediah, the estate had wasted with age. Crown could see Jebediah clearly, in declining health and mental capacity. The house had reeked of it, soiled linens, liniment, molded food and dust. But with Carrie's touch, it had started to look like a house, if not a home. For a day or so after she'd leave, it smelled like her. And for a time, it seemed warm. Then the days would go by, and Crown would be alone and cold again.

Just about Halloween that first year, Jewel had taken an awesome fear of him. Seemed that Troy and Earnest had all but said Crown was the Boogie Man. Jewel stayed clear of him and most days, Carrie said she had to near drag Jewel down to his place. But when Crown suggested that Carrie leave Jewel behind, Carrie wouldn't even consider it. Carrie nursed this unreasonable guilt, blaming herself that Jewel was like she was. It didn't seem to matter that Carrie had been barely knee-high and that Sam and Mae had no right giving a child the responsibility for birthing their passel of babies. All Carrie would say was that Jewel was a might prettier and could have been a might brighter, if Carrie hadn't been so clumsy.

Crown studied his reflection in the ornate hall mirror. Carrie and Jewel had polished it until the brass regained its orange luster. He almost looked handsome. In the dim light his deformity was well hidden behind a finely groomed and oiled mustache and beard. Still he knew it was there, and he couldn't imagine Carrie Giddings would want to kiss what lay behind all that hair.

"You goin' to the dance?" Carrie had asked as casually as if she were asking about the weather.

"Don't think so," he'd answered nonchalantly at the time. But Crown had taken Carrie's inquiry as invitation, and he was fraught with visions of her in his arms.

In the end he'd decided to go. He'd had a time finding something suitable to wear. He'd never been to a dance, but he finally decided it didn't matter what he wore. The only thing that mattered was whether or not he impressed Carrie.

Studying his reflection once more, Crown wondered how Carrie could not be repulsed by him. He sighed, pulled on his jacket, gave it a crisp tug, and left.

The January air was brisk, and he stiffened against it. He'd already hitched the team and laid a pile of fresh blankets in the wagon. He'd ask Carrie to take a ride with him. He'd bundle her in the blankets so she'd be cozy and warm. Then he'd show her McGee Farms like she'd never seen it before. Like it could be hers someday, if she would only be his.

She'd turned eighteen before his eyes, and what had been scrawny had filled out nicely till he could barely contain the fire she ignited each time he saw her. He kept wishing he could get sick just so she could tend to him again. He imagined her hands, tender and warm washing him gently, massaging his skin and ... He sighed. He wasn't sure he could go through with it. If she rejected him, it would hurt like hell. He'd have to crawl back under the rock he'd come out of. He'd have to hate her like he hated everyone else.

He came to the farm too quickly. His fear balled up inside as he passed Sam Giddings' house. It was dark, like all the others. Everyone had left. Crown had hoped Jewel would stay home this time. But it looked like even baby Crown was going to the dance tonight. Crown still couldn't believe Mae Giddings had named that baby after him or that Carrie had suggested it. What he could believe was that Sam Giddings had pitched a fit though to no avail and Crown had dug one more pit out of Sam's pride.

The night was dark, the moon absent, the stars distant and dim, augmenting Crown's solitude. He had always felt at peace with it, until he met Carrie. She made him want the mundane things that common men wanted—a woman, a child, a family. He turned into the farm where lights danced, titillating him with promise he knew could only bring regret.

He'd walk through the doors and people would nod respectfully, though without warmth or welcome. He'd hold his head high satisfied with the warm greetings he'd get from Carrie and Mae. He'd watch Carrie dance, and when she was tired, he'd take her out in the cold and cover her in his blankets and take her for that ride.

CHAPTER 8

▼

Crown didn't think Carrie would ever get tired of dancing. It seemed every widower, bachelor and boy wanted to swing her around that floor. She was dressed like usual. They all were. There was no such thing as a change of clothes or a decent pair of shoes. But they all wore happy like they didn't scrape their scanty living on Crown McGee's farm.

Carrie wore happy better than the rest. Crown had never seen her unhappy, peeved yes, and usually at him, but never unhappy. She seemed to take life like it was a game and she was winning no matter what happened just as long as she was in the game.

But tonight she looked different, like she was some damned fairy tale princess, and this was her ball except the fairy godmother wiped the smut off Carrie's face then forgot to give her that carriage and gown and the glittery slippers.

Crown stood on the edge of life wishing he could sweep Carrie Giddings into his arms and take her home with him. Instead he had to endure Karl Johnson's endless chatter about rice and weather.

Finally Carrie stopped dancing, and she headed to the table spread with yams and rice dressing and pecans and greens and punch and rice pudding. She headed right to the end with the punch where Crown had staked a place. She headed toward him with her eyes on a lanky boy half a head taller than Crown with a year or more of growing yet to do and a face he didn't need to hide.

Irritated, Crown jabbed at Carrie with a cup full of punch to ease her thirst and take the shine from her brow that half-grown boy had put there.

The boy frowned. Carrie's eyes locked with Crown's. She smiled. He melted. Sweat beaded his brow, and his heart skipped when she laughed.

"I swear Crown, it looks like you need this more'n I do. But thanks."

She put the mason jar to her lips, and it could have been a goblet filled with ruby wine, the way her lips pressed to the glass and her throat lifted revealing the line of her neck and a hint of her nubile breasts.

She lowered the glass and fanned her hands at her face. "I know it's January, but I swear it's July in here."

Seizing the opportunity, Crown reached for her. He threaded his arm in hers before the fear could paralyze him, before the boy could even fathom what she'd said let alone what to do about it. Crown started walking, leaving the boy standing with a puzzled look on his face.

"Crown McGee, what's got into you?" Carrie asked taken aback.

Crown didn't answer. He just headed for the closest door. It led out back, which wasn't the right direction since the wagon was parked and waiting out front, but Crown was as hot as he'd ever been, and if he didn't hurry and get out of that place he'd suffocate.

Out back, Troy and Earnest tended a hog gutted, stuffed with onions and apples and pitted end to end, a twine of sugar cane and wild onions its final indignity. Earnest stoked the fire, while Troy turned the spit and basted the pig with a sticky concoction of molasses and moonshine. Roasted skin hung from its loins, dripping juices that sent the flames roaring up toward the puffed, spitted carcass. Men and boys, mouths salivating, gathered round, enduring the heat and sparks.

Crown took a quick detour around the granary. "Too hot here," he grunted.

Carrie strained to keep up with him. He was walking so furious and fast her feet barely touched the ground. He felt like he'd lifted her into the air and was flying away with her.

"Crown, slow down. I'm hot as hell, and you ain't makin' it any betta. What the devil is wrong with you?"

On the north side of the granary, the wind cut through his jacket and stole some of his warmth. Crown slowed so Carrie could feel it too. So she'd want to sit close to him in that wagon, all snuggled under his blankets. So she'd ...

"Well Crown McGee, you took me from hot to freezin', and you ain't said a word yet."

"You said you were hot, so I thought you could use some air. I thought you might take a ride with me. You know to see the farm."

"So you're doin' my thinkin' now. Well I seen this farm every day of my eighteen years. What you go'n' show me on this moonless night I ain't seen b'fo'."

She was teasing, and Crown knew it. His face burned beneath his bearded, sable skin.

"I s'pect you seen it enough too by now. So what do you really want, Crown?"

Crown lowered his head. He didn't know how to tell her. He didn't know what she'd say, and he couldn't face it here so close to people the way they were. He wanted her alone, where she'd be the only one who could hear his words or see his shame when she rejected him.

"Ne'er mind. I'll take that ride with you. I just need to find Jewel that's all."

"No, I … I need to talk to you private. Please, Jewel'll be fine. Just a few minutes. I got blankets in the wagon to take the bite out of this chill. I won't take you far. I won't keep you long. Jewel'll be fine till then."

"Can't it keep till tomorrie? We'll be out at your place first thing. Soon as we recover from tonight anyhow."

From the pity in Carrie's eyes, Crown knew he looked desperate. He hated pity, but he couldn't help himself.

"All right," she consented, and he hadn't uttered a word, just stood there with his arm in hers and his hands in his pockets and his head down against the cold.

"Wagon's out front."

Crown had lost his ability to say more than a few words at a time. How'd he ever tell her how he felt? How'd he ever ask her to come home with him and warm his bed and make him feel human every day, not just once a week when she came cleaning?

As they walked, Carrie chattered, throwing in the occasional barb.

"Crown, when you go'n' git a car? Pap says when you go to a town like Boone that's all you see. Course you'd have to do somethin' to that road. Why Karl Johnson just bought him the latest Model T. Danny said he'd give me a ride some day, soon as he learns how to drive her."

Crown stiffened at the mention of Danny, then Carrie melded into him. He didn't care that it was just for his warmth. He just knew it warmed him deep down inside to have her near him. It warmed him in a place he'd never been touched before.

It took an eternity to reach the wagon, and when they did he tried to lift her up but his hands were numb and nervous and he was clumsy, and she finally just did it herself. Her dress brushed his face as she rose, and he stood there for a moment just remembering it.

"Come on, Crown. It's freezin' up here!"

Her words bit into him, destroying his reverie. He climbed up beside her and fumbled with the blankets. She finally wrested them from his hands and stuffed them around her. It wasn't going as he planned. But then she leaned her head on his shoulder, and he forgot how cold he was. Crown had wanted to go slow, and he knew Less would hurry the evening, so he'd given More the lead. He gave the reigns a jerk, and More nudged forward happy to be moving instead of standing still in the chilled night air.

Crown turned down a side road that wound through the rice fields and back. The only sounds were the wind whistling unencumbered over the barren fields and the rhythmic plod of hooves on the cold hard ground.

When he'd gone far enough, he pulled to a stop and for an instant, it seemed his heart stopped too. Then his heart raced ahead of him, so when he talked he was breathless.

"Crown."

"Carrie."

"Can't see much in the dark."

"Didn't think to bring a lantern."

"Oh."

He turned to face her then, his heart nearly popping out of his chest. He leaned toward her and lifted her chin so he could see her eyes.

Carrie straightened abruptly. She turned away from Crown, causing his hand to slip from her chin.

"I should'a told Mama and Pap whar I'd be. They'll be worried. Jewel too."

"I just needed to talk to you private, Carrie."

"You said that already, Crown."

"You got a steady?"

"A steady?"

"You know, a beau?"

"Well, not that he's said so in so many words, but far as I can tell, that Danny Johnson likes me somethin' fierce."

Crown cringed. It was the second time Carrie had mentioned Danny.

"Karl Johnson's boy? You like him?"

"He's all right, I guess. I mean he's good lookin' and all and his papa's the most important man on this here farm, that is if'n we don't count you."

Carrie swung around suddenly facing Crown. Thrown off balance, he grabbed her arms to keep from falling backwards. Again Carrie shrugged him off.

"That whut you drug me out in this chill air for? You aimin' to fetch me pneumonie just 'cause you curious?"

With her hands on her hips, her head tilted up at him and her lips in a pout, Crown was tempted to kiss her. But even in the dark, Crown could see the fire in her eyes. He slid, putting a little more space between them.

"I ain't curious. I just think you could do better. You ought to be treated proper, like a lady."

"Ain't that Pap's job, Crown, decidin' what's good or betta? You aimin' to take his place?"

"What fool thing is that for you to say?"

"Who you callin' a fool? I ain't the one drug you out in the cold, lookin' like a puppy with his tail 'tween his legs, wantin' to talk private, then not talkin' at all."

"Damn you, Carrie."

"Damn you to hell, Crown McGee. Take me back where it's warm and folks got more common sense than to take a girl in the night air in her party dress."

"Party dress. Hummph. That's the same damn dress you wear every day, you moron. You think you the queen bee around here. You ain't nothing but a tenant farmer's daughter without a pot to piss in or a—"

"You take me back this minute, Crown McGee!"

Tears stung her eyes, and Crown wished he could take the words back that made her look so small and fragile. But then she steeled her quivering lip and jerked the reigns from his hands and kicked him hard as she could. He fell with a thud, barely managing to roll free of the wagon as the wheels rumbled by him.

Crown stood up slowly, easing into his anger. He dusted himself off though he couldn't see his own hands let alone the dirt that soiled his jacket and pants. He stomped down that road after his wagon and Carrie Giddings. He didn't know if he were angrier with himself or Carrie. But he did know what he'd do when he found her. He'd pick her up none too gently, shake the ornery out of her, then kiss her hard and hungry, so she knew he wanted her more than life itself.

Halfway down that road, he came upon her. She was wailing something fierce and calling him every foul name he'd ever heard and then some.

"Carrie."

She turned and looked at him, snot and tears streaming down her face. Subconsciously she wiped her nose and snorted so he almost laughed. She looked like her dumb sister Jewel that first day he'd come to McGee Farms. But he loved her even like this.

He reached out his hands. To his surprise, she scooted to the end of the wagon and let him lift her off the seat. With her feet dangling half a foot off the ground, she wrapped her arms around his neck, laid her head in the curve of his shoulder and sobbed like a baby.

Crown shuddered. He'd never wanted her more. But he stood still, his arm supporting her dainty figure, cooing softly and brushing her hair and calling her name till she calmed and slid slowly to the ground.

"You must think I'm a fool," she whispered.

"No, Carrie. Anything but that." He whispered back.

"I'm sorry."

"Me too."

"We still friends, Crown?"

He wished she'd said anything but that. He wished he could take back the night and start all over. He wished he hadn't been in such a hurry. But at least he had what he started out with, her friendship. Disappointed, Crown nodded.

"I guess we better get back, Carrie."

"Yep, they'll be worried."

He helped her back into the wagon. This time he didn't fumble. He wrapped her securely. She laid her head on his shoulder. He urged the team on, all the while wishing he could stay in that wagon with Carrie Giddings by his side, swaddled in his blankets, her head on his shoulder.

CHAPTER 9

▼

Crown and Carrie had been riding silently when they reached the last field and something cut through the wind and the plodding and the peace they had made with each other. Crown pulled the team to a stop. Ears pricked, the mare neighed softly.

"You hear that, Crown?"

"Shh."

"That's Jewel! Crown, that's Jewel!"

Carrie leapt off the wagon and tore out into the darkness of the field. Crown lit out after her, following her cries. Something or someone rustled by him, knocking him down. Crown reached, grabbed a panted leg and held for dear life. Then someone kicked him hard to the ribs on the other side. He let go of the leg and cowered as he was kicked once, twice, three times again for measure.

The wind whipped, pants rustled and a flurry of legs ran past him. Crown sat up ignoring his pain. "Carrie. Carrie." He called desperately. "Carrie."

He stumbled through the darkness till he nearly fell over her. "Carrie?"

"Oh, Crown, Crown. I wuzn't sure it wuz you. They hurt her, Crown. How could they do that to someone sweet and kind as Jewel?"

Crown reached for Carrie, but she pushed him away. She had Jewel cradled in her arms. Jewel cowered naked, shivering, scratched and bruised.

"Git the blankets, Crown."

Crown scurried back to the wagon. He grabbed the blankets and called out to Carrie. She called back, and he followed the sound of her voice.

He found them again. With Carrie's help, he wrapped Jewel in the blankets, while Carrie gently questioned Jewel.

Jewel was scared and scarred, but she hadn't really known what was happening. Just that the boys wanted to see her naked, then started pushing her back and forth and laughing like it was a game, till one of them kissed her and it felt good at first, but then they started to touch her funny, and she didn't like the game any more.

Crown felt relief when he realized Jewel hadn't really been ruined. He picked her up, all swaddled in the blankets he'd intended for Carrie.

"You ain't the Boogie Man, are you, Crown?" she asked innocent and childlike.

"No, Jewel. I ain't no Boogie Man."

"I didn't think so."

She put her thumb in her mouth and rested her head in his chest, where Carrie's should have been.

Crown sighed.

Carrie held Jewel's hand as they walked back to the wagon.

"I'm sorry, Jewel. I'm so sorry. I should have never left you. I'm sorry."

Crown stopped then.

"It ain't your fault, Carrie. You take it all in like everything depends on you. Jewel is what she is. What happened, happened."

"Crown, just take us back, please."

They rode in silence, with Jewel and Carrie's guilt between them. They reached the dancing lights. Crown was filled with sadness and regret and the renewed feeling that life was just damn cruel sometimes.

"You stay here with Jewel, Carrie. I'll get your folks."

Crown entered the granary, his eyes sweeping the maze of faces for one familiar. He found Sam Giddings first. He wished it had been Mae. Sam was full of moonshine and madness. He lunged when he saw Crown.

"Whar in hell you been with my daughter? You think 'cause you own this place, you own me and mine? I'll see you dead first. You stay away from my Carrie, you here. She don't want no part of the likes of you."

Crown almost forgot why he'd come. Then Mae touched him softly.

"Everythin' all right, Crown?"

"No. It's Jewel. She's been hurt. She's in the wagon with Carrie."

Sam's expression changed, and Crown couldn't resist the urge to jab at him yet another time.

"If you'd spend half the time tending your younguns as you spend tending that shine you'd a known where Carrie was. You'd a known she was safe with me.

And you'd had Jewel tucked safe 'cause she ain't fit to be left alone. And that ain't Carrie's fault nor burden neither. It's yours."

He said it, and he couldn't take it back, though it hurt Mae as much as it hurt Sam. It hurt them both because it was true and it had come from him.

Mae sobbed hollow and animal-like. Someone took baby Crown from her. Sam took her hand. They both looked at Crown, and he wished he could sink into the ground. Perhaps they were right. He wasn't human.

He followed them outside and so did half the granary. There weren't many who didn't love Sam and Mae Giddings. There weren't many who didn't love big, sloppy silly Jewel, "pretty as sunshine and dumb as a mule."

When they got outside Jewel was sleeping, snug in the blankets Crown meant for Carrie, snug in Carrie's arms where Crown had hoped to be.

Crown offered the Giddings a ride home. Sam refused. Mae accepted. So they all piled in the wagon behind Carrie and Jewel and Crown.

The silence was as thick as the fog that had begun to creep out of the bayou and over the farm. Crown wished again the night could be over. How'd he ever been so foolish as to think he belonged with people?

They reached Sam Giddings' place too soon. They all ambled down, hugged tight like a family with Crown licking his wounds on the wagon seat above.

"Thanks, Crown."

Carrie touched his hand lightly as she spoke. He wished she'd stop touching him. Then he said it, in front of God and Carrie and the entire Giddings clan.

"I love you Carrie, and I aim to have you."

Sam dropped Jewel. She landed safely against Mae's side. Mae cradled Jewel in one arm. She turned to Sam and reached to hold him with her free hand, but she couldn't keep his words.

"Never! You hear me. Never! You git off my place. You stay away from my family."

Crown laughed. "You mean my place, don't you?"

Mae shook her head sadly. Troy and Earnest dragged Sam inside, cussing and kicking and spitting. Only Carrie stood rooted, facing Crown with a look that nearly killed him.

"Damn you, Crown. Why you tryin' so hard to hurt a man ain't got nothin'?"

"He's got something. He's got everything I want. He's got you."

Unable to look at Carrie, Crown looked down staring at his own hands. "I ain't never been nothing, Carrie. My mama's guilt, the nuns' obligation, my papa's shame. You're the first one ever made me feel like more than that."

He sighed. He'd never said that much to anyone. Now he'd all but told her his life story. That he was nothing without her.

Carrie stood on her toes and framed his face with her hands. She brought his face to hers and melded her brow into his. He burned where her flesh touched his. He burned where it didn't. He so wanted to kiss her and for a moment he exhaled and she exhaled and their breaths met.

"Crown, I like you. I liked you from the moment I saw you. My friendship's the one thing you can count on. I swear. But … I don't love you, Crown and I got to love the one I'm with. I gotta have that to keep me goin' when life tries to take me down."

Crown let out his breath so his chest sagged, and he shrunk till he felt smaller than she was. He wanted to tell her she didn't have to love him. She just had to be with him. He got angry instead. It was the only way he knew how to fight.

He sat up tall, his chest pumped hard with venom. "I mean what I say. I'll have you, Carrie Giddings, just like I got Jebediah's land. You mark my words. You'll warm my bed come this time next winter."

Crown turned the wagon around and tore down Cemetery Road, Carrie's look of horror still etched in his mind.

CHAPTER 10

▼

Crown sat up through the night and into the next morning. He waited for Carrie and Jewel but they didn't come that day or the next. Two weeks later, old man Turner died, and Crown had a burial. Troy and Earnest showed up like usual, though they avoided him and he them.

The house grew cold and dusty. Crown kept a small fire lit, a lone lantern dimmed in the study he made home. He couldn't sleep in the bed he dreamed wet with Carrie. He couldn't lie without thinking of her, so he sat and read of politics and finance and rice farming and war. He sat and emptied his head of dreams of love and happiness. He thought only of how he'd possess Carrie Giddings like he possessed all that had been Jebediah's, the farm, the cemetery, the cold empty mansion, and even Jebediah's rotting corpse.

In time though, Crown put worry aside. Not that he'd forgotten about Carrie. Not that he wanted her any less. But he had learned that the things you want and think and dream about come about with time. He had waited nineteen years to get satisfaction from Jebediah McGee. He could bide his time for Carrie.

Crown stayed clear of the farm through the long winter. Then spring came and with it rain, cold and hard at first, then soft and warm. He drove to the farm daily, just to watch the fields swamped with water and dream of the rice piled high in his silos come fall.

He had stolen a glance or two toward the Giddings' shanty, but he hadn't spotted Carrie. It was likely she made herself scarce at the first sound of his wagon, and for the time being, that sat well with Crown. He would never give her the satisfaction of begging again. He would make her suffer, wondering when and how he'd take her.

That was something Crown had not figured out for himself. He just knew that he would, that he had to. His opportunity hit him square and hard midway through the next harvest. The rains had been hard, leaving the creeks swollen and though it hadn't rained in three days, water still dripped like sweat from the trees.

Soggy with mud, Crown had been trudging through the rain soaked cemetery making sure the headstones were secure, the coffins snug in their places. Surprised, he came upon Troy and Earnest digging vigorously near a grave they'd planted just two weeks before. They jumped when he called them, looking back and forth one to the other nervously.

"What in hell you two up to? Ain't nobody died I know of. Answer me! What ya'll doing out here?"

Troy stepped toward Crown, a shovel full of mud in his hand. "Leave us be, Crown. We ain't got nothin' agin you, but it's best you not know this bidnes."

"You planting something in my ground makes it my business."

Crown shoved Troy aside. He spotted the corpse, small, pale, white.

"What ya'll doing with that White boy?"

"Go'n' back to the house, Crown."

"Dammit, Troy, Earnest. What ya'll doing out here? You aiming to get us all killed?"

"It weren't our fault. Pap found out it was Nate Comeaux's boys done that thing to Jewel. She got all crazy like when they come over for some grain for their pap's still."

"Nate? That old moonshiner?"

"Yep. Pap, he lit out after them. Then he spotted Nate's still and got to drinkin' to git his courage up. Nate's youngest found him. Pap smothered him to keep him from hollerin' and tellin' everybody where he was. He didn't mean to. He was just tryin' to keep the boy quiet is all."

"Your damn pap ain't got the sense Jewel was born with. When ya'll go'n' figure out you best off without him?"

"Don't talk agin him like that, Crown, or I'll have to bean you. He ain't near as bad as you make him out to be. He's our pap. You can't talk agin him that way."

Crown shook his head. "So you aiming to plant this one on me. Suppose someone finds him here? Who they go'n' blame, huh? You think about that, either of you? Who they go'n' blame but you boys ... and me?"

"You got to help us, Crown. They go'n' be lookin' for this here boy."

"Help you? What you ever done for me?"

"We ain't never done nothin' agin you. And Ma and Carrie been right nice to you. Nicer than most."

Crown softened at the mention of Carrie's name. He would never get a better chance. Still he wasn't quite ready to play his hand.

"You're right, Troy. They'll come looking for that boy, and you're leading them right here to me."

"How they go'n' find him among the dead, Crown? Even dogs couldn't find him here. And with all the rain, the trail's for sure grown cold."

"You'd best be right, Troy. You best be right or it's our hides. Nothing to be done now but bury him and wait. There'll be a price to pay though. You tell your pap there'll be a price to pay, and I reckon he knows what that'll be. I'll come calling next Sunday night. I'll come calling for Carrie."

"Crown, Pap ain't go'n' let you have Carrie."

"That's what you think, Troy? Well let me tell you what I know. When it comes down to it, he'll choose himself over any one of you. He'll hand over Carrie to save his own rotten hide. I'm sure of that. I'm damned sure of that."

CHAPTER 11

▼

Crown didn't know why he'd put it off till Sunday. Maybe because he wasn't half the man he'd made out to be. Maybe because he didn't know what he'd do with Carrie when he got her.

He'd half expected Sam Giddings to show up on his doorstep, shotgun in hand. And he kept the house locked wary that he might not live to see Carrie in his bed. But Troy came back a day later telling Crown they had a deal, and that he could pick Carrie up come midnight on Sunday. Troy said the rest of them would be clearing out of Colwin County. If anyone got suspicious, they'd be looking for them, not Crown.

Sunday came crawling slow as pine sap on a winter morning. Crown took a hot bath, then shaved. He wanted Carrie to know what she'd be living with till the end of her days or his. He put on the same jacket and coat he'd worn to that cursed dance, washed and pressed best as he could with a flat iron heated on the stove.

Come eleven o'clock he hitched up his wagon and walked down the path to the gate. He turned back and looked. When he returned, Carrie would be with him. He wondered if it would look different then, not so bleak and forlorn and empty.

He opened the heavy gate and led the horses out onto the road. The horses balked a minute, not used to being unsettled so late from their stalls. Crown coaxed Less with sugar. She yielded and More followed. Crown wished it could be nearly as easy with Carrie.

Crown waited on the road till he was sure it was midnight. He approached the house wary, half expecting an ambush. It was dark, quiet. Too quiet. He wished

Carrie were standing on the porch the way she'd been the first time he'd seen her. He wished she'd smile and reach out to him the way she'd done then.

Crown knocked gently. Loose, the door swung open, bathing the one room in pale moonlight. Sweeping the room with his eyes, he entered cautiously. There was no sign of movement, no sign of life. On the table a lantern, barely lit, cast a small circle of light on a hand-scrawled note. Crown grinned wryly. Maybe Sam Giddings was smarter than Crown thought. Sam had left Crown with a White boy's body in his yard. Crown had no one and no way to tell about that body without burning his own hide. Resigned, he picked up the note and read.

> You take good care of our gal, Crown. She ain't whut you wanted, but she's better suited to you.

Not what he wanted. She was all he wanted.

> Sam said he'd kill you before he left you Carrie. But I said we owed you somethin for all you'd done. Didn't matter why you done it. That you just happened on us that night baby Crown was born or the night you and Carrie saved Jewel or the day you found Troy and Earnest buryin Nate Comeaux's boy. Seems our lives keep touchin one way or nuther, lak it was already planned.

Crown didn't believe in fate, but he had to agree with Mae. Since the day he'd met Carrie, something had taken hold of him and led him right to this moment, and he could barely contain the fire that had been smoldering and burning since.

> Carrie's pretty and smart. She can have nigh any man she wants. But Jewel. Well, Jewel's damaged like you. And she ain't afeard of you no more. Not since that night that started all this.

Jewel? Why was Mae talking about Jewel? Surely they hadn't left her too. Would he have to endure her infernal wailing and singing and fidgeting with things she had no right to? And where were they? He scanned the room again. It was empty except for a bundle, tugged snug and secure in that tattered old quilt they'd laid for a bed. His heart jumped. But where was Jewel? Crown couldn't move so he read on.

I know you ain't got much experience. A woman can tell such things. So you be gentle with her. You take her soft and slow, and she'll learn to love you. You plant your seed in the same place you seen baby Crown come out of me.

Crown grimaced. Mae's legs gapped wide and bleeding from a hole the size of a baby's head made Crown stumble back into the lone chair. He couldn't envision his Carrie looking like that. He sat and read on, too frightened yet to wake her.

She'll make ye a good wife. She's born for breedin. She can cook a little and clean too. You have Carrie to thank for that.

Why was Mae talking double? She wasn't making any sense.

God speed, Crown McGee. Haps one day we'll meet agin in this world. I trust you'll be good to my Jewel. If'n you ain't, then damn you. Damn you to hell.

Mae

Sam Giddings had gotten the last word after all. Crown read the note again then held it over the candle, watching it burn slowly until his fingers were singed. He walked over to that bundle on the floor. He looked at it for a long time, wishing, hoping it might still be Carrie. He knelt down and whispered soft, pleading.

"Carrie, Carrie. Please be Carrie."

Crown rocked back on his heels. A chill ran through him. He pulled the covers away from auburn hair, tangled and loose the way Carrie always wore hers. He brushed it back gently, revealing the lobe of an ear, a neck rising and falling with the gentle rhythm of her breathing, breasts too tight and full to be Carrie's and a face pretty as sunshine in the pale moonlight.

Crown shut his eyes tight and swore, his voice barely a whisper. He closed his eyes so he could still the headache straining at his temples, so he could think what to do about Jewel. He opened his eyes because all that squeezing was just making his stomach quiver and his veins tense and his head ache more. He opened his eyes to find Jewel staring back at him wide-eyed, like a doe at the end of a double-barreled shotgun. At the sight of Crown staring back at her, Jewel whimpered and retreated in her covers. Crown stood unsteady, his head in one hand, his belly in the other. He stumbled outside and emptied his stomach on the porch where he'd first spied Carrie.

He shook, half with anger, the other with grief. After awhile, he could feel Jewel behind him, staring at his back perhaps feeling the same thing he felt, anger, abandonment, sorrow. He turned and looked at her seeing her the way Jebediah had seen him and hating himself for it. He could almost pity her, if she weren't just another cruel joke life had played on him. He turned away again. A sob wrenched from his gut, tore through his throat and emptied his soul.

"You miss Carrie don't you? Made me downright jealous, the way ya'll'd talk and I was too dumb to join in."

Jewel took a step closer. The hairs on Crown's neck began to rise.

"I cried too. I cried so my eyes swole. I was hopin' I was a dreamin', but then I woke up and I saw you. Not that I don't like you, Crown. I just miss my Mama and Carrie and the boys and Pap."

Jewel sobbed. "But Mama says I'm to go with you now. She says I'm Crown's Jewel. And not to be a bother and do what you say and stay out yo' way."

Crown turned to face her. He had never spoken more than necessary to her. Mostly she'd been afraid of him until that night. He'd made himself scarce since.

He realized he'd never thought of her as a person. She was just Carrie's dumb sister Jewel. He didn't want to think of her now.

"Well come on."

The words came from nowhere, like someone else was living his life and he was standing by watching. He walked down the porch and climbed aboard the wagon.

Jewel followed close behind. She looked up at Crown, uncertain. Crown looked down at her, wishing one last time she were Carrie. Something left him then, left him hollow and cold. He sighed.

"Get in the back. I'll wake you when we get there."

Jewel did as she was told. She curled up in a ball behind him, like she wanted to get close to something human, even if it was only him.

Muddled by the sway of the wagon and Jewel's unconscious whimpering, Crown couldn't think. Before he knew it, he was home. The moon sprawled headstones across the shadowed ground. Crown dismounted and stood haunted by the notion that he was more comfortable with the dead than the living. He opened the gates and led the horses down a narrow path that wound through the graveyard.

Crown was suddenly tired, too tired to put the wagon up and bed the horses, as he should. When he reached the clearing, he unhitched the horses, shooing them away from the graveyard. Then he woke Jewel.

At first Jewel wouldn't leave the wagon. She looked at Crown as though he really were the Boogie Man. Exasperated, Crown pulled a paralyzed Jewel to the ground beside him. An owl whooed and swooped overhead. Not a second later the owl's supper screeched, and Jewel began to wail piteously.

Crown sighed. Why hadn't he left her there? It would have served Sam Giddings right. But something told him he had won after all. He had something Sam Giddings loved, even if it wasn't his blessed Carrie. Even if it was something Crown despised. It was the thing Carrie loved most.

Less had not gone far. She returned and nibbled anxiously at Crown's pockets, but he had nothing for her. He gave her a slap that sent her scurrying away from the treacherous maze of headstones, then started toward the house. Jewel moved then, clinging to him so he could barely walk.

They entered the house, dark except for the lone lantern he'd left. He turned it up and showed Jewel to the room just across from his. It smelled of emptiness and disuse. She shook her head no and clung to him. He pushed her firmly inside, closed the door and locked it. She wailed, pounding and scratching at the door.

Crown's head pounded too. He turned to his own room, closed the door and crawled into bed. He covered his head with a pillow, but he couldn't muffle out Jewel. He waited her out for an hour. He didn't think it was humanly possible for anyone to carry on so long.

Exhausted, he made her a pallet on the floor at the foot of his bed, then went to fetch her. He fumbled with the key. She stopped wailing. He opened the door, and she looked at him, snot and tears mixing into one fine mess on her face.

"Come on."

Jewel followed obediently. In his room, Crown pointed to the pallet. She went to it, curled in a ball and fell fast asleep. Crown looked at her awhile, wondering how he'd manage with a moron like her, with no more help from Troy and Earnest and not even a hope to warm him at night. He wondered himself to sleep, with his head pounding and his stomach quivering and his heart cold.

CHAPTER 12

▼

There it was again, invading what had at last become a deep if not peaceful sleep. Jewel stopped in the middle of the verse and began again with the chorus. She sounded neither blessed nor assured, but shrill and mournful. Crown groaned and covered his head. A pot clanged against the stove. A spoon licked the sides of a wooden bowl. A dish clattered on the kitchen table.

Crown turned over and rubbed his eyes, glued with matter still thick and wet from too few hours of sleep. He rolled to the edge of the bed and sat up, surprised to find he'd slept in his clothes. Only his brogans lay tumbled on the oak floor.

The odor of coffee, hot and fresh, invited on the gray September morning. A body of clouds hung low and heavy in the sky, promising an early, cold rain. Crown had three burials coming in two days, a young mother and infant, an old widow and a hobo who'd been a mite too slow hitching a ride on the Beaumont freighter. There was no one to dig the graves now but Crown. He should have been up before the cock crowed, but he hadn't worried about that when he thought he'd be bringing Carrie home.

Crown put on his shoes and rolled his head, but the tension would not ease. It gathered at the base of his skull and radiated up to his temples where he could feel his veins pulsing.

Jewel must have sensed it for she looked at him tentatively as he entered the kitchen. "Pap says I kin fix up a mean mess a oats when I a mind to. You want me to fix you a bowl?"

"I'll just have some coffee."

Crown helped himself to coffee while Jewel sopped her oatmeal with a chunk of bread. When she finished, she opened the back door and emptied her bowl into the slop bucket.

She started clearing the kitchen and humming that tune. Crown stood up abruptly, slamming his fist against the table and nearly toppling the cup of coffee. The cup clattered on the table, sprinkling drops of hot coffee on his hand. "You got a right to your mood, Jewel, but you got no right to bore me with it."

Nursing his scalded hand, Crown stomped out of the kitchen and out the back door. He swung the door wide, letting it slam shut behind him. The day loomed heavy beneath a fog so dense Crown could barely find his way. He grabbed the slop bucket and headed across the yard in the direction of the pen. Catching scent of the slop, the hogs grunted. Crown leaned against the fence and tossed the slop into the pen. Reluctant to go back to the house and Jewel, he hung the bucket on the fence and marched around the house and across the front yard. The chickens squawked nervously and scattered to get out of his way. He slowed out of necessity, groping his way to the barn door.

In the barn, he grabbed some feed and went back to the yard, cooing and tossing feed randomly to the chickens. The hens hesitated briefly then pecked voraciously at the food. The cantankerous old rooster was nowhere in sight.

Crown whistled for Less and More. They came trotting. Less was spirited as usual and More was in a good mood. Crown coaxed the horses back to the wagon. Neither horse balked when Crown hitched them to the wagon and led them back to the barn. He gave them food and water. While they ate he stowed the harnesses and raked the barn. Afterwards, rewarding them for their cooperation, Crown brushed Less and More.

By the time he was done, the fog had begun to lift. He donned thick gloves and grabbed a shovel, hoe and wheelbarrow and headed for the graveyard. He didn't mind hard work, but digging and hauling for three graves was no small task, and he had already lost time. He dug the grave for Missy Hebert and her stillborn first. He stabbed with the blade end of the shovel to loosen the compact soil. Soon he eased into the work, breaking the earth and the stubborn roots of trees cleared just a month ago.

He dug the pauper's grave next, just a three foot hole in the back section of the graveyard. The undertaker used the same plain pine box to cart paupers to the cemetery. Rolled in a sheet, the body would be dumped in the grave and the casket returned. Crown dug the hole just deep and wide enough to protect the carcass from scavengers.

By midafternoon, Crown was aching, thirsty and hungry, and he still had another grave to dig. He shadowed his eyes and surveyed the house but with Jewel there, and Carrie lost to him forever, his own house offered neither peace nor refuge. Instead he returned to his labor and the promise of a hot bath when he was done.

It took longer to dig the last grave than it had taken to dig either of the other two. Mrs. Marjorie Provost had picked the solitary spot beneath a grove of trees, just three weeks before her death. She'd paid for three adjacent plots and the clump of trees too, saying she didn't want to be bothered with company or too much sun while she waited for the afterlife. The ground proved hard and unyielding. Crown was worn. By the time he finished, the first shadow of dusk had appeared. He threw gloves, hoe and shovel into the wheelbarrow. Despite a slight chill, he pulled his shirt over his head and tossed it into the barrel. If Jewel weren't there he'd have stripped naked and run back to the house in the chill air, but as it was, he'd have to haul the stench in with him. He imagined that Carrie would have had the sense to draw him a warm bath and set a place at the table with a pot of warm coffee to loosen his stiff joints. He had no idea what Jewel had been doing all day, and he was afraid to find out. He hoped she was at least good for washing.

Crown dragged into the house full of venom from too little sleep and too much work. His head was beginning to pound again. Thankfully, he didn't hear either Jewel's infernal singing or one of the mindless conversations she had with herself. Surprised to find the house quiet, Crown called to Jewel, but she didn't answer. She wasn't in the kitchen or his study or the room he'd given to be hers. He half hoped she'd wandered off. Surely she knew the way home, but then he should have seen her pass. Crown shrugged, only slightly concerned, and assured of his privacy, he dropped his trousers, johns and woolen socks in a heap on the floor.

He lit the fireplace and hung a huge pot of water to boil. He pulled the tub out on the kitchen floor and pumped a foot of water into it. Then he strained the morning's coffee and set it on the stove to warm.

He almost fell asleep in the chair he was so tired, but finally he poured the hot water into his bath. It steamed, warming him all over, even before he stepped in. He danced a bit, then sat down gingerly enjoying the prickle of heat against his skin. He lay back and slept.

Crown awoke to the feel of warm hands, gentle against his back. Everywhere else he felt cold. Groggy, he yawned and opened his eyes. He'd been dreaming of Carrie. Awake, his lust for her struck anew. Reality replaced fantasy. To Crown's horror, Jewel was washing his back. She was quiet for a change. Crown followed the angle of her gaze to the tangled patch of hair between his thighs. Crown's knees shot up to his chest; his palms covered his groin.

"Whut's the matta wit you, Crown? I done seen a plenty of them things before. I got me nine brothers you know. And if dey ain't a seein' who can piss the farthest, dey's a playin' with it, seein' if n it'll stand up stiff and tall like yours. Whut you s'pect makes it do that?"

She sat back on her knees and dropped the sponge into the tub. It plopped into Crown's lap splashing soapy water into his face. He squinted but didn't dare move.

Jewel stood, leaned back into her own hands and stretched. "I s'pect you clean enough now. You want I should wash those ditties for you? I's pret' near as good as Carrie with washin'. I'll scrub a hole in 'em fo' I see em' dirty. Whar's your shirt? I'll clean it too."

"In the barn," Crown whispered shyly. He was fully awake now, and to his shame, he had started to harden beneath the gentleness of her touch and the innocence of her talk. He groaned. She was too damned young and daft to understand.

"Get out of here, Jewel. Ain't you got no sense at all. You ought not be bathing a grown man. You ought not be looking at him naked as the day he was born."

"Why?"

"I said get."

"All right, I'm gittin'. I just thought I'd he'p you out dat's all."

"You want to help, you get those clothes washed and dried before day tomorrow. That's all the help I need."

"Carrie was right about you, Crown. She said you wuz the orneriest cuss she ever knowed. How come ya'll so ornery?"

"Get, Jewel. Go on now. Get."

Crown waited until he heard the screen door creak on its hinges and slam shut. He jumped out of the tub and scurried into his room. He could tell the way the linens were jumbled that Jewel had been lying there. She must have been there asleep when he came in. He couldn't blame her. She'd spent her entire life on a worn out quilt on a hardwood floor. It must have felt good to have a cotton tic and space between her and the floor. He pressed his hand to the covers, but they were long cold. He dressed hurriedly in a fresh pair of long johns and overalls. He was afraid Jewel would barge in any minute and see him stretched full and naked. He blushed a little thinking of it, but he suspected she would think nothing of it.

Crown stood by the door awhile, but there was no sign of Jewel. He settled into his study intending to read a little but his eyelids grew heavy and his arms soon fell idle. After a while, the book slipped from his hands and hit the floor with a dull thud. Crown startled and cursed. The book was bent at the corners. He pressed with his thumbs trying vainly to recover the sharp edges. It had grown dark, and still he couldn't hear Jewel. He walked to the door and called to her.

When she didn't reply, Crown lit the hall lantern bright and stepped out onto the porch that wound around the house. He called Jewel again, but only the owl answered. He looked into the sky, but it was as black as the moonless night, and if there were one cloud or many, he could not tell. Calling to Jewel, Crown walked toward the barn. He was about ten paces from the entrance when she appeared in the doorway. He held the lantern up to see tears streaming down her face. She wiped her nose the way she'd done when he first saw her.

"Jewel, why don't you come when you're called?"

She sniffled and answered, dumb struck that he'd asked. "Ain't you got no sense at all. I'm afeard of the dark."

"Then why didn't you come in while it was still light?"

She shook her head and pointed a finger at him accusingly. "You ought not send me out here all alone so nigh to dark. You ought knowed I'd be afeard. Carrie would never leave me alone. Carrie would never do that."

"Well I ain't your Carrie, and I ain't about to baby sit you every step of every day."

Jewel pouted. Crown cursed.

"Hell. Come on in now. We best get some supper and go to bed."

"Ain't hungry."

"Suit yourself. But I'm not about to stand out here arguing with you. You can come or you can stay. Makes no matter to me."

Jewel covered the ground in seconds, grabbing Crown's arm and throwing him off guard. "I told you I's afeard. I just ain't hungry that's all."

"You been sleeping in my bed?"

Jewel stopped suddenly. Crown could almost hear her heart beat. She peered at him, doe-eyed. "I didn't mean to. I just sat down for a minute. Then the next thing I know I was lying down—it being a bed and all. And once I lay down it just come on me nat'ral. Next thing I knew, half the day was gone."

"You could sleep like that every night if you had a mind to. There's one just like it in the room across the hall."

"I ain't used to sleepin' all alone," she answered stubbornly.

"So you said. But I'm not about to give up my bed when I've offered you a bed of your own just like it. Most folks'd be glad to have a room of their own."

"I ain't most folks."

"No you ain't at that," Crown mocked. "You ain't at that."

Crown led the way back to the house with Jewel clinging to his arm and occasionally stumbling over the backs of his heels. He tried to pry her hands free, but she clung to him, releasing him only when she was safe inside the kitchen. She sat at the table while he fixed a simple supper of bread and canned beans. He filled a bowl with the beans and held it out to her, but she just wrinkled up her nose.

"Ain't you at least go'n' put some salt pork in dem beans? How you eat 'em right outta the can like dat? Gran says dat ain't even real food."

"Where am I gonna get salt pork?"

"Don't you know nothin? Why it ain't nothin' but the fat the rich folks always leavin'. Most of the time dat's the closest we eva got to a piece of meat. Ain't much to it, but boy can it flavor a pot of greens or pinto beans."

"I know what it is. I just ain't got any." Crown answered annoyed. He'd slaughtered his own hog, trimmed the fat and used it to make tallow for more useful things like candle wax, soap and lard.

Jewel rocked in the chair, smiling and reminiscing. "Seems like Pap always knew who was slaughterin'. From time to time he'd come home with some maws or pigs' feet or chit'lin's. Boy would we eat good den."

Crown wrinkled up his nose. He'd smelled chitterlings cooking in the quarters on more than one occasion. His stomach turned at the mere mention of the wiggly concoction. It turned again when he remembered why the poor man's delicacy of pig's intestines smelled so bad.

Crown's austere childhood had been filled with hard work and devoid of play, but he had never gone to bed hungry. The nuns raised chickens and hogs. Seasonally the children baited strings with gizzards and caught crayfish in the local bayou. Grown in the parish's own gardens, fresh vegetables were plentiful. Berries and peaches grew in the orchard. Goats and cows supplied milk, butter and cheese.

Despite emotional hardships, Crown had never gone without basic material things. Jebediah's checks had kept him housed, clothed and fed. Crown didn't know what it was like to crave other people's garbage. At times his bitterness seemed misplaced among the tenants and locals who made their living directly or indirectly from McGee Farms. Like the Giddings, they worked hard and played harder, happy and spiritual in the midst of poverty.

Crown wished he could be more like them, but he wasn't ready to forgive Jebediah. Had Crown been different, Carrie might have been his. The thought nagged him. Crown picked at his food. Jewel reached across the table and tore a chunk off of Crown's bread.

"I thought you weren't hungry," Crown remarked annoyed.

"I ain't. It's just hard sittin' here watchin' another body eat."

While Jewel nibbled on the piece of bread, Crown finished the bowl of beans. "Go on to bed, Jewel," he said when he was done. "I'll clean up here."

"You comin'?"

"I'll be in directly."

He cleaned his plate and put the dishes away. Though he was tired enough to fall asleep where he stood, he didn't hurry. He didn't know which was worse, Jewel's constant chattering or her snoring. By the time he dimmed the lanterns and crawled into bed, Jewel was asleep. Despite her snoring, he soon slept too.

CHAPTER 13

▼

Half asleep, half awake, Crown lay in bed pondering what to do about Jewel. A light tapping on the front door reminded him that he had a funeral. Startled, Crown peered out the bedroom window, but it was still dark outside. Snoring loudly, Jewel did not stir. Crown sat up, swung his legs over the side of the bed and bent to pick up his shoes. With his shoes in hand, he walked quietly out into the hall, checked over his shoulder to make sure Jewel was still asleep, then softly closed the door. Crown lit a lantern, walked down the hallway, and opened the front door. Lanky Ned Turner, the local undertaker, peered back at Crown through the screen.

"McGee?"

Crown stepped out on the porch. In a few hours the mourners would arrive. Afraid Jewel would wake up and wander outside where someone might see her, Crown locked the door behind him. He should have talked to her the night before instead of hurrying her off to bed. They'd have that talk tonight or he'd spend another day dodging and worrying.

Ned eyed Crown curiously. Crown followed Ned's gaze from the shoes Crown still held in his hand down to his bare feet. Embarrassed, Crown sat down on the steps, pulled his socks out of his shoes and donned them. He stood up and stepped into his shoes, then felt a sudden urge. He excused himself and went around to the side of the house to drain his bladder. When Crown came back, Ned looked impatient. Crown led Ned away from the house and out to the graveyard.

Ned followed, walking bow-legged and stooped. "Which of these holes is meant for Missy and her baby?"

"That one over there." Crown pointed to a single grave in a clearing. "They in the same box?"

Ned nodded. "Where's Troy and Earnest?"

"They ain't here."

"I can see that," Ned stated annoyed. "Who's go'n' fill these graves?"

"I guess it's up to you and me."

Ned looked down at his starched suit. "I don't usually do that sort of thing."

"Well I'm short handed for the moment. Unless you want me to rig Less and More to the casket in the middle of the service, you'll help."

Ned swore. "I got to git back to town. We'll be in before noon. If Troy and Earnest ain't go'n' be back, you consider gittin' some help. It just ain't proper me lowerin' the casket. Family needs some separation, a way to know it's time to say goodbye. When the boys lower that casket and shovel that first clod of dirt that tells the grieving it's time to go. I'm the one makes sure they do. Not the reverend, but me. I usher them home so ya'll can do the job what needs to be done. Ain't right any other way."

Ned studied Crown awhile, but Crown had no response. "How 'bout I stop by the farm and rustle up Troy and Earnest?" Ned offered. "Ain't like them to forget a funeral. Hell, the hole's been dug. I reckon they just overslept."

"No," Crown exclaimed, then caught himself. "I told you they were gone. Why don't you send old Ben over. That's all the help I need."

"Suit yo'self. I'll find Ben and send him right over."

"Tell him not to hurry. Like you said, the hole is already dug." Crown watched until Ned's wagon was out of sight, then Crown hurried back to the house to have that talk with Jewel.

Jewel was still asleep, but Crown roused her. He needed to make sure she understood. She woke up and stared at him round eyed and confused. Her auburn hair tumbled recklessly about her head. She rubbed her eyes.

"Mornin', Crown."

"Mornin'," he grumbled. "I got funerals today and tomorrow. I'm waking you so you'll know. You stay to the house. Keep inside. Don't light no fires. You get hungry, there's bread and cheese and canned peaches and milk."

"Who's funeral? Missy? I liked Missy. Feel sorry for dem kids though. They orphans twice over. Well, they still got their pa, but I ain't never met a pa could hold a candle to a ma."

"You listening to me, Jewel? Nobody knows you're here, and I plan to keep it that way. Why you think Sam and Mae cut out like they did? Sam did something bad. If they find you here, they'll start to figure things out. That'll mean big trouble for your pap. You want that?"

Jewel shook her head.

"You hide out here the next two days till I can figure something out. Something better for you and me. Till then you have to hide."

Jewel smiled. "But who's go'n' come and find me?"

"What?"

"Who's go'n' find me?"

Crown frowned. She thought it was a silly child's game. Instead it was his whole life. "I'll come find you when my work is done."

Jewel smiled. "I can hide good. I can hide so good, you won't be able to find me."

Crown ate a quick breakfast and left Jewel to play her game. He locked the door behind him, grabbed a couple of shovels and went to wait by the grave. Ben came down about ten and Crown gave him instructions. The funeral procession arrived at eleven. It was a big one. Missy Hebert was just fifteen years old and pregnant with her first child. Her husband was all of thirty-five, a widow twice over with seven kids already. Missy's family, including her ma and pa, nine siblings and a host of aunts, uncles and cousins made up the bulk of the mourners.

One of Missy's aunts blubbered out a song, Reverend Samuels prayed and Ben sprinkled dirt over the casket filled with Missy and her stillborn baby girl. At the sound of dirt raining against the casket, Missy's mother and sisters went to wailing something fierce. In contrast, Missy's husband didn't shed a tear. With quiet detachment, Paul Hebert turned away with his seven kids, no doubt thinking about the next Mrs. Hebert. Crown looked at those seven kids and considered what Jewel had said. Paul Hebert was their own pa, and even he knew he needed a woman to raise his kids. How was Crown ever supposed to take care of Jewel? While her body said she was capable of more, her mind said she'd be half child to the end of her days.

It was several minutes before Ned could turn Missy's kin folks away. After they were gone, Crown and Ben lowered the casket with two ropes. Crown told Ben to come back again the next morning for the widow Provost and the hobo, then left Ben to finish filling the hole.

Crown stopped at the well and splashed water over his face. He felt dirty though he'd left most of the work for Ben. He looked at the house and steeled himself for another day and night with Jewel.

The house was quiet when he walked in. Jewel wasn't in the bedroom or the kitchen. He called to her, but she didn't answer. He remembered then that she thought she was playing a game of hide and seek. He didn't feel like playing.

"Jewel, I ain't go'n' call you all day."

"You give up?"

"Come on out, Jewel."

"Give."

"I give. Now come out."

Pouting, Jewel crawled out from under the kitchen table. "You didn't look very hard."

"I don't have time for your games."

"Ain't you the one told me to hide?"

Crown shook his head. "Just one more day, Jewel. Just one more day." Crown lit a fire and heated up another can of beans. He didn't have any salt pork, but he had bacon. He fried a couple of slices to flavor the beans and entice Jewel to eat. He considered again what she'd said about those Hebert kids being orphans. That's exactly what Jewel was now, an orphan, a throwaway, and Crown knew just the place to take her.

The irony of it struck him. The thought of returning to Montagne Parish almost made him sick. He'd been afraid to leave. Now he had no desire to go back except he had Jewel, and there was no way he could be responsible for her. Sam and Mae had put her on him like she didn't matter, like she was trash. Crown knew what that was like, but he reasoned Jewel would be better suited to the orphanage than he had been. While Crown had resigned himself to a life of self-imposed isolation, most of the kids there had seemed content if not happy. Crown had heard them laugh and play. Jewel would fit right in.

They'd leave tomorrow night after the mourners were gone, and Ben was done with the burials. Crown would leave Jewel in the care of Father Georges and Sister Abigail. She'd be taken care of. He wouldn't have to feel guilty. He'd be done with Jewel Giddings.

CHAPTER 14

▼

Anxious to get the deed done, Crown rose early the next morning. To pass the time, he repaired the fence around the pig pen where a couple of the logs had slipped and were leaning precariously. He strung new wire around the chicken coop, replaced the roof and the walls, and cleared the rats' nest from the roosting boxes. He questioned whether the latter was worth his while. Accustomed to ranging free and unfettered, the chickens were unlikely to roost there. Crown had found eggs under the front porch, in a hollowed stump in the back yard and between the wood pile and the barn.

Ben came down about noon, just ahead of Ned and the reverend. The widow's funeral was sparsely attended, just her elderly sister-in-law and a niece accompanied the casket to the graveyard. Ned took the Provosts back to town, then returned with the unlucky hobo.

By the time Ben had covered the pauper's grave, Crown was restless and cranky. Ben hung around till Crown realized that Ben wanted to be paid. Crown lied and told Ben he didn't have enough cash at the house, but would pay Ben by the end of next week. Crown figured he'd be back from Louisiana by then and he'd have no more need to sneak and hide. He'd be able to come and go as he chose, and he wouldn't have to worry that Ben or any one else might spot Jewel.

Crown dismissed Ben and put the tools in the barn. He hitched Less and More to the wagon and led them out into the yard. He returned to the house and called to Jewel. She didn't answer. He thought he saw her leg under the kitchen table. She didn't even have enough sense to find another place to hide. Ignoring her, he fried some bacon and eggs and made sandwiches. He sliced some cheese and wrapped the sandwiches and cheese in a checkered cloth. He cleaned the kitchen quickly, grabbed the sandwiches, then went in the bedroom and retrieved the knapsack Jewel had brought with her. Crown called her again.

"Come on out, Jewel."

"You give?"

"I give. Now come on. It's time to go."

She skipped into the bedroom and grinned at him. "Where we goin'?"

"Never you mind. I'll tell you when we get there. Come on."

Less and More were grazing on a patch of grass in the front yard. Crown helped Jewel into the back of the wagon, then covered her with the tarp. It was already dusk. The full moon meant it wouldn't get much darker. Crown didn't expect to run into anyone, but he didn't want to take any chances.

"We playin' hide and seek still?" Jewel asked, fidgeting with curiosity.

"Somethin' like that," Crown lied, deflecting her questions briefly.

Peeking out from under the tarp, Jewel was quiet as Crown drove out of the gate and turned down Cemetery Road. She poked out her head and cheered as he approached the farm.

"You taking me home, Crown? Did my Mama and Pap come back for me?"

Crown pushed her head back under the tarp. He didn't answer, but urged the horses quickly past the tenant houses.

Jewel popped up again, excited. "Turn, Crown. You got to turn."

When Crown didn't turn, Jewel started to whimper. "Whar we goin', Crown?"

Leaving behind all that was familiar, Crown passed the farm and turned on the main road, heading east to Louisiana.

"Whar we goin'?"

"Hush, Jewel and go to sleep."

"You don't want me, do you, Crown? I thought it was funny, Mama and Pap leavin' me with you, seein' as Carrie was always the one that struck your fancy. How come they done that, Crown? How come they done that when you don't want me at all?"

"Don't nobody want you, Jewel. Not Sam or Mae or Carrie and for damn sure not me!"

"I want to go home."

"I'm taking you to a new home."

"Will my Mama be there?"

"No."

"Then I ain't goin'."

Before Crown could stop the wagon, Jewel stood up and jumped. He turned and caught a glimpse of her as she hit the ground and rolled away from the wagon with the burlap sack tucked under her arm.

Crown guided the wagon off the road and ran back in the direction he'd come, calling out to Jewel.

He heard her whimpering and followed her cries. She had rolled into the ditch. "Damn fool," Crown yelled in aggravation. He grabbed her by the arm to pull her back up on the road.

Jewel winced and held her right arm against her chest. "See what you done," she accused Crown.

Crown put his arm under her left shoulder and ushered her back to the wagon. He hoped her arm wasn't broken. He didn't need anyone blaming him for hurting Jewel. There was no use trying to take her to Montagne Parish tonight. He'd have to take her home and make sure she was alright. Then he'd see.

When they got to the wagon, Jewel turned and faced him. Her eyes had lost their humor. "I still ain't goin'. Mama said you might try to git rid of me. She said if you did, I was to tell the first somebody I saw that you got Nate Comeaux's boy." She looked as furious and stubborn as she sounded.

Crown stared at Jewel in disbelief. He felt like a fool. He thought he'd gotten the better of Sam Giddings. He thought he'd get Carrie, but all he'd done was to tie himself to a dead boy and Jewel.

Crown let go of Jewel and climbed in the wagon. "Get in," he mumbled. She scrambled up and took the seat beside him. He didn't bother to tell her to get in the back. He turned the wagon around and headed back home. His head was starting to ache again. Dumb as Jewel was, she could be smart about things that mattered. He began to fear that he'd never be rid of her.

Jewel sat up straight and stiff all the way home, clearly ready to jump again if Crown didn't take her where she wanted to go.

She shrugged him off when he tried to help her out of the wagon. She walked into the house ahead of him. He set the horses free and swatted their rumps. Less and More never roamed far. More followed Less across the yard. Crown followed Jewel inside. She lay curled up on her pallet in a tight little ball. She started to shake and cry. Crown lit a lantern, sat down beside her and folded his legs under him.

"I need to take a look at that arm, Jewel." He reached out slowly, easing the arm away from her side.

"Ouch." Jewel cried and tried to pull the arm away. Crown could see it hurt her, but she let him examine it. The arm was already turning shades of red. He guessed by morning her arm would be swollen, black and blue. Crown felt around the length of the arm, tried to bend it and twist it. Jewel screamed.

Crown let her cradle the arm while he continued his examination. "Anything else hurt?" He examined her, satisfied when his poking and prodding elicited no more cries of pain. "I guess you'll live. That was a damn fool thing to do. I'm going to make you a sling in case the arm is broken."

She was crying softly. Crown left her to find some bedding he could use for a sling and some liquor he could use to ease her pain. When he returned, he sat her up and coaxed whiskey into her throat until her protests turned to gibberish and her gibberish turned to drivel. He set the arm in a sling that he'd made from a pillowcase cut down the side and folded. She didn't utter a sound, but he knew she'd be in pain when the night and the liquor wore off. He picked her up off the floor and put her to bed in the room across the hall. She was too drunk to know or care. She could have a tantrum tomorrow. At least for one night, they'd both rest easy.

After Jewel was in bed, Crown crawled under his covers and tried to sleep. Ordinarily, he was not a drinking man, but his head hurt so badly, he took what remained of the bottle of whiskey and drained it dry.

CHAPTER 15

▼

Crown woke first. He lay in bed awhile listening, but there were no sounds coming from Jewel's room. He wasn't sure whether the pressure pounding at the base of his skull was from the whiskey or Jewel. Still he wished he had another swig to settle his nerves. He reached for the bottle, but remembering that it was empty, he went across the hall to check on Jewel instead. She was sleeping soundly. He sat down on the bed and slid her arm out of the sling. Just as he suspected, the arm was badly bruised and swollen to twice its normal size. He put her arm back in the sling and cradled his head in his hands. His nerves were frazzled. His stomach churned. He felt penned in. He looked at Jewel lying in bed and had to leave.

Crown fetched a saddle from the barn, then he stood in the middle of the yard and whistled for Less. With her ears cocked, Less trotted to him from the edge of the woods. Crown threw the saddle across her back and cinched it. He grabbed the reins and swung up onto the saddle. More whinnied in protest. Crown spurred his heels into Less's sides and rode hell bent away from Jewel Giddings.

At the farm, the tenant houses were deserted, the fields were abuzz. Men bent to the backbreaking work of cutting the golden strands of grain. The women and children followed behind gathering and tossing the grain in bundles into the beds of wagons. Crown rode past the active fields until he reached a field that had already been cut. The grain had been pounded to remove the rice and fresh straw was strewn over the dry cracked clay. In a couple of months, the cycle would begin again. The soil would be broken, the fields flooded, the seedlings nurtured and planted, the grain harvested.

Crown had dreamed of endless seasons with Carrie. Now Jewel was his reality, and he couldn't bear to think more than a day at a time. He had one comforting thought. With Sam Giddings gone, Crown would have to spend more time at the farm, and more time at the farm meant less time with Jewel.

Crown couldn't afford to leave his affairs to Karl Johnson. As well intended as Johnson was and as good as he was with the business end of things, the man knew far too little about the land. Sam knew how to work the land, when to plant and when to harvest, and when to let the land lay fallow. As much as Crown hated to admit it, Sam would be hard to replace.

Crown turned Less toward the granary. The first thing he'd do is get Johnson to start the crop rotation and check on grain prices. He'd love to be able to haggle prices with the mills' agents. Instead he was forced to be a silent owner, handing out instructions and letting Johnson do his talking for him.

Crown spent an hour with Johnson, then inspected the fields. The workers quickened their pace when word got around. With Crown poking about, they worked later than usual, but as dusk settled they stopped and headed home. Crown reluctantly did the same.

As he approached the house, he saw smoke streaming from the chimney. He cursed and spurred Less into a trot. He dismounted in the yard and ran into the house ready to light into Jewel.

The house smelled like burnt popcorn. Jewel was blubbering over a scorched pot of beans. Rancid smoke filled the kitchen. Crown cursed and grabbed the pot of beans with the tail of his shirt. He flung the pot, beans and all out of the back door.

"Damn you, Jewel. Didn't I tell you not to cook? You ain't fit with two good arms. What you go'n' do now with one?"

"I'm tired of beans anyway. Ain't you got nuthin' else?"

Exasperated, Crown stared at her. "What you want, Jewel? A pot of water and a few grains of rice? To my recollection beans is more than you're used to."

Jewel pouted. Crown stamped outside, freed Less from her saddle and stored his gear. Then he grabbed one of his hens and wrung her neck. From a safe distance, the others put up a raucous protest. Crown sat on the porch and pulled the feathers off of the hen. She was old and had stopped yielding eggs a year ago. He chopped off her head with an axe, bled her and washed her carcass by the well. Then he went inside, chopped the liver and gizzards, mixed the organs with rice, added a whole onion, butter and salt and pepper, stuffed the rice dressing inside the carcass, and set it over the fire to roast. Jewel looked at Crown like he'd lost his mind, but she was already licking her lips.

Crown's chores at Montagne Parish had included kitchen duty. While he had washed, chopped and peeled, he'd watched. What he knew of cooking, he'd learned by observation. Now, putting what he'd learned to practice, Crown made biscuit dough. He laid half of the dough in the bottom of the Dutch oven and lined it with peaches. He added sugar and bits of dough to thicken the syrup. He covered the pastry with the other half of the dough, then set it in the oven to bake.

When the hen was done, Crown placed it on a platter and split the carcass in half. The juices spilled out and settled forming a thin gravy around the hen. Rice dressing simmered in the center of the carcass.

Jewel clapped her hands. "Ohh, we go'n' eat good."

Crown fixed her plate, then his. With all the riding he'd done, he was ravenous. He finished one plate and helped himself to seconds. Jewel held out her plate, and he heaped it full with rice and chicken.

"Don't get used to it," he warned. "When it's gone, you'll just have to settle for beans."

Jewel ate till she was so full, she leaned back in the chair with her belly distended. "I got me a stomach ache."

"I got to tell you when to quit eating, too?" Crown asked annoyed. He didn't expect an answer and he didn't get one. He rose to clear off the table. Jewel tried to help one handed, but she was more hindrance than help.

"Why don't you go to bed, Jewel? I'll clean up here."

"I'll wait for you."

"Suit yourself."

Crown didn't want to argue with her. He hoped she was full enough to sleep the night through. She drowsed in the chair even as he finished cleaning the kitchen. He waited till her head hit the table, then he picked her up and put her in her own bed.

He had barely drifted to sleep when she knocked on his door. He tried to ignore her, but Jewel kept knocking. Finally she called his name.

"Crown. Crown."

"What now?"

She opened the door and peered at him, the whites of her eyes barely visible in the moonlit room. "I told you, I'm scared of the dark."

"You got to sleep in your own room."

"I can't sleep. The Boogie Man's in there."

"There ain't no such thing."

"Yes there is, and he's in my room. He's crawlin' on the walls and starin' at me with his face all brown except his eyes and lips, they black as coal and mean, and I can't sleep in there."

"Well you ain't sleeping in here. That's another thing you can get used to."

"Can't you stay with me till I fall asleep?"

"I'm tired and I don't intend to sit up half the night with you."

Jewel walked to the foot of the bed. "I ain't goin' back in there by myself."

"Have it your way." Crown pulled the blanket off the bed and tossed it at her.

"Give me a pillow."

"Dammit, Jewel. Go to sleep." Crown tossed a pillow at her. He lay back and closed his eyes, hoping he could fall asleep before Jewel started snoring.

He slept uninterrupted until Jewel woke him the next morning. He opened his eyes to see sunlight pouring through his window and Jewel standing in the doorway with a cup of coffee in her hand.

Jewel walked over to the bed and placed the coffee on the nightstand. "You sleep, Crown?"

Groggy, Crown sat up on his elbows and shook his head. "I told you not to cook. That includes making coffee."

"I just wanted to do somethin' nice for you. I didn't think you'd mind."

He sighed. "If you're going to stay here, you'll have to give me my rest. I don't expect to have another night like the last."

Jewel answered contritely. "I didn't mean to be a bother. I just ain't used to sleepin' all alone. Always somebody been nearby. More'n one somebody."

"Can't help what you're used to. Sam and Mae threw you away just like Jebediah done me. Ain't no sense in you leaning on a past that ain't got no future. You're here now, and if we're to make the best of it, you'll have to do as I say. Ain't that what Mae told you?"

Jewel nodded.

"I'll be fixing my own breakfast and supper too. I don't need you fumbling around making a mess of things. You can fend for yourself after I'm done. Once your arm is better, you'll sweep and scrub the floors, change the beds, wash dishes and clothes, and otherwise stay out of my sight. That understood?"

"Yes."

"Good then." Crown gulped the last of the coffee and gagged on a mouthful of grounds. "Dammit Jewel, you stay out my way you hear. You stay out my way, or I'm go'n' throw you back where I found you."

Jewel scampered out of the bedroom. Crown wished he could get rid of Jewel as easy as that, but he was stuck with her. Mae Giddings had made sure of that. Much as Crown wanted Jewel gone. Much as he wanted Carrie instead. He had what he had, and there wasn't a damn thing he could do about it. Not one damn thing.

Crown got dressed and gathered some eggs for breakfast. He made a fresh pot of coffee and fried the eggs with some bacon. After breakfast he completed some routine chores. He decided to stay close by, since he couldn't think of one good reason to go to the farm and Jewel seemed bent on cooking no matter how many times and how many ways he told her not to. He worked on the house, picking up the repairs he'd left off when Carrie had spurned his proposal.

Jewel kept nagging him for something to do so he gave her some rags and told her to dust every book in the library. He figured with one arm in a sling that task would keep her awhile.

With Jewel out of the way, Crown started on her bedroom. If he expected her to stay in it and give him some peace, he needed to make it more livable. He scrubbed the pine walls then painted them white. Tilted in its frame, the window didn't close properly. Crown reseated it so the wind wouldn't howl through the window at night and blow the curtains, casting ghostly shadows against the walls. He admired his work. Content that he'd done all he could to get rid of Jewel's Boogie Man, Crown went to work on the attic.

By late afternoon Crown had accumulated a pile of trash including some out-dated moth-eaten clothing and linens too mildewed to consider washing. He took a break and went to the study to check on Jewel. She was sprawled on the floor thumbing through an atlas full of maps and pictures. Content that she was preoccupied, Crown opened the safe and retrieved the key he had put away long ago. Then he went to the kitchen, sliced some salted ham, bread and cheese and called Jewel to lunch.

After lunch, Crown sent Jewel back to the study to dust. He went upstairs and unlocked the door to Jackson's bedroom. He piled the linens, rug, clothes and trophies on the floor in the hall. He left the outdated encyclopedias. The curtains were dusty but in good shape. Crown removed them and set them in a separate pile to wash though he wasn't sure he'd put them back up. He left the door open, so the sunlight and warmth could filter into the hallway.

He stepped around the pile of trash and stood at the doorway of the second bedroom. When he had moved in and was curious, he had opened the room and surveyed its contents. He had quickly locked it and had not entered it since. Now he opened the door and eyed the room he was certain was meant to be his.

The room was frozen in time as though a child had died or vanished and the room had been turned into a shrine. The crib was neatly made, though the bedding was yellowed and pocked with holes. The closet stood empty except for a christening gown stained with rat pee. The small bookshelf held an assortment of books and toys Crown had never received, a blank scrapbook meant to detail a child's firsts, and a photograph. Recognizing his mother in the photo, Crown studied the infant dressed in the gown and cradled in her lap. The child's face was covered; his mother wore a weary smile. She was otherwise beautiful, thin and ethereal, the way Crown remembered her.

Crown tucked the picture under his arm. He put the scrapbook and the small collection of wooden trains, horses and soldiers in the hall and tied them in bundles along with the trash from Jackson's room. He packed the bundles outside and tossed them on top of the trash heap in the backyard. Sneezing from all the dust, he took a moment to breathe the fresh air before he set the pile on fire. Back inside, he stuffed the picture in the bottom of his drawer, beneath two extra pairs of long johns.

In the kitchen, he chopped what was left of the chicken and folded it into a pot of boiling water along with the rice. Then he went to the study to check again on Jewel. She had fallen asleep on the floor, a pile of books strewn about her. Crown returned the books to the shelf then woke her.

She eyed him sheepishly, but Crown simply motioned for her to stand. When she did, he examined her arm. The swelling had gone down, but the bruising was still severe.

"Can you move it?"

Jewel took her arm out of the sling and wiggled it tentatively. She tried to bend it and grimaced.

"I don't think it's broken. It's probably just a bad sprain. In a couple of days, I'll remove the sling. Meanwhile you try to work that arm so it won't go stiff. You hungry?"

Jewel nodded.

"I made soup. We'll eat then go to bed."

CHAPTER 16

▼

Crown woke to the distant sound of dogs barking and the irrefutable crack of a rifle. Fear rushed in heightening his senses. The woods were silent but for the rustle of wind and the rap of the dogs. He listened until he was certain the calls were becoming more distant. Then easing into the pillow, he shut his eyes. With the morning already half gone, there was no reason to hurry the day.

Despite all his work, he'd had another hard night, trying to coax Jewel to sleep across the hall only to have her wake up wailing like a banshee in the middle of the night. She'd said Carrie would read to her when she couldn't sleep and as much as Crown hated being reminded of Carrie or doing anything that might be mistaken for kindness, he'd read. The almanac was the closest thing he had to entertainment, but Jewel had been content enough with the drone of his voice, and soon she'd fallen asleep.

He had covered her with a quilt then locked the door behind him, hoping she'd sleep through the night. He was determined that she not spend another night in his room. After all, he was a full-grown man, and she was a near-grown woman, with a body once and half again as developed as her mind.

The sun danced through the sheer curtains, bathing Crown's skin in warmth and teasing his eyelids open. But in a while he slept again, heavy and tired the way one does when unaccustomed to sleeping in daylight. He woke periodically, a little more worn, a little more beaten as the day progressed. About midafternoon, still weary, he dragged himself out of bed and dressed. He remembered then that Jewel had spent the night and half the day locked in her room. He listened but he hadn't heard a sound and wondered suddenly if she was all right.

Crown fumbled with the key he'd left in the lock. He turned the knob and opened the door slowly, one hand pressed against it so that it would not creak on the rusty hinges he had yet to replace. He half expected Jewel to bolt right over him, but he was met only by the soft flutter of her breathing. He opened the door fully to see her sprawled across the bed, the covers sliding precariously to the floor.

She must have been tired because she showed no sign of waking. He envied her ability to sleep unencumbered by responsibility and time. Pocketing the key, he closed the door softly without locking it.

In the kitchen, he lit a fire under yesterday's coffee. He had no appetite, just a need to shake the weary from his body and the cobwebs from his mind. Refusing to trudge to the outhouse, he stepped out back and relieved himself in the weed-strangled earth that had once been a flowerbed. He peed, gave an absent shake and stuffed his shirt back into his overalls.

He listened again and thought he heard the dogs faint and distant. He wondered if they'd come again, if they'd sniff among the headstones till they found the corpse. He hoped Troy and Earnest were right. That one dead body smelled just like the rest. That dogs couldn't sniff a fresh little White boy amongst the rotten black carcasses.

Crown poured a cup of coffee and sat down to sip it. The warmth spread through his body making him feel better than he looked. He rubbed his jaw where rough stubble had already begun to form. Reminded bitterly how he'd shaved it for Carrie, he grunted.

How did he ever think he'd get a girl like Carrie? How'd he ever think he'd be anything more than Jebediah's trash? But there was no use feeling sorry for what was. Crown could no more change the harelip than he could change his name. He could no more be rid of the hurt Jebediah had left him than he could be rid of Jewel.

Crown stood, straight and tall and pressed the wrinkled legs of his overalls. He stood so he wouldn't feel so small and insignificant in a house that had been handed to him by default. He'd had the worst of Jebediah and none of the best. Still the farm was prospering under his care. Crown had heard the whispers born of fear and ignorance and just plain jealousy, but he was certain of a few things. He didn't believe in luck and he didn't make deals. What he had, he'd made, with no help from God or the devil.

From the bedroom came a thud and cry that shook him back to the present. Jewel stumbled into the kitchen, rubbing her eyes with one hand and her butt with the other. The sling was tangled around her neck.

"Take that thing off before you choke to death."

Jewel unraveled the sling, pulled it over her head and set it on the kitchen table. "It don't hurt much any more," she remarked, wiggling her arm. "How come you let me sleep so long?"

"You got something else to do?"

"I just ain't used to sleepin' in the middle of the day. Tain't right. I should be cookin' or cleanin' or doin' somethin' useful. Want some suppa?"

"Can you cook anything edible?"

"I don't know whut that means. Whut's ed ... edble?"

"The word is edible. And it means, is your cooking worth eating?"

"I don't know nothin' bout whut you talkin' bout, Crown, and I s'pect you don't eitha. Don't you go tryin' to leave me out of my own conversate by usin' them hifalutin' words you know I can't understand. Why don't you just say whut eva it is you mean?"

"Dammit all to hell, Jewel, just hush up. You're about as ornery as that sister of yours, and how I never knew it I'll never know. I ain't hungry. I don't want no supper, no breakfast and no lunch either. I told you I'd fend for myself and I will. I got no use for you, Jewel. I got no use for you, and the way Sam and Mae dropped you on me all quick and sudden, they don't have no use for you neither."

The words cut deep, and Jewel sobbed.

"Jewel, I didn't ... Dammit. I told you to stay out of my way. I ain't got time to tend to a blubbering idiot. You stay out of my way you hear me. Else I can't be sorry for what I say and how you feel. I ain't go'n' spend my day sorry in my own house. You aiming to keep this roof over your head, then you stay far away from me as you can."

Crown reeled pushing the screen door with such force it sprung back rattling against the house with a vengeance. Crown didn't go far, but he wore a circle in the back yard, ranting at Sam and Mae and Carrie for leaving him with poor daft Jewel. He hated himself for being so low to a creature no more responsible for her fate than he was. He hated himself for caring. He looked back to see her standing in the door watching him like a puppy with her tail between her legs willing him to forgive her. He turned away suddenly ashamed and wished there was something to forgive.

He was still there when he heard the dogs again. He tensed even before the hogs began to grunt a warning. A hound dog burst through the woods, baying and sniffing at the ground. Crown froze. The dog tore across the yard toward the cemetery then stopped short, confused. He began to howl pitifully, running back and forth, rolling in the sod. A man called out.

"Jubil. Jubil, boy. Come here, Jubil. Come, boy."

The man burst through the woods, his shotgun slung loose at his side. He spotted the dog across the yard and began to curse.

"Worse damn bloodhound this side of the Mississippi. Couldn't smell his own behind. Get out of there, Jubil."

The dog slunk with his tail between his legs, and his forelegs prostrate. The man grabbed the dog by the baggy skin on his neck and dragged him across the yard.

"Bubba, what you got there?" Another man burst through the woods.

"Nothin'. Just Jubil being Jubil. Caught all up in the scent of the dead. Whar the rest of the boys? We go'n' have to find them and pick up that trail again down by the river."

"You reckon he drowned?"

"Reckon, so."

"Whoo, boy. Mind if we take a drink from your well?"

It was the first time the man had acknowledged Crown's presence. Crown shook his head. The men disappeared around the front of the house. Crown didn't dare follow; although they took their time getting water for themselves and the dog, before they headed back into the woods.

When they had disappeared into the thicket, Crown backed into the house still watching and listening. He heard nothing but the beat of his own heart. He turned and leaned against the door jamb. His legs suddenly quit working, and they began to shake.

Jewel broke the quiet. "You scared as me? I near peed my pants. I thought they'd find that boy for sure."

Crown sank to the floor and put his head between his knees. Jewel walked over and took a seat on the floor next to him. She put her arm around him and whispered. "I'd neva tell nobody. I can keep a secret. I ain't neva gonna tell."

Crown was still shaking. He couldn't stop shaking.

CHAPTER 17

▼

For the next week, Crown would stop whenever the woods got quiet. He'd listen for the bay of the dogs, but they never again came as close as they had that evening. Even when he overheard Karl Johnson say they had stopped searching for Nate Comeaux's boy, Crown couldn't relax. They'd found the boy's fishing rod and tackle down by the river, and everybody just assumed the boy had drowned or worse a gator had taken him. Crown reasoned it was more comforting for the boy's mother to believe he had drowned than to know Sam Giddings had smothered him to death. Still Crown knew the truth and felt guilty for it.

He couldn't forget how Jewel had held him when he'd been so scared. He treated her a little better because of it, and while he was still subject to rail at her from time to time, he could never stay angry with her for long. Though he tried to occupy the day between, she was the first thing he saw in the morning and the last thing he saw each night. He had become used to her "good mornin's" and "good nights".

Idle and alone most of the day and with little to preoccupy her time, Jewel ate sunup to sundown. It was beginning to show in a slight pudginess of her tummy and a not unpleasant spread of her hips. Crown would come home to find she'd tried cooking, burned the meat to a crisp or turned the rice into a soupy mess, tossed it out and started all over again. He could yell her to tears when he'd come in for lunch just to find the same waste at supper. Not that she had any tolerance for his chastisements. She just had an incessant need to please, a weak memory and a large lack of ability. She just couldn't seem to help herself.

Crown had been putting off a trip to town until he'd found the cupboard bare of bread, his coffee low and his bacon gone. Though he knew he couldn't take

Jewel with him, he was afraid to leave her alone. She could wander off or burn the house down or just spend the day fretting that she was all alone.

Crown was more than a little irked that he had a certain weakness for her. She took all the steam out of his need for vengeance. He found himself susceptible to her childlike innocence, her honesty and inadvertent bent toward the comedic. He'd tried to cut her down, but she was already so low he only made himself seem small. She was after all, like him, a victim of life, dealt the bottom card with no choice but to play it.

Crown had lectured her for two days not to cook or leave the house or bother a thing while he was gone. He figured some she'd mind and half she wouldn't, but at least he'd tried. Jewel had plied him till he promised to bring her a surprise, like her pap had done anytime he'd made it to town with more than lint in his pockets which happened about twice a year. Crown had already decided on a book. He hoped having one of her own with more pictures than words would entice her to leave his precious books alone. He'd already spent more nights than he'd wanted reading her to sleep. He didn't relish reading from some sing-song children's book, but reading lulled her to sleep, and that was better than listening to her sing and banter half the night.

Every night, Jewel would curl up on her bed and beg and beg until he relented. Crown would read until he heard the gentle hum of her breathing. Then he'd dim the lantern and go back to his own empty bed and lay back thinking a lot about Carrie and a bit about Jewel. He longed for Carrie, but Jewel cut the sting out of lonely, leaving him tepid if not warm at the end of the day.

Jewel followed him out to the barn, clipping his heels more than once as he gathered the tack and hitched the wagon. Confined to the house and farm since Jewel had come, he had not needed the wagon in a long time. Now he walked the team, letting them grow accustomed to the load. At the foot of the path, he stopped suddenly and Jewel bumped full into him suppressing a giggle. Feigning annoyance, Crown stiffened and stepped away from her, resisting the strange urge to give her locks a tug. She took another step toward him, and he stopped her with the palm of his hand.

"Go on in now, Jewel," he said not unkindly. "I'll be back before dark."

Jewel shuddered. "You promise?"

Crown grunted. He wasn't about to make a promise he was afraid he might not keep. He walked her back to the house and lit the lanterns in the hall and in his bedroom.

"Just in case," he reassured her. "I'll be back directly. You can sleep in my bed tonight if you like. I'll take the floor. You stay out of trouble now."

Jewel looked as though she wanted to cry. Crown hurried outside pretending he couldn't see her tear streaked face pressed against his window. She waved lamely. He looked away. She had him acting like a fool, like some doting father, for a child half grown. She had that affect on people. He didn't know whether to curse her or protect her. He often did both.

Crown was glad to get away from her; although, he had never enjoyed his trips to town. Even though folks like Cooper and Mr. Miles had not been unpleasant, Crown had never felt at ease. He had neither trust nor affection for his neighbors, and it had been a long time since he'd felt the need to strut through Colwin County parading Jebediah's wealth as his own. He had no use for the town at all except that its bank held his funds and the store carried what he needed and couldn't grow or make on his own.

He had missed his solitude or so he thought. Jewel was always there, and it suddenly felt strange without her. He'd found himself watching her more than he cared to admit. She was fuller bodied than Carrie, and all woman from shoulder to thigh. His manhood was calling nightly now, and it was all he could do to stay off her. It was different than his desire for Carrie. He had wanted Carrie not only for sex, but for conversations, companionship, even the frequent battles they seemed to spark. Jewel he simply wanted to ease the urges bombarding him nightly, soiling his linens and causing him to muffle his moans into his pillow. He wanted her body warm and soft against his.

He was twenty-three years old and had yet to know a woman. When Jewel wasn't talking, so you didn't notice how dumb she was, she was as desirable as any woman he'd seen. It had become a nightly trial to leave her be.

He pulled into town too soon. So many people in so little space always made him ill at ease. He could not be done with his business fast enough. He went first to the bank. The more of his money he kept on hand, the better. He had slowly been stashing a bundle in the safe he'd found in Jebediah's study. Crown felt more comfortable stowing his own money. He'd already caught three mistakes in his balance, and he was certain someone at the bank was trying to pilfer what was his.

He had a less than cordial relationship with Mr. Langham who didn't relish being called on an error. Langham stiffened as Crown approached, a full month before his quarterly visit.

"Mr. McGee, I wasn't expecting you. What can I do for you?"

Crown stopped abruptly within a breath of the portly banker. "I'd like five thousand."

"Five thousand?" Mr. Langham stammered so his belly shook beneath the tight layers of his shirt and vest and suspended trousers. "Is this for a special purchase? Perhaps we should discuss a loan. Why don't you come into my office?"

"No time, no need."

"Mr. McGee, do you realize you haven't made a deposit in months? With the farm prospering and the—"

"Are you telling me I can't have my own money?"

Langham bristled while a dozen beads of sweat dotted his brow. "No, of course not. It's just that—"

"Then I'll be back in an hour," Crown interrupted. "And I'd like to examine the books as well."

Crown turned to leave as Langham snapped orders sending clerks and accountants scrambling. Crown felt certain Langham would spend a frantic hour trying to make sure everything was as it should be.

At the mercantile, Crown found an illustrated book of nursery rhymes he thought Jewel would like. Mr. Miles looked at him quizzically as he put it in with the bacon and oats, lard, coffee, beans, and soap. Then he smiled in sudden recognition.

"That for Jewel? I'll throw in a bit of candy for her too. She always liked a stick of peppermint and a big fat pickle. You bring her in next time."

It was Crown's turn to be surprised. "You know about Jewel?"

"Sam told me he'd be cutting out to his brother's place up around Marlin. What with Troy and Earnest marrying Opal and Pearl and that Carrie blossoming into a fine young woman, well he said they needed a bigger place for all the grandbabies he and Mae were expecting."

Crown winced. He had known Troy and Earnest were wooing Opal and Pearl, two big-breasted, gapped-teeth sisters whose pap was a drinking buddy of Sam's. But he hadn't known they had gotten married. That was two more good workers Crown hadn't counted on losing when the Giddings pulled out of Colwin County. And though he tried not to think of it, the image of Carrie with a belly full of some other man's youngun gnawed at him.

"Sam said he was leaving Jewel to settle his account with you. To be honest, I was a little worried at first. But it looks like you and Jewel are gettin' along just fine."

Crown grunted. Damn that Sam Giddings. He was smarter than Crown thought. Crown didn't need to hide Jewel after all. Sam had already planted the seed, and if Mr. Miles knew about Jewel, it was certain there were others who knew too. Sam had left a trail of coincidence so no one would suspect why he had really left. Crown was saddled with Jewel. And though the days past were not as unpleasant as he had supposed, he wasn't sure what kind of future he could have with her, pretty but daft as she was. He grunted.

"She'll be needing a few other things too. She didn't come with much. Maybe a dress in place of those damned overalls she's always wearing, and a pair of shoes, and whatever else a woman needs."

Crown was exhausted having said more in a mouthful than he'd said in three years.

"Don't worry Mr. McGee," Mr. Miles said, suddenly friendly. "I'll see to our Jewel."

Crown grunted and grabbed an armful of groceries to take to the wagon. He wondered what Mr. Miles thought he'd been doing with Jewel. He suddenly felt ashamed for the thoughts he'd been having. She was merely a child no matter how she looked.

The day was beginning to darken though it was still early, and Crown felt a sudden and unwanted concern for Jewel. He could smell rain in the air, and his skin tingled, warning of an approaching storm. He threw the tarp over the wagon as he loaded the last of his goods.

"Looks like rain." Mr. Miles looked skyward, then handed Crown a bundle, tied with a bright red ribbon. "For Jewel."

Crown muttered "Thanks," laid the package under the tarp and climbed aboard.

"She alone?" Mr. Miles asked, concerned.

Crown nodded and jerked the reins. The bank would hold. He needed to get home.

Crown had a difficult time keeping the team on the road, and he wished he'd harnessed them with blinders. They spooked at every crackle of lightning which came about every minute now.

It took Crown longer to get home than it should have. By the time he turned down Cemetery Road, he was drenched. He pulled into the barn so his parcels would have a chance to dry out. He walked the horses to their stalls, tossing them each a mound of hay. Then he checked under the tarp, hoping his goods weren't all ruined. As far as he could tell, everything, except him, was still dry. He pulled the package out for Jewel and stuffed it into his wet shirt. He bent over and ran into the house, skipping mud puddles like a child. When he reached the front porch, he stomped the water off as much as he could, then hit the door with three sharp raps. Not waiting for an answer, he knocked again, though he could easily have opened it himself. Jewel finally appeared, frightened and timid. He pulled the package out of his shirt, and she grinned, shyly at first then wide. She jumped and clapped her hands.

"Whut'd you brang me?"

"You want to let me in out of this rain first?"

She opened the door wide, grabbed the package and ran, hopping into bed and pulling the covers around her. She was breathless as she ripped the package open under the faint light that entered through the opening of her makeshift tent.

"I never been so skeered. I didn't think you wuz comin' at all. How come you take so long? And me all afeard of storms and all."

"The storm came up sudden-like, and the horses were skittish. But I'm here now, and you don't need to be afraid. Maybe next time, I'll take you with me."

She looked at him with eyes full of wonder. The book, a jar of fat pickles and a bundle of peppermints spread around her knees. She dropped the covers and stood, twirling on the bed as a pale blue dress unfolded down her overalls.

"Thanks, Crown," she squealed, her face beaming.

"Settle down now. You get dressed for bed, and I'll read you a tale or two to help you sleep."

"Kin I wash up a bit first?"

"Suit yourself." Crown shrugged, feigning indifference.

Unfazed, Jewel ran off taking her gifts with her. When she was safely out of sight, Crown grinned in spite of himself. At least he'd made her happy. He thumbed through the book trying to find a story that would put her to sleep. But everything he saw was meant to put fear in small children so they'd behave. He didn't see much to soothe Jewel's fears on such a stormy night. He finally settled on a few pages of rhymes, including one about an old woman who lived in a shoe with a passel of kids, that reminded him an awful lot of Mae. Silently reading the mindless rhymes, Crown was soon lulled to sleep.

"You go'n' read to me now?"

Jewel grinned and twirled. A crisp white gown, ruffled down the middle and on its hem, outlined her figure nicely.

Aroused and not at all happy about it, Crown nodded and rose. Jewel pulled back the covers where he'd lain and climbed into bed. He sat down beside her. She nestled between the book and him. She felt warm against him. He gulped and began to read, soft, slow, until he felt her sag against his chest. Crown lifted her head and laid a pillow beneath her. Gently releasing her head, his hand stroked her cheek. He intended to leave her there, sleeping peacefully. But she grabbed his hand and wouldn't let go. He nestled in beside her, the length of his body folded against hers. Her hips fit into his groin.

"Jewel?"

He wanted to wake her, and then he didn't. He wanted her so it hurt. He was afraid how he'd feel if he took her, innocent and sweet as she was. He should have eased his hand out of hers and left her to sleep in peace. But stronger urges were calling, and he found himself grinding against her.

"Jewel," he called more urgently.

She turned toward him.

"Jewel."

He rolled on top of her though she was only half awake, looking at him puzzled. He moaned.

"Whut you doin', Crown?"

"I need you, Jewel. Didn't Mae tell you to do what I said?"

"Yes," she whispered so he could barely hear her above his own rapid breathing. "Whut took you so long? I was afeared you didn't want me, Crown. But ain't we 'posed to git married first? Mama said we should."

He moaned and unbuttoned his trousers revealing his erection. Jewel eyed him curiously. He wiggled till his pants were below his hips, then began plunging between her warm moist thighs. Her heat traveled through him making his body tense and forcing his mouth open between ragged breaths.

"You ain't doin' it right," Jewel moaned, straining against him.

"What?"

"You ain't doin' it right."

He raised up on his palms and stared down at her in disbelief. She relaxed and opened her legs, raising her knees so they embraced his hips. She took hold of him then, none too gently and placed him against a small opening between her legs.

"Jewel." Crown shuddered and collapsed upon her.

"There now," she said calmly guiding him. "Try again. Mama said it might hurt me at first bein' neither of us never done it before. She said I wouldn't like it much, that I wasn't 'posed to. But I do like it, Crown. It feels real good."

"Hush, Jewel. Hush." Crown whispered urgently and pressed into her with mounting intensity.

Jewel moaned softly answering each plunge of his groin. Crown's desire heightened at Jewel's unexpected pleasure. Overcome by sheer intensity of feeling and an utter lack of self-control, he heaved until he was spent.

CHAPTER 18

▼

Crown slept hard. When he awoke he was alone. The smell of lilacs and sex permeated the room, arousing him. He was sticky and crusty and he needed a bath. Next time he'd know to wash up after.

"Jewel. Jewel."

She appeared at the door and frowned. "Whut you want now? Whut we done last night ain't meant for daylight. Ain't you got chores to do?"

"I just wanted a towel so I could wash," he lied badly.

"Don't you know whar they are?"

"Jewel!" He was harsh, but he could see she was stealing the last bit of power he thought he'd had. He wasn't about to let her make him feel guilty.

"You draw me a bath, you hear?"

He stood, pantless, his shirt barely covering his desire. It did not go unnoticed, and she skittered away to do as he'd asked.

Crown found his pants tangled in the covers at the foot of the bed. He pulled them on and sat down again heavy. He shouldn't have done what he did. But then Mae had schooled Jewel well, and there was no turning back.

As if he could easily discard his feelings of guilt, he stood up, shook himself and walked into the kitchen. On her knees, her back to him, Jewel was sniffling over a warm bath. Despite feeling guilt and pity, Crown stepped out of his clothes and eased into the tub. She handed him a towel and started to stand, but he grabbed her hand instead.

"You wash me, please," Crown urged gently.

He cupped her chin in his hand. She tried so hard not to look at him, her eyes crossed.

"What's the matter, Jewel? I thought you liked it."

"Mama said, I ain't 'posed to like it. She said we 'pose to marry first. You makin' me a sinna, and I ain't go'n' sin no more."

As if her pronouncement made everything right again, Jewel knelt down beside him and started to sing. It didn't bother him for once; though, he knew she only did it so she didn't have to think of him. She washed him quickly, then rose.

"I got work to do," she said, dismissing him. "Your breakfast's on the table. You best git a move on if you tend to git anythin' done this day."

Jewel swished out wearing that damned dress and no shoes and making Crown wish she'd come back and stroke him just a little bit longer. He splashed water on his face and tried to think of something else beside Jewel, but he couldn't. He ate his breakfast of burnt toast and clumpy oats in a hurry, then went to clear the graveyard.

With Troy and Earnest gone and Jewel to worry about, Crown had twice the work he'd had before. He hadn't been able to maintain the yard, doing only the spot work that had to be done before each burial. The weeds had multiplied and with all the rain last night and the sunlight burning, new weeds had already begun to sprout. Crown hoed and pulled, till his arms were tired. At noon, he unloaded the groceries from the wagon and watched as Jewel put them away. He settled on bread and cheese for lunch while she sucked loudly on a peppermint and pickle. Finally, Crown returned to his chores having had too much and not enough of Jewel.

The hard work helped him quell the fever he had for Jewel. Then reminded of what they'd done, he thought instead of Montagne Parish, of Father Georges and Sister Abigail, of the girls who came and went, the bloodied rags and the babies who stayed. He didn't want that for Jewel.

When he came in for supper, he found a stew warming on the stove. Sometimes she wasn't half-bad in the kitchen, and he found the meal more than palatable. When he was done, he dumped the last bit of stew to the hogs, washed his plate and the pot, and went to check on Jewel.

Curled up on her bed pretending to sleep, Jewel stiffened as Crown approached.

"Jewel."

"Whut?"

"I reckon we ought to get married."

"I reckon."

"Next time I go into town, we'll see the preacher, you hear."

She didn't answer. She didn't need to. He knew that wouldn't make it better for her, just certain. But he'd feel less guilty about having her. He'd feel like it was half way right.

"Night, Jewel."

"Night."

CHAPTER 19

▼

Crown had never considered himself religious. However, he had been reared in a Catholic orphanage and could not escape being molded by it. He figured that was why he had the insane notion to ask Jewel to marry him and why he was hell-bound to go through with it.

Despite and because of their pledge to marry, Crown stayed away from Jewel for nearly a week, hard as it was to do so. He tried to make her feel comfortable with him again, but she stopped asking him to read to her, and she hurried to bed long before he came in from a day's work. At night, he'd lie awake thinking of her, feeling guilty for what he'd done and for wanting to do it again.

There were nights it was all he could do to lie plastered to that bed when he really wanted to coax her across that hall and lay her down next to him. He wanted her there, but he wanted her to come of her own accord, so he wouldn't have to feel so filthy after. He'd been thinking how he was going to make that happen and trying his best to make her his friend again, to no avail. So he simply decided he'd have to beat her at her own game. He'd get to bed before she did.

Early one Monday morning, after a weekend of planning, Crown told Jewel he was going to the farm which he wasn't and that he didn't know how long he'd be which he did.

It was planting season. He'd heard they were doing plane seeding at a farm over in Chambers County, just outside of Winnie. If Crown got an early start, he could get there and back in half a day. He didn't know how he'd get into bed without Jewel seeing him, but he figured a plan would come to him when he needed it.

Crown's face relaxed, though he tried hard to keep any hint of mischief from Jewel. He packed a light lunch and headed out riding saddle. He'd have a better chance sneaking back home if he left the wagon. He chose Less, the faster of the two horses, so he could make better time there and back. It infuriated and amused him that he was sneaking around his own house, for a sixteen year old girl half his intelligence. Still she had a certain hold on him that he couldn't deny.

Crown would have given anything to have been in that room while Mae was telling Jewel how to be a woman. He wondered if Carrie had known, had been there too, had felt the slightest bit of jealousy imagining what he was doing with Jewel now. It gave him immense satisfaction to think so, even if it wasn't nearly true.

Crown hit Chambers County about sunup, the light shimmering on mile after mile of rain soaked paddies. The rows had been dug, the levees piled high to hold water and the rain of the last week had made short work for the bayous that normally fed the fields. He was wondering how he was going to find the exact field where the seeding was going on when he heard a buzzing overhead. Spurring Less to run, he followed the plane south then east until he came upon what could have been a Fourth of July picnic. There must have been twenty trucks lined up along the roadway, a half-dozen saddle riders like him, three rigs and a substantial number on foot. About half of the spectators were curious neighbors, wagering bets on whether or not the fool notion would work. The other half were hapless tenants hoping it wouldn't else they'd soon be out of a home as well as a job. Crown could see the fear and worry etched on their brows and in the nervous way they kicked the dirt at their feet.

Crown surveyed the ragged batch of tenant farmers with contempt. In his opinion, they were spineless men without ambition. They had resourceful women who loved them and too many children to count or feed. They had honest work and roofs over their heads, but squandered their money on alcohol. They'd die young and penniless leaving nothing to their families but their debt to the company store. McGee Cemetery held plenty like them buried one atop of the other.

Their way of life was ending, but Crown had no sympathy for them. He was gathering ideas for change, making the farm, now heavily dependent on manual labor, more mechanized. Plane seeding was still too expensive for most of the farmers, including Crown, but he had plans for mechanizing McGee farms. He knew he'd have to if he wanted to stay competitive. He'd already bought a second thresher, which meant most of the women folk didn't have work in the fall. He'd seen tenants come and go, giving way to migratory families who were better able to handle the seasonal work.

He stopped Less on the fringes and watched excitedly as the plane swooped and dove. From where he sat, he couldn't tell whether or not seeds were falling on that fertile soil, and he certainly couldn't fathom how dropping tiny seeds on open ground could replace the backbreaking work of transplanting seedlings from nurseries to the fields. Half the seeds were blowing God only knew where and the other half would never take root. His workers stooped and bent all day in the hot sun, poking seedlings into the ground with nothing but their fingers. It just didn't seem possible that this effortless method could replace all that.

Still Crown made note of a few landmarks, hard to find amidst the flat monotony of the paddies, so he could be sure to revisit the field come fall. He'd seen enough to know that if it worked, it could save him a heap of time and money. He'd seen enough to know that if it worked, he'd have to follow. Turning the horse around, Crown enjoyed a rare and private smile, pleased with himself for keeping up with the time, for being progressive enough to consider what others thought only foolhardy.

Anxious that he complete the other half of the day's mission, Crown urged Less to a steady trot. He ate in the saddle, cursing the chirping birds in the sparse trees along the way. He wondered how many would be feasting on those seeds come nightfall. It was early afternoon when he reached Cemetery Road so he decided to jog through the farm instead of heading straight home. The workers had just begun the tasks required for planting, using horse driven plows to break the ground where the rice would be planted. Near the granary, the women were tending young seedlings until they were prime for planting.

All appeared well and there was no sign of Johnson at the granary or the nearby fields, so Crown plodded home. He stopped and dismounted as he neared home and considered the best approach to the house. There was no way in except through the front gate so he took it hoping Jewel wasn't staring out a window or standing on the front porch at just the wrong time. He walked the horse through the cemetery, then cut around back to the barn. He saw no sign of Jewel.

After returning Less to her stall, he circled around keeping to the fringes of the woods so Jewel wouldn't spot him. He came upon her hanging wash in the back yard. Her hair was blowing gently in the wind and she was singing or perhaps talking. Crown couldn't tell which. He stepped back into the woods and circled back to the front of the house. He crept across the yard, onto the porch and in through the front door. He felt like the wolf waiting for Little Red Riding Hood. It was a tale Jewel never tired of no matter how much it frightened her. She'd huddle next to him clutching him till she could fall asleep only to dream of wolves in her own Granny's clothing.

It was early yet, but Crown had come in once before on a late afternoon and found Jewel abed so he hoped he wouldn't be waiting long. He stripped down to his shirt and crawled into bed. He felt silly getting in bed so early. He felt stupid sneaking around like he was, but then he heard the back door open and shut and Jewel singing at the top of her lungs. He smiled, turned over and pretended to sleep.

By the time she came into his room, he was no longer pretending. She must have been shaking him awhile, because when he looked at her groggily, he saw nothing but concern.

"You all right, Crown? How come you back so early? You sick or somethin'?" She felt his forehead. "You want anythin'?"

He shook his head no. He felt unnaturally tired, like one feels when they're unaccustomed to sleeping in the middle of the day. He was trying to wake up so he could tell her he just wanted her, but he couldn't keep his eyes open no matter how hard he tried, and he was so incoherent even he didn't know what he was saying. The last thing he remembered was Jewel climbing into bed with him and pressing a towel to his head and rubbing his belly like he was one of her little brothers with a tummy-ache. He curled inside himself content to sleep and have her near him.

When he awoke, it was dark and he still felt strangely tired. Jewel lay next to him with one arm across his chest and the other under her head. She looked pretty with her eyes closed, and he lay there awhile just looking at her. She woke then like a mother who knows when her sick child's fever has broken. Crown swallowed, guiltily. She stroked his forehead softly.

"Feelin' betta?"

"Yeh. I guess I got too hot or something."

"Ain't never known you to sleep so hard or so long 'cept that time me and Carrie found you all full of fever."

"I'm all right, Jewel."

"I see you are." She tried to slip out of bed, like she was suddenly conscious that she was lying in bed with a half-naked man who'd made a woman out of her just days before.

Crown grabbed her hand. "Don't go, Jewel. Don't be afraid."

"Ain't afraid."

"What is it then?"

"I told you Mama said I was 'posed to be married. I ain't 'posed to like it, and I ain't go'n' do it no more."

"If it's so bad, how come Mae and Sam done it so much. They must a done it all the time to make all you younguns."

Jewel smiled. "I reckon Pap didn't know much else besides moonshine and Mama. We used to lie awake gigglin' 'cause he'd come home full of the shine and trash talk and Mama would try to make him hush and well you know …

"Mama never really seemed to mind though, seemed like the next day they'd both be a mite happier."

Jewel relaxed a little. Crown raised up so he could look at her. He brushed her hair from her eyes. "If you tell me what to do, I'll do it, Jewel. I just gotta have you again. I told you I'd do right by you, and I will if that's what's keeping you."

"It ain't that. I figure you mean what you say, bein' as you don't say much."

"What then?"

"Feels like when you done that. Well it feels like you just reached down deep and took my soul."

"Mae tell you that, too?"

"Ain't nobody have to tell me that."

Crown laid back, his hands behind his head.

"I guess you're right, Jewel. 'Cause you know what it feels like to me?"

"Whut?"

"Like I just gave you my soul."

"You ain't joshin' me are you?"

"No. That's what it feels like. And I don't like being weak, Jewel. I don't think I could share that with anyone else."

"Not even, Carrie?"

"Why'd you have to go and ruin a good thing?"

"'Cause I want to know if it's me you want or Carrie you're make-believin' with."

"Where do you get such dumb notions."

"Ain't dumb. Ain't you the one asked for Carrie 'stead of me? And ain't you the one damn near peed in your pants when you found me instead?"

"I don't want to hear about, Carrie."

"Sorry I ain't her?"

"No."

"You mean that?"

He didn't know any other way to shut her up so he kissed her, not on the forehead or the cheeks but on that mouth of hers. She sucked in her breath and a little bit of his, and he thought he really was about to lose his soul.

He rolled on top of her, and she raised her knees like it was something natural instead of something she'd been trying to avoid.

CHAPTER 20

▼

Crown was finishing off a cup of coffee and a half-decent plate of cracklings and oats Jewel had managed to cook. At the rumble of the wagon, he glanced across the table at Jewel only to find her looking back at him with surprise. The only people who came within a hundred yards of his place were the dead and the grieving. Crown walked to the front door, slipping his coveralls over his shoulder with each long stride. It had been over six months. Still, Crown wondered nervously whether Nate Comeaux had come to collect his boy. He pushed the door open cautiously. To his relief, the wagon was full of Colored folk.

Crown leaned against the door jamb and held the door slightly ajar. A buxom girl with a broad grin and a raucous voice bounded onto the porch. Crown recognized her as one of his own tenants, though to his recollection, he had yet to see her do any work.

Without introduction or a customary hello, the girl pronounced, "I come for Jewel. Granny Giddings said ya'll'd had more 'n enough time to git to know each other." She eyed Crown defiantly and called past him to Jewel as though he had no right standing in his own front door.

"Jewel, it's cousin Lenetta. Come on to church."

"You're Jewel's cousin?"

"You deaf? That's whut I said ain't it. Come on now, Jewel. We ain't got all day."

"That all right with you, Crown?" Jewel asked sweetly.

Crown looked back to see Jewel slip into the bedroom. He stood holding the door uncomfortably while Lenetta looked him over like she'd already made up her mind he wasn't fit for Jewel.

It felt like forever before Jewel stepped out of the bedroom wearing the blue dress. She sidled up to Crown smelling like lilac powder. He might have mistaken her for a comely young woman if she weren't barefoot with a fat peppermint in one hand and a silly grin on her face.

"Lawdy, Jewel, where'd you git that dress?"

"Crown bought it for me from the town sto'. Ain't it purty, Lenet? Ain't it the purtiest dress ya'll eva saw?"

Jewel dipped under Crown's arm and out onto the porch. She twirled a time or two and for a moment, Crown thought she looked pretty too.

"It's purty, Jewel," Lenetta echoed Crown's admiration. "Now come on. We go'n' miss Deacon Bibee and that's the best part."

"It all right with you, Crown?"

But Lenetta swept her off the porch with a defiant look at Crown that dared him to tell Jewel any different. He shrugged his shoulders and watched them ramble down the road in that rickety wagon full of Sam Giddings' nieces and nephews and Jewel.

He had all day to consider Jewel's people and their strange ways. They'd dropped her on him months ago with narry a word in between. Then suddenly they appear on his doorstep, just when he'd settled in, getting used to the two of them. He suspected that Mae had orchestrated the whole thing, leaving him alone with Jewel just long enough for his body to overcome his better judgment. Rattled, he had the feeling that nothing would be the same.

It was near dark before they returned. Crown had been out to the farm and back, weeded a small corner of the cemetery and replaced the hinges on Jewel's bedroom door, though she never slept there now. He was pacing the kitchen floor when he heard the wagon coming down the drive. He stopped his pacing then ambled into his study, grabbed a book and settled into his chair as though he'd been reading without a moment's worry about Jewel.

The book lay on his knee unopened except for the index finger he'd jammed absently between the pages. He listened to Lenetta howling and Jewel answering in return.

"Crown! Crown!"

Two sets of footsteps echoed down the hall. Doors opened and shut. They called again, and before he could decide to answer, the door to his study opened.

"He's in here, Jewel. Ain't you heard us callin' you? I brought Jewel back home. Least you could do is ansa, so a body'd know she'd be all right."

Crown grunted and turned back to the book he'd pretended to read. Jewel squeezed past Lenetta and squealed. "You go'n' read to me tonight, Crown? I'm go'n' put on my nighty first then you can read me to sleep. He reads good, Lenetta. Better than Carrie even. He knows all the words. You want to stay and listen?"

Crown looked down at the book he'd been pretending to read and felt the blood rush up his neck to his cheeks.

Lenetta grinned. "Naw Jewel, I got a wagonload of folks waitin'. I best git back."

Crown stared at the book in his lap. Jewel had him pure daft. How'd he ever pick up that damn book of rhymes and fables. Lenetta and that wagonload of Giddings would be howling at his expense all the way home.

Crown was still staring at the book when Jewel reappeared holding the white gown, her hair hanging to her shoulders and her lips massaging her thumb.

"You go'n' read to me now, Crown?"

"I'm too tired to read, Jewel."

She looked disappointed, and he almost relented, but he'd made a fool of himself enough already. "You get on to bed now."

"You mad at me for stayin' gone so long. I didn't mean to. It's just that—"

"What in hell makes you think I care whether you come or go? You think I'm sitting up waiting for you. I ain't gave you the last thought since you walked out that door. You here, but it ain't my doing. Nobody cared if I wanted you, Jewel. Nobody cared if you wanted me. They just threw us together 'cause we the ones nobody wants."

"I … I like you, Crown."

"You don't know what you're saying, Jewel. You don't even know what that means."

"I do know. I know you ain't near as mean as you make out to be. I know you just as scared as me sometimes, maybe more. And I know I ain't half bad company, 'cause there's times I seen you smile and there's times I heard you laugh, and I knowed it was me 'cause there ain't nobody else."

"Jewel."

Crown shook his head and let the book fall to the floor. He left her standing there staring at it, like him dropping it meant more than any mean word he'd said. He wished he could take it back, but he couldn't.

He walked out the door into the night without even bothering to light a lantern. The moon was full, illuminating the barren yard and the silvery headstones and the barn he'd painted rust instead of red. He walked to the cemetery like the dead were calling him. Like anyone who'd hurt a creature like Jewel wasn't fit for heaven or earth. He kicked at a root that poked up from the ground below, the tree it had rooted long gone. Something small scurried scratching through the leaves piled two inches thick. Crown looked up not at all apologetic as the owl screeched angrily overhead. He leaned back against a headstone. Ignoring the way the concrete scratched through the thin sleeves of his shirt, he slid down until he was sitting with his back against the marker and his legs outstretched.

He sat looking back to the house, to the window where Jewel undressed slowly, unaware of his audience. He sucked in the still, moist air as he watched her cup her breasts and stroke her belly timidly as though unsure of her own worth before she pulled the white gown over her head and lay down alone on the bed. He took another breath, but he couldn't quell the burning in his groin. Closing his eyes, he groped, stroking so he wouldn't need to have her when he'd made her feel lower than the dirt he was sitting on. He stroked till the burning escaped and left him feeling low and dirty and ashamed.

The sun rose up even with the moon before Crown stood stiffly and ambled back to the house. He eased the door open and closed it softly so he wouldn't wake Jewel. He was chilled from the night air and sticky. He warmed a pot of water and washed up then tiptoed into the bedroom to lie beside Jewel. He crawled under the covers still dressed so he'd have to work hard to bother her. He sneezed, and she stirred turning to face him till her warm breath met his. He turned away.

"Crown." Jewel whispered, registering contentment in the soft whisper of his name. She snuggled up behind him till his hips nested into hers. Her arm came around him. Her breath tickled his ear. He closed his eyes and let her wrap herself around him.

"You didn't mean it did you, Crown?" she whispered. He edged close as two people could get without being one.

"I know you didn't mean it."

She slipped back to sleep, the quiet rhythm of her breath massaging his neck until he felt the guilt ease away and the fear fade and his eyelids lower to his cheeks.

CHAPTER 21

▼

Morning came bright and warm rousing Crown. He lay there awhile just watching Jewel from the hair that matted and curled in chaotic mounds atop her head to the gentle rise and fall of her breasts to the way she drew her knees up till her toes touched her bottom. With his thumb, he wiped the light drool dribbling over her pursed lips resisting the urge to kiss them. Finally he sighed and eased out of bed, leaving her sleeping, a slight smile on her lips.

He washed and changed so no one would suspect his night had been so hard. Then he headed to the farm not quite ready to face Jewel though he suspected she'd forgotten already. It seemed like hurts pricked her quick and sharp leaving no scars. Still he fancied he'd stop on his way back from the farm and pick her a patch of those wildflowers lining Cemetery Road all pink and white and yellow in that funny way that life and death entwined mocking each other. He laughed out loud.

Crown dawdled about the farm for half the morning, but things were going quite well enough without him. Fact was the work came to a stand still everywhere he appeared till he figured he was doing more harm than good. Squirreled away in an office, he scanned the books for over an hour though he could not concentrate on inventory, receipts or outlays when all he could see was Jewel sleeping in their bed. About noon his stomach grumbled, piercing the eerie quiet that had settled over the farm. He looked up and realized he had been asleep dreaming of Jewel and a night of fevered closeness.

Crown rubbed his eyes and leaned back in the chair. He twirled around till he faced the window and the flat expanse of McGee Farms. The lush fields waved under a steady wind. Everywhere water glistened like rivers of jewels bending the sun's rays in iridescent shimmers of blue and purple and gold. Here and there workers gathered, idling over cold lunches and small talk. Crown sobered at his own success. There was little for him to do at the farm most days. So little he felt compelled to stay away. So little he felt confined to that house at the end of Cemetery Road and that field of corpses. He was more comfortable there, after the mourners had gone and he was left alone to plant the body and cover it with earth and mound the soil just so. How could he resent the only place that made him feel necessary? How could he deny his own kinship to death? Except there was Jewel, making it a place of light and life, a place worth coming back to, a place he could call home.

A sharp knock interrupted his thoughts. Karl Johnson poked his head in the doorway, a worried grin failing miserably to mask his concern.

"Everything all right? You been at those books awhile. The wife's always got a warm lunch if you care to join us. With our oldest boys off to college, she's always got more than the rest of us can eat. We'd be happy if you'd join us."

Crown's brow arched, but Johnson's invite sounded sincere. Except for the fact that he always had a nose up Crown's butt, Johnson wasn't a bad sort. He was an ambitious man, and Crown found it hard to find fault with that. Johnson had apologized in advance in case Crown found some honest mistake but Crown had found nothing. Still Crown didn't relish sitting across the table from the Johnsons, and he shook his head politely.

"I best get home."

Johnson grinned too familiar, and Crown shuffled uneasy.

"I guess Jewel'll have a little something for you, too. It ain't good to keep a woman waiting."

Johnson laughed at his own joke, then left, leaving the door open and a trail of laughter turning Crown's mood from pensive to bad. Crown sat there awhile waiting for the laughter to stop reverberating in his head, but it remained as if it had been lying there dormant just waiting for the right moment to torment him again.

By the time he got home, he was brooding. He passed by the patch of wildflowers, scoffing at the idea he'd ever thought to come home with a bouquet for anyone, let alone Jewel. He took his time watering and brushing down the horses, then found a myriad of odd jobs around the barn before he ambled into the house. His hunger had turned to a stabbing headache at the base of his neck. His stomach had grown queasy having been too long denied, still he headed straight to his study closing the door and settling into his chair with the Farmer's Almanac, just two months old and already well worn.

After a while he heard Jewel outside the door. She shuffled then opened it without bothering to knock. He didn't look up; though, he was well aware of her presence there. He could feel her eyes on the back of his head. Her scent invaded his space, making him want her even while he denied her a simple acknowledgement.

"Crown."

He grunted.

"I made you some lunch. I been waitin' for you. It's nigh suppertime now, and I'm hungry."

"Any fool would have eaten already."

"You et yet?"

"No."

"Then I'll warm you a plate."

"Suit yourself."

"You come along when you ready, you hear."

She was pleading and he softened. How could he hurt her when he wanted her so?

"I'll be there directly."

She closed the door, and he closed the book. He shut his eyes and rubbed the back of his head and hoped a little food and a little Jewel would ease the tension gripping his insides and making him feel like earth turned inside out before a planting.

CHAPTER 22

▼

By the time Crown had reason to make another trip to town, Jewel had told him she was pregnant. He wondered how she knew, but then it seemed Mae had told Jewel a lot of things in the week before she left.

Jewel had grown more than willing when she remembered that Mae had said their nightly tossing was what brought babies and would give her a certain power over Crown. She'd used that power, though not maliciously, which made Crown believe she was a lot smarter than he'd ever thought she was.

She'd let him ply her before he read to her each night. She'd fall asleep in his arms, and he'd have to wake her because once was never enough. She was beginning to enjoy the power over him so much she had taken to teasing him, like the way she delighted in asking dumb questions she already knew the answer to just when he was least interested in talking.

She had a lot of Carrie in her too, some of the same feistiness, and she could make him just as mad. Funny but he hadn't thought of Carrie much. He was fond of Jewel. She kept him company, and she was the first and only woman he'd ever had. It was hard to think of Carrie when he worked all day and thought of Jewel all night.

As they rumbled into town, Crown hoped no one else could tell that Jewel was pregnant. Women had a sense for such things. He left her at the mercantile while he went to finish his business at the bank. When he returned, she was chattering away. He hoped she hadn't told Mr. Miles too much.

At the first sight of Jewel garbed in a satiny white dress with a fringed hemline, Crown gaped. She looked beautiful and silly in cream colored netted hose rolled down just an inch or two below her hemline, one leg garnished with a blue garter.

Without the garter, the hose kept crawling down her other leg. When she wasn't pulling up her stocking, she twirled a solid gold band around her finger, one of several just like it from a velvet box beneath the glass topped counter in Mr. Miles' store.

Without waiting for Crown to ask, Mr. Miles explained, "We can't have a wedding without a ring and a dress."

Crown looked down at his feet, aware that Mr. Miles was grinning at him. He walked over and slapped Crown on the back.

"Congratulations, son."

"I ... I best get the wagon loaded."

"Never you mind that. You and Jewel get over to the church. I'll take care of these things for you. Go on now. Get out of here."

"Come on, Crown." Jewel linked her arm in his. "Tain't nothin' to be ashamed of."

She led him outside, parading the two blocks to the church, not once hesitating to tell anyone they encountered where they were headed and why. By the time they got to the church, a small crowd had surrounded them.

Crown and Jewel were ushered inside by whoops and whistles, back slaps and congratulatory hugs. Jewel was giddy with all the attention, but Crown felt two feet tall. Unaccustomed to so much excitement, he clung to Jewel.

The commotion drew Reverend Samuels out of the parsonage, just two rooms attached to the church. "What's going on in here. That's no way to carry on in the Lord's house."

"Jewel and McGee here's gettin' married Rev," someone shouted from the crowd.

"You go'n' marry 'em ain't you, Rev?" chimed another.

Reverend Samuels eyed Crown suspiciously. "Perhaps. Let me have a few words with Jewel."

Reverend Samuels took Jewel aside. Crown was left uncomfortably in the midst of all the well wishers. He watched Jewel nod yes, then relaxed when the reverend smiled back at him. To Crown's relief, Reverend Samuels motioned for Crown to join them.

Crown was glad to be at Jewel's side again. She linked her arm in his and grinned up at him. He offered her a strained smile. He had hoped for a quiet and private ceremony, symbolic of the way he hoped to live his life with Jewel.

"So you aim to marry?" Reverend Samuels looked down at Jewel's belly. Crown shuffled uneasy, but he didn't see how the reverend could know that Jewel was pregnant.

"Normally there's a waiting period," he continued. "But I realize ya'll don't get to town much. I'll talk to the circuit judge and have the papers ready for you the next time you come in to town. Meanwhile I'll marry you, but it won't really be official until you get the papers from the judge."

Reverend Samuels leaned close and asked Crown if he knew what that meant. Crown said he did, though he knew he had no intention of stopping what he'd already been doing for three months, and with Jewel already pregnant he reasoned that it wouldn't make a damn bit of difference to the Lord. It was the intent that mattered, and Crown intended to do right by Jewel and what was his. He had stayed away from Jewel for nearly a week once and that had nearly been the end of him. Now even if he were angry, Crown couldn't stay away from Jewel for more than a day or two.

Nettie Cooper stepped forward. "Ya'll need a witness, Rev?"

"That all right with ya'll?" Reverend Samuels queried Crown.

Crown nodded. No one else would have suited him better except Cooper himself or Mr. Miles and neither of them were there.

Reverend Samuels hushed the crowd. No one bothered to sit. There was no marching down the aisle, no organ or flowers or solo. Still Jewel looked as though she would never be happier. The ceremony was over in ten minutes. Thankfully Jewel declined Nettie's invitation to dinner. She seemed as anxious as Crown to get home.

The crowd followed them out of the church, down the street and back to the store where the wagon was waiting. Mr. Miles met them outside with a package for Jewel. Crown endured another round of congratulations, until Mr. Miles pulled Jewel from the crowd and helped her into the wagon.

Crown nodded thanks and climbed in beside her. The crowd parted reluctantly, still yelling their congratulations, a few running alongside the wagon.

When they were out of town, Jewel opened the package from Mr. Miles. It contained a brand new jar of pickles, another bundle of peppermints, and a small white blanket trimmed in lace. Jewel must have told Mr. Miles everything. Crown shook his head, but he couldn't be angry. Jewel had wanted to buy something for the baby, but Crown had told her that would arouse suspicions and it was early yet and they'd best wait till it was closer to her time.

He had been acting like he knew more than he did. All he really knew was that girls would come to the convent all small like Jewel. In a matter of months they'd balloon to twice their normal size, all of it in their bellies, then mysteriously, their bellies would go away, and the girls would go back home, and the orphanage had one more mouth to feed. Until Crown had happened upon Mae and Carrie that night, he had no notion of how those babies got into this world. Remembering that night made him frightened for him and Jewel.

"Mae tell you what to do when the baby comes?"

"Some."

"Some?"

"Enough. Don't you fret about that. That's my worry. You just be there when the time comes. We ain't got no Carrie to bring this one in the world. It's just me and you, Crown. So don't you go runnin' off like Pap."

It was the first time she'd ever said a disparaging word against him. Crown grunted. He was nothing like Sam Giddings.

"Ain't I always been there when you needed me?"

This time Jewel grunted. "And a plenty times when I didn't."

Crown laughed. He liked the sound of his laughter, and he laughed again loud and long. Jewel looked at him and giggled till they were both laughing. All the noise they were making spooked More and Less. Crown jerked the reins to assure them he was still in control. He looked at Jewel and smiled.

"You ain't half bad, Jewel Gid ... I mean McGee."

"You ain't half bad yourself, Papa."

Crown got serious then. He was anxious for the months to pass and the child to come. He hoped the child would have his smarts and Jewel's looks. Only then would Crown feel like he and Jewel had a real chance in this world.

CHAPTER 23

▼

Crown had grown accustomed to their routine. Up early six days a week, he would feed and water the horses, slop the pigs and feed a small roost of chickens he let run wild. After breakfast, if he didn't have a funeral or trip to oversee the farm, he would clear land, come in for lunch then go out again till supper. Afterwards he would enjoy a late coffee before joining Jewel in bed.

On Sundays he rested, sleeping late till the smell of bacon wafted into the room sometimes crisp and inviting, sometimes burnt. Then Lenetta pounced in taking a little piece of his Jewel and leaving him steeping in his own company for most of the day, every loathsome Sunday of every week.

Lenetta took to coming weekly picking Jewel up on Sunday mornings and bringing her back much too late to suit Crown. He sent Jewel off with her passel of cousins and his tithe so the God he had never trusted would send her back home to him.

Jewel would make him breakfast and leave him a little lunch to tide him till she got home. He puttered around the house, doing a little reading and a lot of worrying. He mostly wore out the floor from the front hall to the study to the kitchen till Jewel got home. She would never know it though because he made sure to be in that chair in the study pouring over the latest Farm Journal when she returned.

Even at the convent, Crown had been given Sundays to rest. He found it hard to work and harder still to read with Jewel gone. Yet when Jewel urged him to go with her he declined. Nineteen years in a convent was more church than Crown could stomach even though he was curious. Church the way Jewel recounted it was a far sight different. Jewel always came back laughing and clapping and singing and humming some earthy gospel that was etched for the moment in her memory. Lenetta would walk into the house imitating Deacon Bibee and they'd howl in delight like he didn't perform the same perfunctory song and dance twice every Sunday, once for the morning service and again for the evening. Crown envied their enjoyment. He believed in heaven, and he believed in hell. He figured he was worse than some, better than most and headed for the latter no matter what. He had a Bible that he read occasionally, finding comfort in Psalms and Proverbs though he'd never admit it.

He would read a little just to get him through those Sundays, till Jewel breezed through the door with a grin on her lips and a song in her heart and eyes that smiled he was sure for him.

Granny Giddings had taken a liking to Crown, even though they had never met. She always sent Crown a plate of food and some wisdom Jewel felt compelled to recite. It made Crown feel like he was part of something bigger, even if Jewel was the only one he dared to share it with.

He would settle down once she was home and Lenetta was gone having eyed him over like she could see clear through him. Jewel would warm his supper and get ready for bed while he ate. Then he'd watch her while she cleaned up after him. It gave him comfort to know she liked doing things for him. It gave him something close to joy to know she came back to him at the end of the day, filling his empty belly with food and warming his cold bed with her body. It gave him something close to peace to curl up with her at night and know she'd be there come morning, fixing him breakfast, lunch and supper, sometimes edible, sometimes not. It gave him something beyond pleasure to know she was the one thing that was his, that had never been anyone else's. But he was watching her change. Her breasts were swollen, her hips were spreading. Her waist had grown thick and her belly distended. She had taken to rubbing her belly and talking to it like there was a little person inside already formed, with little ears pricked to her every word. She had tried to draw Crown in too, but he pulled away when she reached for him, urging him to caress her rounded belly. He scoffed when she suggested he might have some words for the life they had created. He could see her changing, and he hated it. It was the only thing he feared.

CHAPTER 24

▼

The spring rains had been especially heavy, the roads so bogged down, Jewel had missed her Sunday-go-to-meeting two weeks in a row. Crown had been happy to have her to himself again, though he'd never admit it. But four days ago, the skies had cleared, making the roads dry and safe to travel again.

With supplies low and travel postponed, Crown was overdue his quarterly trip to town. Jewel had hounded him for two days about the trip till he'd relented to take her with him. Early that May morning, Crown went out to hitch the horses to the wagon. He thought for a moment to sneak off, leaving Jewel behind. He'd never seen her angry, but he suspected he'd have hell to pay if he left her. Jewel's boldness had grown since she'd been filled with his child, and she wouldn't be left behind.

As Crown led the skittish mare out of the barn, Jewel came bounding out of the house. Crown wasn't sure who was more restless, Less or Jewel. The trip would do them both good. As for Crown, the trip to town was even less tolerable because Jewel would be with him. If he were alone folks would pay him no mind, but with Jewel so obviously pregnant, they'd get more attention than Crown could stand.

"You trying to leave me, Crown McGee?" Jewel teased.

Ashamed that he'd had that very thought Crown turned away from her and secured the harnesses. Jewel hooked an arm under his forcing him to look at her. She was a contradiction with her extended belly and her pigtails and an oversized pair of Jebediah's overalls she'd salvaged from the attic. It was another reason they needed this trip. Jewel was bursting out of things to wear.

The drive in was pleasant. The countryside, green year-round, was lush in spring, with squirrels playing and birds singing and wildflowers blooming. Pine forests hugged the farm to the north, coating everything in the yellow down of mating. In the low-lying marshes south of the farm, cypress dominated. Fragrant purple and white honeysuckle lined Cemetery Road, wrapping around the trunks and stretching up to touch the chains of Spanish moss hanging from the cypress. As warm as it was, Jewel huddled close to Crown, wrapping her arm in his and singing one of her little ditties.

Crown slowed a little near the farm, taking in all that had become his in so short a time. It was the season Crown liked best. He could smell the rain-soaked earth changing. Soon his crop would rise up from the earth adding tints of gold and green to the landscape.

Jewel laughed as a squirrel ran across the road in front of them, an offended cardinal diving at his head. Crown smiled, knowing contentment for the first time. He found himself leaning into Jewel and enjoying her song. He straightened though as they neared town. Jewel tugged at him, looked up and smiled but he didn't look back. Not even she could ease the tension he felt as he pulled up in front of the mercantile.

They spent the day with her shopping for baby things and him trying to hide from all the people who suddenly wanted to pat him on the back and grin at him like they knew what he did with his nights. Jewel was the center of attention because everybody loved her, and no one could believe she was pregnant and married to Crown McGee. But she seemed happy enough, and folks tended to like Crown better because of it.

She was about five or six months pregnant, and her belly was nearly as big as Mae's the day Crown had come to Colwin County. Jewel's cheeks were fat, and she said she couldn't see her own feet, which made her laugh out loud every time she looked down. Crown had worried about her making the trip to town, but their papers had been in for two months.

Even Jewel could count high enough to know the numbers didn't add up, so she said there wasn't any use of them hiding it anymore. She'd smiled, quoting the gospel according to Mae, "Half of the first borns and half and half again of the seconds come long before the weddin'."

Later that evening, they sat at the kitchen table over the last remnants of supper, looking at the Sears catalog Jewel had gotten at the mercantile and fighting over the pages because all Crown wanted to look at was the farm equipment and all Jewel wanted to see were the fancy clothes Crown said they couldn't afford to buy. Jewel jerked the book and held it to the far side of her belly. Crown tried to reach around but couldn't, so he reached behind her. She screamed and giggled and nearly fell to the floor she leaned so hard. He stopped reaching for the book because he was afraid he was going to hurt her.

"Whut you 'fraid of, Crown? Baby ain't go'n' break."

"Stop fooling around, Jewel."

She stopped laughing and reached for his hand.

"Oh Crown, she just kicked. Mama always gathered us around her about this time so we could feel the babies. Said you could always get a feel for how they go'n' be that way. I think this one's not go'n' be a bit of trouble. She just lies there all peaceful-like most of the time. Then now and again she'll kick, once or twice, just to let me know she's all right.

"Give me your hand, Crown, in case she kicks again."

"No."

Crown slid his hand away from Jewel, afraid he'd jinx the baby more if he touched it. Afraid that baby would come out looking and acting just like him.

"Come on now. Don't you want to feel her?"

"Leave me alone now, Jewel and give me the damn catalog."

"No."

"Jewel."

"Come git it."

"I can't. Your damn belly's in the way."

"Never stopped you before."

She stood up and popped him square on top of his head with that book, then ran. She looked like a whale out of water, and Crown was suddenly laughing too.

She turned at the door of the kitchen with one hand over her belly and the other dangling against her plump hip. She looked silly and beautiful standing there.

"I never laughed, Jewel, till I met you."

"That's the nicest thing you eva said to me, Crown."

She smiled at him, then turned down the hallway and disappeared into the bedroom. When he didn't come right away, she popped her head out again.

"Well, are you comin' or ain't ya?"

CHAPTER 25

▼

It was near harvest time again, and as much as Crown hated to leave Jewel, he needed to be at the farm. Reluctantly, he'd hired Lenetta to sit with Jewel till the baby came. Still, he was prone to worry. As her time grew short, Jewel had become fat and heavy. She waddled like a duck, and Crown found her less desirable, his thoughts turning guiltily to Carrie. A time or two Jewel had caught him fondling himself and offered to relieve him. Ashamed, he'd declined saying it probably wasn't good for the baby. Jewel said Mae had told her to expect him to be less willing, and though Jewel sounded certain when she said it, she'd looked hurt. Crown wished the baby would come so things could go back to the way they were when just looking at her was enough to get him going and having her was enough to keep him through the night.

Crown shook his head. It wasn't the time to be thinking about Jewel. He'd neglected the farm enough already, worrying about leaving her alone, yet ashamed to bring her along with him, despite the fact that everybody in Colwin County already knew he'd taken her for his wife.

He didn't know how much Sam Giddings did on the farm until he was left with Karl Johnson's big ideas and no one with common sense to balance them. Crown had nearly fired the man when he caught the women planting early. Johnson had finally persuaded Crown to let him plant one field. Crown had relented just to shut him up. Whether it was the flocks of migrating birds that too often overstayed their welcome or the bugs and mildew that followed the spring rains, the crop didn't come up, and there wasn't enough time to plant another. It was just one field, but with a child on the way, it was good money lost, and Crown couldn't afford that.

Crown passed the farm and turned onto the main road, riding over to Chambers County first to check out the field that had been seeded by plane. He had heard the plane seeding had been a success, but he wanted to see for himself. Crown expected the rice to be sparse and scattered, but to his surprise, the field looked as plentiful as any other he'd seen.

Crown headed back to the farm eager to discuss what he'd seen with Karl Johnson. If prices held, Crown thought he could plant a field or two by plane as early as next season. It would be expensive, but would mean fewer laborers and less cost in the long run.

With machines more common and farms consolidating, Crown couldn't tell how many hapless souls had been displaced. Most had already headed to California, but that still left more than enough filling the towns and back roads of East Texas looking for work. Crown couldn't use any more help than he had. When the angry, out of work men weren't drinking moonshine and fighting, they lined up outside the farms and mills begging for work. Crown had hired a few of them as watchmen, just to keep the others off his land. That didn't keep their tired women and half-starved children from squatting along the river and bayous in camps that were dirty and desolate and mean.

Crown often found them camped out on Cemetery Road as though they were waiting for someone to die so they could take their place. He had to chase whole families off his land, often after they'd squatted in one of his own cabins with a distant cousin who had the fortune to be employed albeit as a tenant on Crown McGee's farm.

Crown pulled up to the front of the granary and tied his team to the post. Inside the place was humming with activity, and he could smell the rice dust in the air. The weather was dry for harvest, and he was grateful for that. The last thing he needed was for the rest of his crop to rot.

Johnson hailed him from the far side of the building. Crown hoped the man didn't have any more fancy ideas. He followed Johnson out back where a half dozen men gathered around one of the two threshers. Smoke—black, oily and thick—poured from the engine. Crown cursed. He had hoped to add a combine next season and he wanted to try plane seeding next spring. He didn't need any more expenses. Johnson had already cost him enough.

"Damned thing. What is it this time?"

"Blew a gasket, Mr. McGee. Second one today and we're all out of spares. Somebody'll need to go into town and get one. My boy would be glad to go for you."

"No. I'll do it myself. I'll get Cooper to come out and take a look at it. It shouldn't be blowing gaskets like that. You flush that engine before you started her up? It's been sitting since last harvest. It should have been flushed then and again for measure."

Johnson looked sheepish. Crown didn't expect an answer, but he couldn't stop thinking that Sam Giddings would have taken care of things without being told.

"I'll be back in four hours, meanwhile double up on the one that's working and keep that grain moving."

"What about Jewel? You want somebody to ride up and tell her where you're off to?"

Crown grunted. "She's got Lenetta to keep her company."

Crown returned four hours later with Cooper and three brand new gaskets. Cooper looked over both machines before he left.

"You been running them hard. I need to overhaul the engines, the blades are dull and the belts need changing too. Meanwhile I'll flush the engines good. You're done for the day. I'll bed here tonight and have them up and running by tomorrow morning."

"How much?"

"A small fortune."

"Can I get by the harvest?"

"You'll have to. It'll take a while to get the parts. I can see what I can scrounge around. With all the speculators losing their farms there's parts a plenty if you don't mind second hand."

"I don't mind. You just mind you give me a second hand price."

Crown looked down at the watch that had been Jebediah's. He'd taken the picture out though he couldn't quite bring himself to throw it away. After all his mother was half of it, and he hadn't quite settled how he felt about her. Someday Jewel would be there and maybe this baby they had on the way.

"I got to get home. Any more trouble Johnson, you know where to find me. Your boy can take Cooper back to town in the morning."

Crown left them there talking about threshers and combines replacing the need for good field hands just when there were hands aplenty. He headed back down Cemetery Road certain that Jewel would light into him for taking so long. She'd grown bossier with her new girth. At times she'd break down crying though she swore there was nothing wrong. He slowed in no hurry for Jewel's unpredictable emotions or Lenetta's ribald ribbing. By the time he turned into the cemetery it was dark. A lone lamp lighted the way to the house.

He took the time to give Less a good rub down, then tossed her a mound of fresh hay. He made his way across the yard noting the sliver of moon and the absence of shadows.

The house was quiet. Crown crept inside so he wouldn't wake Jewel. It was early yet, but he wasn't surprised that Jewel had gone to bed. She'd been plumb tuckered out lately, and Lenetta would sleep day and night if he let her.

He opened the bedroom door slowly. To his surprise, Lenetta was sitting straight up in his bed. Jewel was lying beside her. Crown walked over and peered into Jewel's moonlit face. She looked content, like she hadn't been worried about him being late at all. He shook Lenetta gently. She jumped, and he pressed a finger to his lips.

"Shh. Don't wake Jewel. I'm home now. You can go to bed."

Lenetta shook her head then startled in recognition. With her teeth barred she whispered, pulling Crown so close her rancid breath brushed the hairs in his nose.

"You ain't about to sleep here with her nursin' an infant, and you liable to squash her like a bug. I'll step out so you can see your daughter. You holler when you're done."

Lenetta released her hold on Crown, then stepped out of the room, yawned and closed the door behind her. Crown stared after her as though he had no idea that one day a baby would actually come. He looked at Jewel again. She looked so peaceful, and Lenetta had said he had a daughter. He hoped wistfully that the baby was as beautiful as Jewel. He pulled the covers back gently. Sure enough a tiny bundle lay suckling, more for comfort than nourishment from the hollow sound of it. Crown pried the baby gently from Jewel's breast. The baby protested softly, and he gave her a finger to suck.

He felt the ridge of her mouth, the soft folds of her lip massage his skin. Uncertain, he walked to the window so he could see her in the faint light. She grabbed his finger with a tiny fist all her own. He stared at it amazed it was so tiny and strong. Then he looked at her for the first time. The wisp of auburn hair, the skin like sunshine, the wheat colored eyes, the tiny but broad nose and lips.

"Loooorrd." Crown choked back his agony even as the plea erupted from his throat.

He held her up to see her better. The tiny coverlet dropped to the ground, and she was stretched naked and cold in the sparse moonlight. She was otherwise perfect, ten fingers, ten toes, fat little bowed legs, a distended belly, and arms that kept reaching for something Crown didn't have to give. She started to fuss, and there was no mistaking it. He had cursed her, beautiful as she was, with a lip she'd never be able to hide.

He hugged her against his chest. His sorrow, held for a lifetime, escaped in one hollow breath. He had loved her before she was born, but despite all his wishes and hopes and prayers, she was defective. He bundled her, so she wouldn't be cold, looked twice at Jewel sleeping peacefully and eased out into the night.

Crown didn't really think about what he was doing. He just couldn't bear for her to have the life he'd lived, to suffer the way he had. He grabbed a shovel and trudged to the cemetery, stopping only when he stood over Jebediah's unmarked grave.

He laid her down and muttered, "I'm sorry". Then he cursed Jebediah for making him loathe himself and her so. He started digging. Tears coursed down his cheeks.

"Whut you doin', Crown? You give me that child! You give me my baby now!"

Crown had been so absorbed he hadn't heard Jewel and Lenetta approach. He looked up at Jewel leaning on Lenetta like it had taken all her strength to give birth to the life he had the audacity to take.

"It's no good, Jewel. Did you look at her?"

"I looked."

"And you … you still want her?"

"I want her much as I wanted you, at least till now."

That hurt him. He hung his head.

"It's no good, Jewel. She's got no place in this world. She'll be all alone. People will taunt her and call her names. She'll end up just like me, hateful and mean and no damn good."

"You been good to me, Crown, but ain't nobody go'n' hurt her long as I breathe. Not even you. I'll see you dead first."

He looked up to see the long barrel of his twenty gauge staring back at him with an angry, intent Lenetta on the other end. Jewel was smart enough to give Lenetta that task. Jewel might not have been able to pull the trigger, but Lenetta would not hesitate.

Crown laid down the shovel and picked up the child. He handed her to Jewel and stepped back.

"I'm sorry, Jewel."

"I s'pect you are. But you stay away from her and me from now on. I'll see you dead 'fore I let you harm her. I'll see you dead."

Crown watched Jewel shuffle back to the house, tired, worn and a little bit older. He should have known he'd take the sunshine out of her if she hung around him long enough. He should have known.

CHAPTER 26

▼

Feeling small and lonely, Crown stayed away from Jewel. She'd moved into the room across the hall, leaving him with an empty bed. Only her scent lingered in the room. He'd been angry as hell the day he'd come home to find Lenetta had washed his linens and was hanging them on the line to dry. Lenetta spat at him and yelled that she wished Jewel had let her kill him. Crown yelled that he'd wished she had. Jewel had stared at them from the back door and turned away when he looked at her. Crown felt he would die if Jewel kept looking at him like that.

Lenetta left two days later. Whether she'd had her fill of him or Jewel had asked her to go, Crown didn't know. He watched from the barn while they parted tearfully.

He had offered to drive Lenetta home, but she'd sworn she would rather walk than ride with the likes of him. Lenetta said Jewel deserved better, and Crown knew she was right. Still he had been glad to see Lenetta go, and he had hoped without saying and with no one to say it to, that there'd be peace in the house again.

In the days that followed, he admired Jewel from a distance, reluctantly estranged from the one person who had accepted him unconditionally. Jewel had been brought up with babies all her life. Mae always had two or three in diapers, and Jewel took to mothering easily. Crown envied her time and gentleness with the baby. Despite Jewel's attentions, the baby fussed day and night. It seemed she was forever at Jewel's breast, and while it would comfort her momentarily, she would soon be wailing piteously again. It was wearing Jewel down, till she hardly had time to eat or sleep herself, let alone time to care for Crown if she'd had a mind to. Jewel had never been thin, but in the days after their child was born, both Jewel and the child were wasting away.

Crown was worried. He wished then that Lenetta had never left, but he didn't dare ask her to come back. He knew what was wrong. He'd seen it in the orphanage three times before. He'd seen two baby girls die within days of their births, buried them himself in the small cemetery they used for the changelings that didn't make it. He'd seen a male child live awhile. Crown had strained the goat's milk himself, boiled it half and half with water, then soaked a towel in it, until the towel was sloppy with milk. When the milk had cooled, Sister had shoved a corner of the towel none too gently into the infant's mouth, and squeezed with wrinkled fingers till the milk dribbled down his reluctant throat. The baby had gotten fat and might have survived, but then the orphanage had a run of the fever and he'd died anyway, leaving Crown alone with his affliction.

Crown wondered whether he should just let their child die like the others had died, starving to death even while she fed voraciously at Jewel's ravaged breast. But his daughter had suffered enough at his hands, and he didn't have the heart to do her any more harm. Besides, the sleeplessness, worry and fear were taking a toll on Jewel, and he couldn't bear to lose her too. So he woke up early one morning and milked the cow and strained the milk and mixed it half and half with water brought up from the well. He strained it again because the salts were known to settle after a while. He set the milk on the stove to boil, mindful that the child might be fussing for breakfast any minute. He soaked a fresh cloth in the mixture then ladled the cloth and a bit of the milk into a small bowl.

He knocked gently at Jewel's door. When she didn't answer, he opened the door slowly. Jewel was asleep in the rocker with the baby cradled at her breast. She was uncovered from her shoulders to her waist, the bib of her overalls laid down and her blouse swaddling their daughter. They both looked weary, like they'd been warring with each other and had collapsed in the midst of the battle, neither winning nor acknowledging defeat.

Crown lifted the baby gently, pausing when Jewel stirred, exhaling only when she settled to sleep once more. He took the child into the kitchen, still swaddled in the blouse that had begun to smell more like her and less like Jewel. Crown laid his daughter easily in the crook of his arm, pried her lips open with his finger, till he could feel the cleft in her mouth. He lifted the rag drenched in milk and squeezed it gently. Then probing, he forced it into her mouth till she began to gag. Her eyes opened wide, and she looked at him. When she opened her mouth wide to fuss, he squeezed the rag against the roof of her mouth. He felt the warm milk drain over his finger. She cooed, then relaxed and closed her eyes.

"Whut are you doin', Crown?"

Crown turned to see Jewel self-consciously slipping the bib back over her shoulders. It did little to hide her milk-laden breasts. Their eyes met then averted. Jewel crossed the room quickly and reached. Apologetic, Crown handed her the child, the rag still dripping milk from his oversized hand.

"I'm not hurting her. I'm feeding her."

The baby fussed, and Jewel rocked her, though to no avail. Jewel checked her over, then peered suspiciously at the rag in Crown's hand.

"It's cow's milk, but it will have to do. She can't nurse with the harelip. She'll die, Jewel. I know. I've seen it before."

Jewel nodded in acknowledgement. Crown handed her the cloth.

"Just slip it in her mouth and squeeze."

Jewel nudged a small corner of the moist rag into the baby's mouth.

"Further down, Jewel, till you think you'll choke her but you won't," Crown coached. "You'll have to do it each time she feeds. It will seem a lot at first, but she'll start to fill up, and you won't have to feed her so often. She'll gain weight, and you'll be able to rest."

Crown shuffled after he said it, aware that he had little business speaking of the welfare of any child, let alone the one he'd tried to kill only days before. Jewel sat down at the kitchen table doing as Crown instructed. The child lay peacefully, her eyes closed, her throat undulating as she drank. Jewel looked at Crown with eyes wet and full.

"Thank you, Crown. I never been so wore out and weary. How come you know so much?"

Crown didn't answer, just grunted suddenly uncomfortable. "You want me to fix you something, Jewel?"

"Whut, you go'n' cook for me too?" Jewel smiled wanly. "I'm too worn out to eat, Crown, but I thank you. No, we just go'n' lie down and rest."

Jewel rose stiffly. Crown helped her to her feet and walked her to the bedroom door, where she turned only to dismiss him, still uncertain. Crown went up the stairs and unlocked the door to the nursery. He'd spent a lot of time dressing up that room in anticipation of the child. Intending to keep it a surprise, he'd worked alone on Sundays, while Jewel visited her folks. He picked up the crib, leaving the room with its freshly painted walls and dimmed hopes, and shut the door behind him. He was afraid if Jewel saw the room now, she'd move upstairs with their daughter. That was more distance than Crown could bear.

He wrestled the crib down the narrow stairs. He knocked on Jewel's door and opened it without waiting for her answer.

"I thought you could use this. She'll rest better and so will you." Crown walked in the room and set the crib down within an arm's length of Jewel's bed.

Jewel looked like she wanted to cry. "Thank ye, Crown. I reckon we can both get some sleep now." The baby was nestled in the crook of her arm. Jewel rose, careful not to wake her, and placed her in the crib. Jewel touched Crown ever so lightly on his arm and walked him to the door. "Thank ye." She shut the door, and he left them to sleep while he went about his chores.

That night Crown kept his door open so he could hear Jewel cooing to the baby. He realized he didn't even know the baby's name, and he wanted to. Jewel was singing, and Crown crept to the door and listened. He wanted her as badly as he ever did. He wondered if he started acting like the cuss he was if she'd leave the baby long enough to come to him. But he realized he didn't want her that way. He knocked on the door, and the singing stopped. The rocker creaked then fell silent.

"Jewel?"

He opened the door timidly.

"Jewel?"

"Whut you want, Crown?"

"What you call her?"

"Sela."

"Sela?"

"Sela Mae McGee."

"I like that, Jewel. I really do."

A breath of silence passed between them.

"Night, Crown."

"G'night."

CHAPTER 27

▼

Crown had slept atop the covers with his clothes on. He woke up ruffled and weary. He'd lain awake till nearly dawn wondering how he'd ever make things right with Jewel. Outside his window, a cold heavy fog draped the yard. He peered across the hall, but Jewel was already up, and the bedroom was empty and dark. Crown jolted up like he'd suddenly remembered the difference between night and day. He pulled on his boots and listened, filtering through the sounds of marsh and morning, till he could hear Sela's faint gurgle and Jewel's gentle humming. The scents of warm milk and hot coffee drifted from the kitchen.

Passing Jewel and Sela with a nod, he followed the smells to the stove, where he helped himself to a cup of coffee that tasted half as good as it smelled. Between sips he paused, his back against the counter.

"You go'n' be all right, Jewel," He stated more than asked. With her back to Crown, Jewel simply nodded. Crown finished a bad cup of coffee, then mumbled under his breath.

"You say somethin', Crown?"

"I'm going to the farm. Be back directly."

"Kin you send Lenetta this way?"

"What for?"

"I need help, less you aimin' to do the washin' and cleanin' round here."

Crown had no use for Lenetta, and he had only just gotten used to her gone, but he couldn't deny Jewel the help. He grunted his agreement, then left so Jewel couldn't see the disappointment he knew was etched across his face. Outside he swore just loud enough for God to hear him, then crossed the yard to the barn. He hitched the wagon and laid the axe under the seat because he intended to cut some firewood while he was out. It would be another month before they'd need it, if at all, the way the seasons tended to blend mostly summer and spring with a little fall and just a tease of winter. Still one could never be sure, and it was wise to have an ample supply of firewood good and dry stored in the wood bin in the barn until then.

Crown turned onto Cemetery Road and headed for the farm. He didn't see Lenetta, but he spread the word that Jewel was looking for her. By the time he left for home early that evening, Lenetta was headed back to the farm.

Crown met Lenetta on Cemetery Road. She was looking dead at him when he pulled to a stop a little too close for her comfort. Lenetta jumped in the ditch and cursed.

"You damned fool. You almost hit me."

"You ought not be walking down the middle of the road."

"Whar else I'm go'n' walk? You too damned cheap to widen the road."

"What I'm go'n' widen it for? Dead don't need but one road in. Living don't need but one road out."

"Hmmph. Jewel had any sense, she'd take that road."

"What you know about it? Jewel ain't complaining far as I can see."

Her yellow legs freckled with mud, Lenetta climbed back onto the road. She grabbed the harness in one hand and wagged a plump finger at Crown.

"I know you up to somethin', Crown McGee. You ain't fooled, Jewel, and you ain't fooled me. You up to somethin'."

"I don't know what you're talking about, and I suspect you don't know either."

"I'm talkin' 'bout you, Crown McGee. How come you helped li'l Sela? How come you got a soft spot in your heart all a sudden, when I'd swear you didn't have a heart at all?"

"Get out of my way, Lenetta."

Crown jerked the reins, and the horses lunged sending Lenetta backwards into the ditch. Crown reigned in the horses and called out to Lenetta. Lenetta climbed out of the ditch and charged at him shouting a string of expletives. In no mood to fight and certain Lenetta was alright, Crown signaled the team to drive home. Lenetta was still standing in the road and cursing when Crown turned into his gate. He pulled inside and came to a stop, letting his anger boil over, then steep. He didn't head for the barn till his anger was lukewarm. He didn't head to the house till it had fizzled, and he didn't have to worry about pushing Jewel down that road.

CHAPTER 28

▼

With Sela feeding and sleeping about every three hours, Jewel soon began to look herself again. Crown had not asked for anything; he had expected nothing. Though Jewel had warmed a little to Crown, she had not forgotten. Crown knew it by the way Jewel stopped whatever she was doing to fold her arms over Sela and position herself between Crown and Sela whenever he came near.

Still Jewel had asked Crown to chop down a tree for Christmas, had walked out to the woods with him and picked it out herself, and gotten all misty eyed when he propped it in the parlor. She burned two batches of popcorn before Crown relented and popped a good batch for her. Then she stayed up half the night stringing those white flowers of corn all along the green branches of that pine. It still didn't look like much so she rummaged through the attic until she found a box of red satin ribbon and green glass balls. Crown couldn't imagine Christmas even with the tree he'd set in the parlor and Jewel wailing Christmas carols and that damned box of ribbons and bows his mother must have used on some other tree in that house once a long time ago.

Jewel said the tree needed presents and the fireplace needed stockings and she wouldn't rest till Crown took her to town to get them. Crown hadn't been to town since before Sela was born, but as soon as they arrived in town, Crown was convinced most folks knew what he'd done to Sela. Folks weren't so friendly this time. Lenetta must have enjoyed blabbing all over the county. Crown was certain the women doting over Jewel, oohing and aahing over Sela to Jewel's face were whispering behind Jewel's back that the poor thing was too dumb to know her child was ugly. Of course Jewel knew it; she just loved Sela anyway, the same way she might have loved Crown if he had let her.

At the mercantile, Mr. Miles struck up a real friendship with Jewel once he realized she could make Crown part with his money. The storekeeper delighted in showing her all the things Crown said they couldn't afford and wouldn't have wanted to spoil Sela with if he'd had any influence in raising her.

Crown left to run his errands. Afraid of the damage she might do to his wallet, Crown cut short his quarterly trip to the bank. He made a modest withdrawal so he'd have sufficient cash for all the things Jewel would talk him into buying from Mr. Miles. When he returned, she was leaning over the counter with Sela cradled comfortably between her arm and her hip. She watched wide-eyed as Mr. Miles turned the dial on a brand new radio. It crackled and popped until he turned it just right and the popping became the whiz of bullets and the plodding of hooves and a cacophony of voices that seemed to come out of nowhere.

Watching her, Crown knew just the thing she'd want for Christmas, and he wondered how he'd get her away from it long enough to buy it and then get it in the wagon and home without her knowing. She had him doing the craziest things like cutting down pine trees and popping corn so she could string it around the tree making the house smell like Christmas and filling it with all the things Crown had missed growing up. He wished he could gain her trust as easily as he could get the things she wanted.

Still it made him feel good to do something for Jewel, like maybe there was still a chance for him to salvage what they'd had before Sela. Cooper's wife, Nettie took Jewel off to a church supper, and Crown used the chance to get the radio. Crown bought Sela a rag doll with tomato red lips and hair of black yarn and burlap skin and overalls like the ones Jewel was wearing again.

Crown bought more than he needed, throwing in a few large items, like two new shovels, chicken wire and posts for the pig pen, just so he wouldn't have to explain to Jewel why the wagon was piled so high. Thanking Crown for his business, Mr. Miles eagerly helped Crown load the wagon. Crown threw a tarp over the goods and sat back to wait for Jewel. There was nothing else to do in town; unless, he went to talk to Cooper about farming and machines, and Crown didn't feel like talking.

It was hot for December. The sun was high in the sky and Crown hoped it would cool down so he could light the fireplace on Christmas Eve and sit next to Jewel beside the fire with a book and a bowl of popcorn. It was wishful thinking he knew, but it was all he wanted for Christmas. Before long Jewel came back with a sleeping baby, a full belly and a plate for him. She offered to drive while Crown ate, but he wasn't hungry, and he needed something to concentrate on besides Jewel. On the drive back she fell asleep, but even in that mindless state she kept jerking her head up like his shoulder wasn't fit to lie on.

CHAPTER 29

▼

Christmas morning was warm and if it weren't for the scent of pine, Crown wouldn't have known it from any other. Lenetta woke them up before sunup, saying they were invited to Granny Giddings for the day. Jewel looked so excited, Crown couldn't say no. But he couldn't go either, not with everyone eyeing him like a dog for the things he'd done and knowing the invite was never meant for him anyway.

It was lonely in the house with Jewel and Sela gone. Jewel even took Sela's presents with them like she didn't think Crown cared about Sela or Christmas, but Crown did care. He was angry at Jewel for leaving him like he didn't matter, and he was angry with himself for caring.

He'd had Johnson string a line from the granary to Cemetery Road and along the road to the house. Far as Jewel knew they were getting lights for Christmas. After Jewel and Sela were gone, Crown went to check on the radio where he'd hidden it in a corner of the barn behind a pile of hay. Sela's doll, still swaddled in the plain brown wrapper from Mr. Miles' store, lay on top of the radio. Crown lifted the doll and polished the radio with the tail of his shirt so it would look shiny and new when he put it in Jewel's room.

The radio was heavy so Crown wrapped it good in Jewel's newly washed sheets and lifted it into the wheelbarrow so he could get it to the house without bruising it. He laid the doll back on top and headed for the house. Leaving the wheelbarrow on the porch, he lifted the radio and dragged it across the floor on those same sheets. He didn't dare scratch the floor Jewel had polished on her hands and knees. He managed without scratching the floor or the radio.

Furnished with a bed, a chest of drawers, Sela's crib, a rocking chair, and a throw rug, Jewel's room was nothing more than practical. The radio made a nice touch positioned against the wall so the light from the window caught the shine on the wood. Crown admired his own work, then turned on the radio, but all he got was static.

Crown turned and turned that dial just like Mr. Miles had done. He wanted things just right for Jewel, but nothing was working out like he planned.

Just when Crown thought he would have to give up trying, he finally got something on the radio besides static. It was just the news out of New Orleans, but he suspected anything would be all right this first time. He didn't dare go searching again. He turned the sound up, then lay on Jewel's bed awhile remembering how excited she'd been and hoping he'd see that look in her eyes again.

The day was long in passing. Crown paced the floors from Jewel's room to the parlor to the study. He tried to settle down to read, but not even that could ease the anxiety of waiting. Crown kept imagining the sound of wagon wheels turning, but no one came up the drive with Jewel. He was lonely and desolate and angry for feeling that way. By the time Jewel and Sela got home, Crown was seething. He could hear Jewel laughing on the porch and Lenetta laughing back, and he wanted them to stop and feel what he felt.

Crown stepped out on the porch. His mood must have shown because Lenetta froze. He grabbed Jewel under the arm and ushered her into the house. He lifted her so high, her toes barely touched the ground. Lenetta was screaming obscenities, her hands filled with presents and plates. Packed into a rickety wagon, Jewel's cousins emptied into the yard.

Crown slammed the door and locked it. He lifted a sleeping Sela from Jewel's arms. Jewel panicked, trying to reach Sela, but Crown held the baby high above his head where Jewel couldn't reach. Jewel started to cry and punch at Crown. He grabbed her arm and dragged her into the parlor.

Lenetta pounded on the door. "Jewel! You alright in there? Answer me, Jewel?"

Jewel tried to run back to the door, but Crown grabbed her bib and slung her down right in front of the tree she'd made him pick especially for her. Sela was asleep, looking peaceful and sweet up above his head, with no idea her papa was about to go crazy on her mama.

"Whut you go'n' do, Crown? Don't hurt Sela. Don't hurt my baby."

"Why you make a fool out of me, Jewel? Have me cutting down trees, like it's go'n' be Christmas round here. Have me buying presents for you and Sela like it matters. Why you make me out to be a fool?"

"I … I didn't."

He pushed her down so her face scraped the tiny needles of the tree. Sela's doll lay at her knees.

"Wh.. whut's this?"

"Open it."

Jewel fumbled with the plain brown wrapping. She let it fall away till only the doll was in her trembling hands.

"This for Sela? I know she'll like it. Let me give it to her, Crown?"

"Get in your room."

"I'm sorry, Crown. Just give me Sela now, please."

"Do as I say, Jewel."

She walked to her room, not saying a word. She looked so small, but he couldn't feel sorry for her when he was so full of his own pain.

Lenetta was still pounding on the door and with all Jewel's cousins calling her name, Crown's head was beginning to pound too. He stopped Jewel just shy of the bedroom.

"Tell them to go away, Jewel."

Jewel walked to the door. She looked back at Crown like she wanted to bolt, but then she looked at Sela.

"Go on home, Lenetta. We alright. You go on home now."

"You sure, Jewel?"

"Go on now."

It must have sounded reassuring outside to Lenetta and the rest of Jewel's cousins, because Crown could hear them shuffling off the porch. Inside though, in the space between Crown and Jewel, there was nothing but hurt and fear and anger.

In the bedroom, the radio was playing static again. Jewel stood in the door like she was hearing it for the first time.

She walked into the bedroom then of her own will, following that sound like she couldn't understand how it came to be there. She stared at that radio all shiny and new, and then she began to cry.

"I didn't know, Crown. I didn't know."

"I thought about you, Jewel. I thought about you and Sela all day and me here all alone, just thinking till I plumb went crazy."

"I'm sorry. I didn't mean it. I just didn't think, Crown. I'll make it up to you. I'll do whateva you want. Just put Sela down."

"What you think I want, Jewel?"

Jewel backed against the bed, while Crown watched her from the doorway. She pulled the quilt down, then walked toward Crown slowly, her hands outstretched.

"Just hand her to me, Crown. I'll lay her down in her crib all nice and gentle. Then I'll do whateva you want. I swear I will."

Jewel reached up, and Crown let her take Sela from his arms. She laid Sela down then started to undress. Crown watched her undress and lie down and spread her legs and open her arms like she wanted him when her face said she didn't.

He followed her to the bed. He stood over her looking at her reaching for him and wished she meant it. He leaned over her and grabbed her narrow waist, lifting her to his chest. Her head hung back, her hair brushed his arm. She sobbed.

Crown loosened his pants and let them fall to the floor. He pressed against her thighs all soft and warm and raised her hips to his. He slid inside but it was too easy for her so he started to hump her hard and fast and furious like he felt and she cried and he heaved and lay on top of her and kept her there into the night till his anger was spent.

Crown woke in the night alone. Sometime while he slept Jewel must have rolled him over and gathered Sela and turned off that damned radio.

CHAPTER 30

▼

It was a while before Jewel would listen to the radio or look at Crown. She had a way of saying she was sorry though, and Crown realized she hadn't meant to hurt him, because it wasn't in her to do so. She was sweet and good and much like a child herself, so when she'd gone off and left Crown alone she'd had no bad intentions.

Crown understood that now, but it was too late to take back what he'd done. So he said he was sorry by keeping his distance from Jewel and Sela. He tuned the radio each day hoping Jewel would take to it, and eventually she did because she loved to talk and the radio gave her something to talk to. It sang with her and gave her music to dance to and times to laugh. Crown would lie in his room at night and listen to the sound of her laughter, glad for her but saddened that he wasn't part of it. He'd open his door, and sometimes she'd open hers too, and he'd watch her dance in the moonlight to the jazz out of New Orleans. He wondered if she'd ever want him to touch her again. The more impossible that seemed the more he wanted it and the more their separation pained him.

Jewel was listening to the radio and tickling Sela's fat feet one night when an announcer came over the radio sounding like the world had gone to war. From the kitchen, Crown strained to hear, but Jewel was keeping up a lot of racket playing with Sela and fussing at the announcer to get off so she could get back to her show. Crown put down the knives he'd been sharpening and walked to the bedroom door.

"Hush up, Jewel. I want to hear this."

She hushed when she saw the look on his face, but Crown could tell she didn't understand why the man was so excited or why Crown was so concerned. After awhile, when it was clear the man wasn't going away, Jewel took Sela outside to play with the lightning bugs. Crown stayed, pulling the rocker up close to the radio so he could hear better.

He sat around the radio listening to all the talk for two weeks not understanding most of it except that things were bad and as much as the politicians and big businessmen tried to make like everything would be all right, things were getting worse, not better. Crown finally figured there was nothing to do but to keep working hard, to use only what was necessary and to put away what he could, so he'd have what his family needed when they needed it. To keep up with the latest news, he took to listening to the radio before he headed out each morning and again in the evening after supper. Jewel pouted that Crown had taken over the radio and was keeping her from listening to her favorite shows. He'd shush her till she tired of nagging and stormed out of the room.

Back east jobs were eroding along with business profits. Crown knew enough to figure it would soon trickle down to places like Colwin County and to people like him. He heard about runs on banks and the funds not being there, and he was glad he had stashed a sizeable amount of his own wealth at home. Still in May of 1930, he went into town to withdraw the rest of his funds. Mr. Langham panicked and sweated and locked the door and tried to persuade Crown not to lose confidence for fear everyone else would follow suit.

Crown wasn't concerned about anyone else. He owned a few stocks as well, and as far as he could tell, now they weren't worth the paper they were printed on. Crown just wanted to make sure he got what was his and that he and Jewel wouldn't have to worry if what he expected came true—that the worst of times were headed their way.

Truth was Crown had wanted an excuse to take his money out of the bank. After years of poor bookkeeping and lame excuses, he didn't know if Mr. Langham was a thief or just incompetent. Regardless, Crown didn't trust anyone dumb enough to keep making the same mistakes.

When Crown could not be persuaded to leave his money behind, Langham closed the bank, locking the doors and pulling the blinds. But Crown had no intention of announcing that he had a fortune in the back of the wagon. He loaded up in the alley and headed straight for home with his shotgun across his lap.

Crown had never been so jumpy or so glad to get home. He'd made a recess in the wall of his closet and covered it with a false panel. He moved the safe there so it would be harder to find if other kinds of trouble ever came calling. Colwin County had never been known for that sort of thing, but the worst came out in the best of folks when times got bad, and Crown had the feeling that things were going to get very bad, real fast.

CHAPTER 31

▼

Most years, winter came to Colwin County in January, stayed a brief spell then quickly gave way to spring. But winter had come late and March had been gray and wet and unseasonably cold. After three weeks of cold, dreary rain, the clouds had finally broken; the roads once flooded and impassable had begun to dry out.

Confined to the house, Crown had grown restless. At least Jewel had her chores, but without her Sunday outings to break the monotony, she was as anxious as Crown. Saying only what was necessary, they had stepped around each other afraid to break the fragile peace. Wednesday morning, Jewel broke the silence with words that cut Crown more than she could have imagined.

"Ooh, I ache for company," she complained to Sela. "Wouldn't you like a trip to town, sweetums?"

Crown found a half dozen reasons to go to the farm instead, mumbling them off to Jewel as she sat feeding Sela at the kitchen table. He had cut back on his trips to town and now regularly used the farm's store. The store mostly carried staples for the tenants, things they needed and couldn't easily get and would be beholden to Crown for. Bought surplus, the quality was fair to poor, but in these times, the goods would do for Jewel and Sela as well.

Jewel answered without even talking directly to Crown. "I guess we'll have to wait till Sunday, then. We'll see Lenetta and Granny Giddings and have us a good ole time, then."

Crown stared at the two of them awhile, but Jewel never looked up. Crown sighed, suddenly tired. He left Jewel and Sela and went to saddle Less. Crown could no more abide a lonely ride on a wagon built for two, than he could abide the solitude in a house half filled with people. He wondered if the house had ever been lived in the way he had imagined. It didn't seem possible that it had ever been anything but dark and lonely and cold.

Crown turned onto the road and shuddered. In his hurry to leave the house, he forgot to get a jacket. Now he was chilled to the bone. Stubbornly, he leaned closer to Less and nudged her to quicken the pace.

He passed the deserted tenant quarters with barely a glance and continued a quarter mile down the road to the fields. It was planting season at the farm, but all the signs said they should wait. For all his shortcomings, Sam Giddings would have known that. Sam would have plowed the fields but waited for better weather before planting.

The men had already broken the saturated ground and moved on to the next field. Other farms dragged logs across the fields or used livestock to trample seeds into the soil, but McGee Farms held steadfast to one last vestige of human labor. Now women and children, barefoot and ankle deep in mud, prodded tender shoots into the moist earth with their fingers. At any given time, half of them were bent over, the other half bent back nursing sore spines and spreading the latest gossip. Lenetta was among the latter, though Crown suspected she'd spent more time straight up than bent down.

Crown rode on, unaccustomed to giving orders to women. He'd find Karl Johnson and make him straighten out his own mess. A quarter of a field would already be planted, but at least they'd save the rest.

At the next field, two teams surged side by side, dragging the earth beneath horse and plow. Crown dismounted and stuffed his overalls in his boots. He left Less to drink from the rain ponded along the levee while he searched for Karl Johnson. The foreman, a dark burly man with long spindly legs too thin for his massive body met Crown halfway down the field.

"We go'n' get the east fields done today, then start on the west acreage first thing come mo'nin'," the man volunteered.

"You tell the women to start planting?"

"Naw, suh. Mr. Karl, he said it'd be warm enough come midday, and they might as well get started. I told him we might get another week or more a cold, but he paid no mind."

"Where's he now?"

"He's in his office I s'pect. He ain't one to tarry in these fields any longer than he has to."

Crown looked up and squinted, the full sun catching him unawares. Crown had stopped shivering and many of the men were shirtless. Johnson could be right this time. It'd be a first, but even the almanac predicted a short winter.

"You want me to send the women-folk back?"

"No. No. Carry on."

Crown walked back to the levee and mounted the mare. He followed the levee to the end of the field then turned down a narrow dirt road that led back to the granary. He found Karl Johnson in his office, gazing out of the window, with his head leaned back in his hands and his feet crossed at the ankle and propped against the windowsill. Crown cleared his throat, and Johnson nearly fell out of his chair.

"Mr. McGee. I guess I should have known the weather would bring you out today."

"I guess you should have known to ask me before you set the women to planting my fields."

"You don't agree?"

"I don't disagree. Just you mind these are my fields and if there's ever any question, I'm the one you should ask."

"I didn't mean."

Crown held up his hand. "I could use a few things from our stores. You have the boys load up one of the wagons out back and deliver these things to Jewel."

Crown reached in the breast pocket of his overalls and pulled out a list he'd jotted down just before he left the house. He wanted just a few bare necessities, like cornmeal, coffee, matches, canned beans, rice and lard. There was no telling how long these hard times would last, and they had to learn to live with less. He handed the list to Johnson.

"I want to get back before dark," Crown emphasized as Johnson scrutinized the list a bit too long.

Crown waited till Johnson left the room, then he took the seat Johnson had warmed and looked out the window toward the south fields.

Crown wondered how many times Jebediah had sat at that same window. In the distance the people looked like ants, small and mindless, their lives filled with Crown McGee's drudgery.

Crown didn't doubt that Jebediah had been a shrewd businessman. The farm had profited heavily during the war and then survived the surpluses of its aftermath. Crown had entered the business during a time of prosperity. When farmers further north and west were losing their lands to drought or overproduction or debt, coastal farms were thriving. Crown had the right crop at the right time and no real test of his worth as a businessman. A few days in a town further from Colwin County than he'd ever been could change all that.

Crown had tried to tell Jewel that things were different. That there'd be fewer trips to town and no more orders from the Sears Catalog. Though 1929 had been a good year and prices for grain were better than fair, Crown was wary. He couldn't see beyond tomorrow and that had him worried. There was no telling how long his prosperity might last.

The work was seasonal and the cabins were empty most of the year. The old families had moved on as Crown came to rely on tenants less and on machines and migrants more. He'd bought the combine outright when it looked like things might get bad, and it worked well most of the time so he wasn't short on labor. He was still having trouble with the two threshers though, replacing parts on one or the other or both every season.

With most of the tenants gone, the population of the county had dwindled, though on any given day there were just as many people as before. The trouble was most of them were just passing through, on their way from destitution to any place that offered hope. Some were on their last dime and unable to go any further than the nearest relief office where the lines were long and the help equally long in coming.

The cemetery had become a drain, with most of Crown's burials coming from the county, pauper's graves for those too poor to pay. The county fees were barely enough to justify the holes Crown dug, so he started burying them double and triple to cut down on labor and land.

Crown was doing better than surviving though and trying not to show it so no one would get the notion that he had more than his share. His land was paid for. He had a garden and livestock and ample stores to feed his family through hard times. He had cheap labor, folks willing to forgo wages for a place to pitch a tent and two meals a day while the seasonal work lasted.

Still worried, Crown spent his days between the farm and home, finding more comfort in the former than the latter since Jewel still wouldn't have much to do with him.

He didn't know how much longer he'd abide the distance. All he had was his hunger for her. Without it he didn't see the sense of the two of them except there was Sela and no denying that she was his.

They had settled into a routine with Jewel preparing his meals and drawing him a hot bath at the end of a hard day, but otherwise making herself scarce. The house was clean, and Crown had little to fuss about except that his bed was still lonely and cold. On the rare days Jewel would let him get close enough, he'd smell her all sweet like milk and lilacs and babies, and he thought he'd die if he couldn't touch her again. Her breasts were fuller, her hips rounder, and he'd had to buy her two new dresses for fear she'd burst out of that blue drop-waist dress that was still her favorite and he'd have to jump her right where she stood. Instead he kept his distance, much as he wanted to hold her close.

He was a stranger to Sela too. She was growing up, and he wasn't a part of it, and he wasn't sure if Jewel would ever let him be. Sela had taken to pulling up on things and liked to sit on Crown's boots holding onto his pants while he rocked his foot up and down like a horse. He bent down to hold her once, but Jewel scooped her up protectively. He didn't know how to make Jewel believe he wouldn't hurt Sela again. He wished he'd never tried. Then he would have Jewel and Sela and some semblance of a life again.

Anyone would have thought that Sela was the prettiest baby ever born the way Jewel was always kissing her and telling her so. It hurt Crown that Jewel had all that love for Sela and none for him. And it was his own fault, because he'd been afraid that Sela would end up just like him—ugly, worthless, mean.

He wondered if Sela would grow to hate him the way he'd hated Jebediah. At least, Crown relented, Jebediah had given him a chance at life. Crown had intended to kill Sela. He didn't expect Jewel would ever tell Sela, but with inter-lopers like Lenetta buzzing around Colwin County, it was only a matter of time before Sela knew.

Crown was still thinking of Jewel and Sela when Johnson returned. Crown thought of them all the way home wondering how he'd ever get back what he once had. The gate was open as he pulled up; though, he was certain he had closed it before he left. He could have sworn too that he'd seen his new grounds man, Ben, at the farm when he left. On the way back, there'd been no sign of Lenetta though, and he could only guess she'd taken advantage of his absence to come calling.

Crown jumped down cautiously and closed the heavy metal gate. He looked out over the cemetery, toward the barn and then the house. To his surprise there was a car parked out front. His heart jumped. He wondered if Jewel had gotten someone to come and get her. It would only serve him right, and he resigned that she was probably leaving him that night. At least he wouldn't have to suffer much longer. She'd be gone and soon there'd be nothing left of her, not a whiff of lilacs or the hum of her voice or the way she smiled all crooked and childlike.

Crown took his time, in no hurry to say goodbye. When he finally walked up to the house, he noticed with a start that the car was from Louisiana. It was sleek and black with a roll-down top and shiny chrome trim and lights that looked like eyeballs.

From the house, Jewel's laughter flittered like butterflies, soft and light. Crown followed her laughter into the house. He ached just knowing he couldn't make her laugh any more. He heard a man's voice then, silky like mud, sweet like pure cane.

"Jewel!" Crown bellowed in anger and surprise.

She came out of the kitchen, still smiling.

"Crown, how come you never told me 'bout Jackson?"

Jackson peered over her shoulder with his arm around her waist where Crown's should have been. He looked like Crown had always imagined, smooth sable skin, thick, perfect lips, a broad nose and dark round eyes. His smile cut from ear to ear.

"Nice to see you, brother."

Jackson slipped his arm from around Jewel's waist as though he was perfectly comfortable with it being there. Crown frowned. Jackson extended his hand and grabbed Crown's in one fluid motion. Crown stiffened. Jackson shook his hand vigorously.

"You done all right, Crown. I went by the farm today, but you seemed busy, and I heard I had a sister-in-law and a niece almost brand new, and I had to see them. Yes sir, you done all right."

"Where you been all this time?"

"Oh, I been about. New Yawk, D.C., Chicaga, N'Awlens."

"What brings you here?"

"That anyway to greet your brother?"

"I ain't got no brother."

"Crown!"

Jewel glared at him, but Crown ignored her. What was she doing anyway letting a stranger in the house, laughing and flirting with him like she'd known him all her life when she wouldn't even share the same room with her husband?

"Jewel, you take Sela and get into your room."

"Go on now, Jewel." Jackson whispered smooth as butter. "Me and Crown, we got business to discuss."

"I got no business with you. I don't know you from Adam. You best get on your way."

"I got a right to what's mine, Crown. I'm Jebediah's too."

"Then how come he didn't see fit to leave you nothing?"

"Never you mind that. He'd have burned it to the ground before he let you have it. But you just mark my words. I intend to have what's mine and maybe a little taste of what isn't."

Jackson turned his eyes leeringly toward the door to Jewel's room. Crown's fist opened and closed as Jackson brushed by him.

Jackson turned back to face Crown before slipping into the night. "You'll see me again, brother," he promised.

"I'll have to get a lock for that gate," Crown mumbled in reply.

Crown was so shaken he stood there for a while listening to the sputter of the car as it pulled out of the yard. Certain Jackson had gone, he pounded on Jewel's door. On the other side, Sela began to cry. Jewel opened the door and cursed.

"Dammit, Crown. I just put her to sleep."

He didn't mean to but he grabbed her then and pressed his lips to hers. She kneed him in the groin, and he fell to the floor with a whimper.

She slammed the door on him, banging his head in the process. He cursed. He stood, leaning on the closed door for support. He twisted the handle, but she'd locked it.

"You're still my wife, Jewel. Next time you let a strange man in my house and sidle all up to him like a trollop, I'll whip you like the whore you are."

He'd said it before he knew it. The door opened, and she glared at him.

"I ain't no whore, Crown. You take that back."

He glared back at her as much as he wanted to say he was sorry.

"You ain't nothing but a poor little tramp, pretty as sunshine and dumb as …"

"Dumb as a mule." She finished for him, letting the words steep between them. "I know whut I am, Crown, and it ain't never bothered me, till now."

Pain, silent and deep pooled in her eyes. She closed the door, slow, deliberate. He could hear Sela wailing on the other side and Jewel trying hard to sing and sob at the same time. He leaned against the door wanting to hold her and tell her he was sorry. And he cried for the futility of it. All he seemed to do was push her further and further away when he knew there was no one else who'd take her place—no one who'd share a meal or a book or a bed with the likes of him. And even if there were, he only wanted Jewel.

CHAPTER 32

▼

Crown left for Boone in the middle of the night while Jewel and Sela still slept. Stopping by their door and assured by Jewel's shallow rhythmic breathing, he tip-toed out quietly.

It was a longer journey than either horse was accustomed to. Crown had made the trip only one or two times a year since he had settled in and not once since the Crash. Although More was strong, Less was younger, lighter and swifter. Crown wouldn't have to leave Jewel and Sela alone so long.

Less flinched as he saddled her. Crown waited for her to calm, then walked her down to the gate in case she got skittish when he mounted.

Outside the gate, he let her nibble sugar from his palm while he stroked her mane. Then he mounted her cautiously. She pranced for a bit. He let her dance then eased her into a trot. It might have been pleasant alone with the horse and his thoughts and the song of the woods, if he'd had something more pleasant to think about.

He decided to take a detour through town so he could check on Jackson. He pulled into town and slowed as he tried to spot Jackson's car in the moonlight. From the looks of Jackson, Crown didn't figure his brother to be up before noon. If he made good time, he'd be back home before then. Still he worried about leaving Jewel alone. He tied the horse at the livery where she could drink at her leisure. When he spied Jackson's car inside, he stopped worrying about Jewel and concentrated on the problem at hand.

Jackson was greasy slick with hair conked and smoothed back on his head, shiny skin and a smile that slithered slow and crooked over his teeth. It was a look that appealed to women, a look that seemed to appeal to Jewel. It was a look that made Crown wary—too smooth, too easy, a little too sweet to be real.

Crown was tempted to ferret Jackson out of the hole he'd crawled into and end it that night. Instead, Crown led Less across the tracks and headed down the narrow trail that crossed the woods to the main road. Boone was thirty miles south on that deserted road.

Crown mounted and let Less choose her own pace, knowing that if he rushed her, she might not be any good for the trip back. Without the burden of the wagon, Less quickened her gait and two hours later, Crown rode into Boone. He skirted the county jail and courthouse, dark and closed, and headed straight for Judge Bishop's house.

The two story frame house was one street over and two blocks down from the courthouse. Leaving by his back door, the judge usually took the alley to the courthouse. Crown remembered the first time he'd met the judge. Father Georges had sent Crown there with a letter of introduction and a small hope that he wouldn't be left entirely penniless. Now Crown was back fighting once again for the fortune Jebediah McGee never meant for him to have.

Crown turned down the alley. He tied Less to the fence, opened the gate, walked up the brick-lined path to the back door and knocked. The housekeeper cracked the door open. She was a tall thin woman with a pointed nose and exaggerated chin that made her look like the illustration of the wicked witch in Jewel's book of fairy tales. A scarf revealed only a hint of gray streaked brown hair. A pair of wire rimmed glasses sat on the end of her nose.

"Who's that this time of morning?" she asked impertinently.

"I need to see the judge."

"That's not what I asked. What's your name?"

"McGee. I need to see the judge."

"I heard that the first time. Judge didn't tell me he was expecting anyone."

"He's not expecting me. I just need to see him."

"Well he doesn't take appointments at the house. You can see him directly at the courthouse."

She slammed the door shut. Crown was tempted to knock again but thought better of it. He leaned against a tree just out of eyesight of the housekeeper as she warmed the stove and started breakfast.

It was another hour before Judge Bishop left the house. Without the sweeping black robe, he was a short portly man. With a straight back though and a high forehead, he exuded a confidence that made him seem a foot taller. The judge opened the gate and turned toward the courthouse and Crown. Crown stepped out from behind the tree. Judge Bishop stopped short.

"What the hell."

"I … I'm Crown McGee. I need to talk to you. It's important."

Annoyed, Judge Bishop veered around Crown. "I know who you are. Did you make an appointment?"

"No. I … I don't get to Boone much, and … and this thing just came up."

"You mean this thing with Jackson?"

Crown stopped. "So you've seen him?"

"He's been by the office, yes. If you want to know more than that you'll need to make an appointment. And this time young man, may I suggest you get a lawyer."

"I … don't know any lawyers."

"Try Thomas Coleman. Tell him I sent you. He's about the best there is in this county." Judge Bishop smiled, suddenly amused. "You'll need an appointment with him, too."

The judge walked away leaving Crown unsatisfied. Crown had hoped to get answers. All he'd gotten was assurance that the problem with Jackson wasn't going away quickly or easily.

Realizing he had no idea where to find Thomas Coleman, Crown ran to catch up with the judge.

"Judge." Crown called, interrupting the judge's walk once more.

Registering a slight smile, Judge Bishop stopped and waited for Crown to catch up. "I guess I can spare the time seeing as you've made good my decision and shown more man than most."

Crown shifted uncomfortably. "I never said thank you."

"You needn't thank me. Far as I'm concerned you only got what you had coming."

"You think I should share it with Jackson?"

"That can't be answered here and now. Jackson's got a right to be heard, same as you. Like I said, you'll need a good lawyer."

"Where can I find this Coleman fellow?"

"He offices in the courthouse. Doesn't open till nine though, but I'll let you in so you can wait."

Crown grunted thanks; the judge nodded in reply. They walked on quietly, neither with the penchant for talk. At the courthouse the judge rang the bell, and a janitor opened the door.

"You're late, Judge."

"I was detained. Show Mr. McGee to Mr. Coleman's office. He's determined to wait the hour till we're officially open, but if Tom comes in early as he is apt to do, let him know the boy is waiting."

The janitor eyed Crown suspiciously, but he did as the judge asked, taking Crown up the narrow staircase to the second floor and pointing him toward a lone bench to wait.

After a while Crown dozed lightly until the courthouse began to bustle as secretaries and clerks and finally the lawyers began to arrive. Thomas Coleman dragged in clearing his throat and nursing a sore runny nose. He walked straight to Crown, apologized for his lateness and ushered Crown into the office in deference to the other two clients who had arrived with appointments.

"I hear you're looking for a lawyer. You want to tell me about it?"

"There ain't much to tell."

"Well let me see if I can sum it up for you. Jebediah died. His will said only that he didn't want Jackson to get a dime. The will was silent with regards to you. You came out of nowhere to contest it. It was well known that Jebediah's health and mind were in a sorry state when he died, and no one had heard a word from Jackson, that is until two weeks ago. Judge Bishop sided with you, ignoring Jebediah's trustee and lawyer, me."

Crown looked at Thomas Coleman. The drooping eyes and handkerchief concealed the angry man that had nearly bowled him over five years ago. Recognition shadowed his eyes and creased his forehead.

Thomas Coleman patted Crown's shoulder reassuringly. "You needn't worry. Prudence has taught me to accept Judge Bishop's decisions. He's usually right."

"Now about this thing with Jackson. I suppose he plans to contest the will."

It was stated more than asked, and Crown saw no need to answer the obvious. Coleman continued.

"I've already made an appointment with Judge Bishop on your behalf. Jackson's got a lawyer named Minnick from Baton Rouge. He's one good lawyer, but he's not local and that's to our advantage. We've got the will obviously, and we can always use character. I'll get my man Hawkins to run a background check on Jackson. Anything I need to know about you?"

Coleman said it matter-of-factly as though he didn't really expect an answer from a man who'd spent most of his life in a convent. Crown hedged, Nate Comeaux's boy, pale and white and dead and lying in his ground as vivid as the day Troy and Earnest had put him there. Crown shook his head, but Coleman wasn't even looking his way.

"We'll set up a deposition with Minnick and Jackson as soon as I can get a wire off. Till then there isn't much to do but wait. Anything else I can do for you till then, you let me know."

"That all?"

"That's all for now. You go on home and try not to worry. You've got time on your side. The same time Jackson has against him. Jebediah disowned you the day you were born. If Jackson had shown up five years ago, I wouldn't have given you a chance. Now your chances are good, better than most."

Coleman escorted Crown to the door. Crown looked away, his face contorting with the old hurts Coleman had raised so deftly.

"My secretary has some papers for you. You'll need to sign them. My retainer is five hundred dollars. This whole business will cost you, no more than customary though, and I suspect it's worth it to keep what you've built out of Jackson's slimy hands."

Crown grunted in agreement. Coleman stuck out his hand. Crown took it awkwardly, his own grip limp to Coleman's firm one. Crown pulled his hand back quickly not quite ready to trust a man who had admittedly been his opponent.

When Crown stepped outside the courthouse, the sun blinded him. It was nearly straight up, and the day's business had taken longer than he had hoped. He mounted the mare, digging his heels firmly into her haunches. She rose, but he leaned over her and hung on urging her toward home and Jewel.

Less was unaccustomed to being ridden so hard. By the time Crown reached home, she was sweating and breathing so hard her nostrils flared wide. Crown jumped down leading her urgently over the rough ground.

Crown stopped cold at the edge of the clearing. Kicking up dust and driving the chickens into a mad frenzy, Jackson's car made circles in front of the house. Jewel was at the wheel with her head hung back, and her mouth opened in a delightful squeal. Jackson was sitting a little too close to her, one hand on the steering wheel, the other draped over her shoulder.

Crown wanted to fly across that yard and rip Jackson's arm from its socket, the same arm draped around Jewel. But he didn't want to give Jackson the satisfaction so he turned away instead.

Crown led Less into the barn. His anger festered while he removed the saddle and gave Less a much needed rub down, some water and hay. By the time Crown came back outside, Jackson's car was gone, and Jewel was rocking Sela on the front porch. The delight Jackson had put there was still etched across her face. Sweet and innocent, she beamed up at Crown.

"Jackson taught me how to drive, Crown. I ain't barely even rode a horse, and today I drove a car. I declare that Jackson is sumthin'. You should try it, Crown. I bet he'd teach you."

"Ain't nothing Jackson can teach me, except not to stray too far when I got a snake for a brother and a harlot for a wife that ain't got the brain of Eve."

"I don't know what a harlot is, but it don't sound nice. Why don't you talk plain so I can know whut it is you're sayin'?"

"You make me sick, Jewel. You understand that?"

Crown glared at her, then stalked into the house, wondering why he even bothered. Maybe he should just let Jackson have her. It would be one less thing to worry about. Crown swore Jackson would never get the money and he'd never get the land and he'd never get Sela even if he did have Jewel eating out of his hand.

CHAPTER 33

▼

Crown should have been working; instead, he sat in the study brooding. Outside the wind howled hauntingly under a gray overcast sky. According to Ben, Jackson had been to the farm on two or more occasions, chatting up Karl Johnson and making out with any young thing in a skirt. With Jackson prowling around Colwin County like he owned it, Crown was afraid to leave Jewel. He kept close to the house, letting Ben keep him posted on the comings and goings at the farm.

Crown shivered though the window was closed; the early spring days though windy were far from cold. Jackson had brought back too many memories—memories, Jewel, even as distant as she was now, still somehow helped Crown to forget.

There was a time when Crown thought nothing could hurt him. For sixteen years he had lived and worked at Montagne Parish under Sister Abigail's strict rule. She was firm but fair, albeit a bit quick with the corporal punishment. Crown had a bed, ample food, daily religious instruction, and relentless chores, but nothing anyone could mistake for affection. He had learned to live without the latter, to swallow his tears and keep his feelings, if he had any, to himself.

Twice a year he endured his mother's visits with practiced detachment. Then, on his sixteenth birthday his mother didn't come. Had he known at Christmas, he was not to see her again, he might have had the courage to ask her why. He had dined alone with her in his room on a meal she had brought with her, ham and cornbread and rice cakes. It was always the same. They both picked at their food. She chatted aimlessly about Jebediah and Jackson and the farm as though hearing of their lives without him should bring Crown some comfort. As usual he said nothing, grunting a reply only when asked and wondering if she thought he was addled as well as ugly.

Before she left, she handed him his usual gift, a card with some sentiment Crown would never read, a single silver dollar he had no practical use for, and a pound of hard candy Crown had never acquired a taste for, perhaps simply because his mother had given it to him. When she'd gone, he'd place the dollar on the night table for Sister Abigail and leave the candy outside his door. Later, he'd lie back on his bed listening to the children swarm around after supper fighting over the hard rock candies until Sister Abigail shooed them off to their own beds.

Sister Abigail would knock then and open the door without invite. She'd take the silver dollar from the table lecturing, "Shore up, Mr. McGee. You are the lucky one you know."

The year Crown turned nineteen the checks stopped coming as well. Jebediah McGee had died without leaving any provisions for Crown. It was the first time in years that Crown had cried. He'd tend the livestock he argued, watch the younger children, wash the clothes, clean the kitchen, anything Father Georges asked.

"You're a man now," Father Georges had replied. "The other children can take over your chores. You must think of your future. You can't stay here forever. The parish simply can't afford it."

Father Georges had rebuked every argument, leaving Crown with the feeling he was less than necessary and had no choice but to take the next train to Colwin County.

Still the convent had been home, and the day the gates to Montagne Parish closed behind him, Crown had been afraid. He left with the clothes on his back and to his surprise, thirty-one silver dollars Sister Abigail had saved for him.

Sister Abigail escorted him to the train station. Inside the station, she motioned Crown to sit. As always, he did as he was told. She left without explanation. Crown thought for the first time he was totally on his own, but she returned in a while with a ticket and a bag lunch.

"Stand up, Mr. McGee."

She had never called him anything else, not when he was a too curious boy of four, not now that he was nineteen and barely a man. Sister tucked the ticket in Crown's coat pocket and the bag lunch in his hand.

"Your train leaves at ten. When you get there, you are to ask for Judge Bishop."

"Don't go," he had wanted to say. Instead he'd hung his head low as the tears began to well again and his lip trembled.

"Shore up, Mr. McGee," Sister Abigail had chastised not unkindly. "You would soon be leaving us anyway."

Crown stood, pacing the floor in frustration. He had waited nineteen years for a man he didn't know to decide the father he'd never met owed him something more than his name. Now Jackson threatened to take all Crown had fought for.

Crown sighed. He'd given Jackson as little thought as possible over the years. Admittedly though, it had given Crown more than a little satisfaction to know Jebediah had disinherited his chosen son. Crown could only imagine why. Jebediah had been dead six years, yet there'd been no sign of Jackson. There'd been notices in newspapers in every major city from New York to San Francisco. Judge Bishop had made certain of that, forcing Crown to wait an agonizing six months before he'd even consider Crown's petition. Either Jackson didn't read or he didn't care and from the looks of him, Jackson cared about money.

Crown ground his fist into his palm. He had a constant headache from all the worry. It seemed that Jebediah McGee would never let him be.

The sound of footsteps on the porch startled him. He hadn't heard a car pull into the yard though, and he soon recognized Ben's polite rapping. Crown opened the study door and looked down the hallway. The back door was wide open. It was midmorning, and Jewel was already out back taking clothes off the line, while Sela played in the basket beneath her feet. The clothes whipped frantically in the wind, and Jewel laughed as she got tangled in the sheets.

Ben knocked again. With his eyes still on Jewel, Crown motioned Ben to enter. Ben opened the screen door, and poked his head inside the front hallway.

"Coop sends word, suh. Yo' parts are in. You want me to pick 'em up?"

"You seen Jackson around?"

"No. Rumor is he lit out two weeks ago. Said something about going over to N'awleans for the Mardi Gras."

Anxious and restless, Crown was glad to have something to think about besides Jackson. "You go on back to the farm. I'll pay Coop a visit myself. Tell Johnson, he'll have those parts by tomorrow morning."

Crown headed for town, reluctantly leaving Jewel and Sela behind, but he didn't pass any shiny black convertibles on the way into town, and he saw no sign of Jackson once he got there. Reassured, he took the time to pick up a few items at the mercantile, some lilac soap for Jewel and a licorice for a teething Sela. Then he went to see Cooper.

Cooper wasn't home, and Nettie wasn't sure where he'd gone or how long he'd be. By the time Crown found him behind Sadie's swapping tales and sipping moonshine, half the day was gone. Worse still, Cooper swore he hadn't told Ben or anybody else that Crown's parts had come in because they hadn't.

Crown grabbed Cooper and lifted him off the barrel he was riding. It took three men to pry Crown off. Crown stumbled back to his wagon, his brow bleeding from a cut put there by a bottle of moonshine. He didn't know who was lying, Cooper or Ben, but Crown knew who was behind it.

Crown crawled aboard the wagon and yelled to the team to get. They didn't move fast enough so Crown stood, whipping the reigns like a madman. He rode that way out of town and ten miles down Cemetery Road.

When he reached his own place, the gate was open. Jackson's car sat in the clearing. Crown didn't even slow down as he rounded the corner and barreled down the narrow path to the house.

Jewel and Jackson sat on the porch, swaying back and forth on the swing Crown had yet to sit on. Jackson jumped up when he saw Crown coming. Shirt open, chest bare, Jackson bounded off the porch. Laughing, he jumped in the car and gunned the engine. The horses balked. The wagon lurched. Crown fell backwards.

Crown cursed and turned the horses around chasing futilely behind Jackson's speeding car. The wagon nearly turned over as Crown rounded the gate a second time. The frightened horses reared and Crown was thrown hard, landing shaken but unhurt in the muddy ditch along the side of the road.

Crown stood up and tried to brush himself off. He'd have been better off walking the other way, but he wanted to know what Jackson was doing at his house in the middle of the day half-naked with his wife. He marched back to the house muttering obscenities and calling Jewel every name but the one God had given her.

When he reached the house, Jewel had locked the doors front and back. Crown finally got the shovel and broke a window. He crawled in cursing as he cut himself on the jagged edges of glass. Crown pounded on Jewel's bedroom door. Sela screamed. Jewel whimpered.

"Go away, Crown. We ain't done nothin' but talk."

"Don't you lie to me, Jewel."

"You got no cause, Crown." Jewel yelled back, behind the closed door.

"Then how come he hi-tailed it out of here? How come you hiding like you think I got all the cause in the world?"

He pushed his shoulder into the door. The door shook but held fast.

"Go away, Crown!"

"What you done with him, Jewel? If you laid with him, I swear I'll kill you."

"Crown, git away from that door."

The blast peppered him with buckshot. He screamed, madder than before and hit the door with such force it shattered. His shoulder popped out of joint, but he didn't stop till Jewel leveled the gun at his head and threatened to shoot him dead on.

"I said I ain't done nothin'. Jackson just come to talk that's all. That's all."

Crown stood there not knowing whether to believe her or not. He wanted her to be his again, so he didn't have to worry about sweet talking Jackson. Sela was sitting in the middle of the bed crying and reaching for her mama. Crown sank to his knees. Jewel lowered the gun to her side and reached for him.

"You skeering me, Crown. You ought not act like that. You skeering me. You hurt?"

He nodded yes. She walked to him timidly. He grabbed her waist with his one good arm and buried his head in her belly. He could smell her, and he ached for her. He tried to raise his injured shoulder, but the pain was too great. She leaned on his shoulder and pulled. He yelled, as the shoulder popped back into place. It hurt like hell. Jewel put her shoulder under his good arm and helped him up onto the bed. Sela was still crying, and Jewel picked her up and rocked her, soothing her with her sweet voice.

"Jewel, I need to know."

"I told you, Crown, ain't nothin' happened with me and Jackson."

Jewel put Sela on the floor to play then left him lying there pained and bleeding. She came back shortly with a basin of hot water and rags to clean his wounds. Gently, she took off his shirt and bathed him where buckshot and splinters had pierced through to his skin. It was mainly superficial, and he figured he'd live. He lay there grateful to have her tending to him like she cared again.

Jewel swung his legs up on the bed and lifted his head so she could lay a pillow beneath him. For a moment her hair brushed his face, tempting him to touch her. He stared up at her, but she turned away. She lifted the quilt and covered him, then tucked it squarely beneath him.

"I swear, Crown sometimes you act like you ain't got the sense God gave a flea."

"Well, Jewel sometimes I ain't."

She laughed then, and he smiled.

"Made you laugh."

"Didn't."

"Did."

Ignoring the pain in his shoulder, Crown reached for her and pulled her on top of him. Jewel sobered then and tried to rise, but Crown held her tight.

"When you go'n' forgive me, Jewel? It's been a long time. I miss you."

"I ain't mad at you, Crown. It's just that. Well you tried to hurt the one thing that was mine and yours, and it was like we didn't matter anymore, if we eva did."

"You matter to me, Jewel. You and Sela are all that matter to me."

"You mean that, Crown?"

He nodded. She laid her head on his chest. He wanted her badly, but he felt it was too soon, and he didn't want to lose her again because he did the wrong thing, so he just held her. Then Sela began to cry, and the moment passed. Jewel patted his chest and rose to tend to Sela. Crown felt a pang of jealousy, he knew in his heart he shouldn't. He turned his face to the wall and grimaced. His shoulder ached reminding him what a fool he'd been. He heard Jewel leave the room. He wanted to call her back. He wanted her to lie with him and hold him and tell him it would be all right, but he didn't call her. He just lay there till it was clear she wasn't coming back and his head was pounding from all his worrying and there was nothing left to do but sleep.

CHAPTER 34

▼

Crown woke to the incessant tapping of light rain on the roof. He couldn't tell if it was day or dusk with the curtains drawn. Rubbing his shoulder, he rolled over and groaned. The door was still hanging on its hinges, and Crown wondered if he should fix it or just leave it there. At least Jewel wouldn't be able to shut him out anymore. He touched his forehead, scratched raw where he'd butted against the door. Jewel must have thought he was near insane. But when he was hurt she'd come to him, nursed him, treated him better than he deserved. He sat up woozy, the headache of the night before still pounding. He wondered where Jewel and Sela had slept. He rose, steadied himself and walked into the kitchen straight as he could with his head and shoulder hurting him like they did.

Jewel was there feeding Sela a tepid gruel of rice and milk and talking to herself like always. She looked up at Crown and shook her head.

"Sometimes Crown, I think you're dumber than me. Only a fool would butt heads with a door."

"When you're done telling me what a fool I am, you can get me some breakfast."

"Git it yo'self."

"You getting mighty full of yourself since you made friends with my brother."

"This ain't got nothin' to do with Jackson. It ain't about him. It's about you and me."

"What's the matter now, Jewel? I ain't touched you. I ain't touched Sela. I ain't even allowed in the same room with you, so how can I do anything wrong?"

"You forgittin' bout last night? Just 'cause I tended to you don't mean I forgive you."

"Then why didn't you just shoot me dead? It would have been a lot better than this. Then Jackson could have the land and you could have him and—"

"I invited him to dinner."

"You did what!"

"I said I invited him to dinner on Sunday."

"What made you do a fool thing like that?"

Crown's voice was getting louder. Sela started crying, and Jewel started bouncing Sela on her knee. The louder Crown shouted, the louder Sela cried and the faster Jewel bounced.

"You so worried he go'n' take somethin' from you. How you eva go'n' know what he wants if you don't talk it out with him?"

"Dammit Jewel. How come you meddling in men's business? This ain't got nothing to do with you."

"Ain't I been tellin' you that all along? You the one keep houndin' me 'bout Jackson. He's just nice to talk to that's all. He's been places, and he tells me things."

"I don't want you talking to him no more."

"There's some things in this world, Crown McGee, you ain't got no control of."

"You sound just like that damn Carrie only not near as smart."

Jewel lifted Sela to her shoulder and rose, her jaw trembling. "You can say any ol' mean thing you want, Crown. Won't change how I already feel. Won't change what I already know. You as ornery as Jebediah eva was. You his son through and through."

Jewel turned her back on Crown and stamped out of the room. Crown put his head in his hands. How'd he get to the point where he couldn't even talk to her? How'd he let everything go so wrong? And he couldn't blame Jackson, much as he wanted to, easy as it was, because it started long before Jackson. It started the night he took Sela out in the night and laid her on that cold ground. It started when Jewel looked at him like she wanted him lying in that ground instead of her Sela. When she turned her back on him and told him he was the nothing he'd always known he was.

CHAPTER 35

▼

Much as he'd hated Lenetta when she'd been there, Crown stopped by the farm and asked her to spend the night on Saturday, just to be sure he had someone between Jackson and Jewel. Lenetta wasn't bad to look at, just lazy and trifling that's all. Crown didn't expect Jackson had ever done a lick of work either so he guessed Jackson and Lenetta would get along just fine.

Crown puttered around the house all day Sunday, getting madder by the minute every time Jewel put another pot on the stove. Though she had never complained, she'd never treated cooking for him like it was more than a chore. Foregoing church, Jewel and Lenetta spent that Sunday cooking and cleaning like they thought Jesus himself might show up for dinner. Enjoying his situation, Lenetta egged Crown every chance she got, and he was beginning to wish he'd never asked her to come.

Jackson came tooling down the road about seven, almost too late for supper, but Jewel didn't seem to mind. She'd put on her powder blue dress, which fit her just fine since she'd slimmed down a bit and lost her tummy. Sela had long been put to bed, and Lenetta had taken her supper early and retired to the room with Sela.

Crown was sitting in his study pouting and considering whether or not he even wanted to bother to eat. The door opened, and Jewel stood there grinning.

"Jackson's here, Crown. I'm go'n' heat up the supper while ya'll talk, Jackson."

Jewel waved Jackson in like it was perfectly natural for him to be there. He bowed like some fancy Frenchman and took her hand and kissed it and said he'd much rather talk to her. Crown almost rose out of his chair when she blushed.

He was beginning to wonder if this was just part of his punishment, letting him think the worst of Jewel and Jackson until he had to kill one or the other or both.

"Brother."

Jackson stretched out a hand that didn't look like it had ever done work or ever would. Crown set his book on the table. He stood because he didn't like the idea of Jackson towering over him.

"Just 'cause Jewel invited you, don't get the idea you're welcome."

"Now, now little brother."

"I told you, you ain't no brother of mine. I didn't have nobody when I was growing up in that orphanage, and I don't need nobody now."

"Now, Crown. Is that any way to be?"

"Maybe it is. Maybe it isn't. I've known folks like you. Think you can talk your way into anything. Wouldn't know hard work if it stood up and hit you in the face. I reckon that's why Jebediah left you out of his will. It ain't my fault you squandered what came easy."

"You listen here, Crown," Jackson gritted, the mirth slipping away behind cold, dark eyes. "Jebediah never meant for you to have anything of his. He'd have taken his name too if there was any way he could have."

Crown stared back, hoping he mirrored the hate he saw in Jackson's eyes. "I know what I meant to Jebediah. I don't need you to tell me that. And I know he'd stand up and holler right now if he could see me with all that was his. And that's the beauty of it. 'Cause I got it, and he can't do a damn thing about it."

"But I can. I talked to a lawyer. He said I might have a case for at least half seeing as toward the end old Jebediah wasn't in his right mind. I might have settled for that too if you weren't so cussed ornery. Everybody round here knows I was his favorite. Hell, 'fore you come along, I was his only. Jebediah should have killed you out right. Then I wouldn't have to bother doing it for him."

"You threatening me, Jackson?"

"I'm telling you, Crown. I'm go'n' have what's mine."

Jewel tapped on the door and opened it. She stepped between the two of them, locking her arms in theirs. Crown pulled away and frowned.

"Suppa's done ya'll, all but the eatin'."

"Not hungry."

"Suit yo'self. What about you, Jackson? You hungry?"

Jewel looked up at Jackson and smiled sweetly. Crown felt like he wasn't even in the same room.

Jackson slipped his hand over hers. "So hungry I could eat you."

Crown watched them leave, too angry for words. What else could he say? Jewel made it all too clear that Jackson was the one she wanted.

Evening slipped into night with Crown brooding in that chair to Jackson's melodic exaggerations and Jewel's giddy laughter. Then silence. Crown sat up; his ears perked. All his fears came unbundled and swirled tornadic.

When Jewel finally opened the door and announced that Jackson was leaving, Crown's knuckles were ashen. His hands still gripping the chair, Crown didn't even bother to look her way. She left the door ajar while she walked Jackson outside. Their footsteps were reluctant, synchronous. Crown's heart was hollow. He imagined her walking off that porch and getting into that car with Jackson and never coming back, but then there was Sela. Crown heard Jewel sigh and shut the door and ease into her room without saying goodnight.

The next morning there was silence between them and a faraway look in Jewel's eyes. Crown puttered around outside, finding one small job after another, just so he wouldn't have to see that look.

Lenetta woke up about noon, took another hour to come to, kissed Sela and Jewel and headed home on foot. Crown was nailing a loose board on the porch when Lenetta left, making a point to step on the precise board he was working on just so he'd have to stop. She looked down at him defiant and smug, but he ignored her. She seemed small compared to his problems with Jackson and Jewel.

About five, Jewel called Crown in for supper. Reticent, he went in and washed up, watching her from the corners of his eyes. She had cooked cornbread and greens with onions and bacon and a slice of ham. He'd half expected her to warm over the leavings from her dinner with Jackson, but he saw no evidence of the night before. The greens were tough and greasy, the cornbread flat and thick but Crown didn't mind. He didn't look at her though. He couldn't. He ate in silence wondering if it were his last meal, one last gesture of kindness before she told him she was leaving. Jewel had even baked a pie, a runny peach cobbler that looked more like soup than syrup. She set a piece in front of Crown just when he was about to excuse himself. He looked up at her then, and her face looked a lot like the pie, all weepy and runny, and he felt a pang in his heart, and he held his breath and closed his eyes and prayed she wasn't about to leave him now, 'cause he wasn't ready.

Jewel sniffled and sat down. Sela stirred in the bedroom, but Jewel didn't budge and in a minute Sela comforted on her own. Crown looked at Jewel, and Jewel looked back. Her lips trembled. Crown rose suddenly and the chair fell back, hitting the floor with a thud. A startled Sela cried again. Jewel jumped up and ran to the bedroom. She came back shortly cooing softly with Sela cradled in her arms.

Crown had picked up the chair and stood trying to figure how he'd get past her without hearing her tell him goodbye. He took a step forward, but she stood in the doorway, blocking his path.

"Crown, I'm sorry 'bout Jackson. I ought not do you that way. I didn't mean to, Crown. I'm sorry that's all."

Crown took a step back. She was apologizing to him. For what? For being human? For liking a man that knew how to wile a woman? Even Crown knew Jackson was good at it. What chance did poor, dumb Jewel have?

Crown nodded. "Thanks for supper, Jewel. It was a good supper."

Jewel laughed. "That's a lie, Crown McGee, and you know it. But I did try. I did. If it's any comfort, Jackson's suppa wusn't much betta."

Crown grunted, and Jewel laughed again. "How come you so shy for words?"

"I ain't no Jackson."

Jewel blushed.

"Heard him offer to take you up near Marlin, see your folks."

"Yeh."

"You considering?"

"Don't know, Crown. I would like to see Mama and Pap, Carrie and the boys. You'd never take me, would you, Crown?"

Crown looked at his feet.

"I didn't think so."

"I got some more chores to do."

"I'll wait up for you, if you like."

Crown looked up again, surprised and answered with a slight nod. Jewel smiled, but she looked sad. It was a look that made Crown afraid.

CHAPTER 36

▼

One day turned into another, just like the one before. Crown and Jewel seemed content, as far as anyone might have told, if anyone had been there to see. They had picked up old habits and before they'd put Sela to bed they would read. Jewel knew most of the rhymes by heart, and she'd clap Sela's hands and recite them sing-song while Crown turned the pages. He didn't need to talk with Jewel chattering happily and Sela gurgling nonsense.

Other nights Jewel and Sela would listen to the radio while Crown read his almanac and farm journals. Jewel would stand on her knees and dance with Sela till Sela could barely hold her eyes open. Sela would fuss and fight because she couldn't stand to sleep and miss out on anything, but Jewel would settle her down, and before long Crown and Jewel would be alone again.

Jewel was back in his bed with Sela sleeping peacefully across the hall most nights. Even when Sela didn't sleep through the night, Jewel would come back to him, and he would have her again because he'd missed her for so long.

Jackson had been noticeably absent. For a month Crown was ill at ease, but then he started to relax and with harvest approaching, he often left Jewel at home so he could take care of the farm. He'd fired old Ben. Crown suspected Ben had lied about Jackson's whereabouts, but now Crown had no one to help with the cemetery and no way to know if Jackson were coming or going. Still he stayed away from town, sending Johnson's boy to fetch supplies when they needed them. He even started letting Jewel spend an occasional weekend at Granny Giddings, just so she could be more content with him and less lonesome for home.

Sela had a birthday and a mouth full of sharp little teeth and learned to walk though she still didn't say much except "Mama" and "no-no" and "mine". Jewel was starting to trust Crown with Sela, but he didn't know quite how to play with her so he simply let her play with him. She'd climb up his pants or sit at the table tugging on his beard or play with the buttons on his shirt or cuddle up in the crook of his arm and fall asleep while Jewel cleaned the kitchen. Crown wished he could play with her like Jewel, but he didn't know how, even though he spent most nights just watching them.

They had settled in one evening when they heard wheels turning in the drive. Jewel looked at Crown. Her eyes were big, and he could see her heart pounding over the bodice of her dress. He stood up slowly, his heart pounding too, but he was sure it was wagon wheels he'd heard, not a car.

The front door was open because it was still hot even though they were in the middle of October. Crown walked toward the door, peering through the screen until the man was in full view. Crown settled down a bit. It was just Danny Johnson. Crown had forgotten that he'd asked him to go to town, but then he usually didn't come by this late. Crown swung the door open and stepped out onto the moonlit porch.

"Why you come so late? Couldn't wait till morning?"

"Mr. Miles give me this here letter for you. Said it wouldn't keep."

Crown looked at the letter in Danny's outstretched hands, but he didn't reach for it.

"You seen my brother Jackson around?"

"Seen him when I give him a letter just like your'n. Said to tell the missus hello."

"That right?"

"Yep."

Danny thrust the letter toward Crown again. Crown took the letter, noted it was from Judge Bishop and stuffed it in the pocket of his overalls. He looked back for Jewel, but she was clanging pots feverishly in the kitchen. He wondered if she'd heard.

"Might as well unload while you're here, Danny." Crown called out to Jewel. She appeared in the doorway, her hands covered with suds, her face grim.

"Jewel, Danny's brought supplies. I'm go'n' help him unload. You put Sela down to bed."

She nodded and turned, but she looked as troubled as Crown felt. He considered that a minute with his fist in his pocket crumpled around the Judge's letter.

"Come on, boy. Those supplies ain't go'n' unload themselves."

Sela was asleep and Jewel was waiting in the kitchen when Crown returned with the box of groceries. He set the box on the table, and Jewel began to empty it, putting things away with a quiet efficiency Crown admired.

Jackson's sudden reappearance made Crown feel ill at ease. Crown left Jewel alone so he could lock up the house and read the judge's letter.

It wasn't a letter, but a summons to appear in court a week from Friday. Jebediah's will and the judge's decision were being contested. Crown had known it was coming even while he hoped it wasn't. His gut ached, cramped two times over with the fear he'd lose it all to the likes of Jackson. Cramped with hatred for Jebediah who undoubtedly was laughing in that dark place he now called home and for Jackson who dared waltz in to claim the one place Crown had carved out for his own. Crown paced in the study, certain he'd never last the nearly two weeks until he could face Jackson.

"Crown?"

Crown turned to see Jewel standing in the doorway. She was biting her nails, a gesture he'd only seen when she was very nervous.

"That 'bout, Jackson?"

She was pointing to the letter he had let fall to the floor. He nodded.

"Whut it say?"

"Says he wants what I got."

Jewel backed away. "Whut you mean?"

Crown looked at her. Her eyes were pensive, but otherwise blank. "Means he wants the land, the farm, the money, this place. What you think it means?"

His worry had turned to anger, and she backed away from him. "Don't know whut it means, Crown. Why you think I'm askin'?"

"You knew about this, Jewel?"

She shook her head and stepped back again. Crown reached her before she could bolt. He grabbed her arms and lifted her off the ground till her face met his.

"You knew about this, Jewel?"

Jewel shook and began to weep. "No, Crown. I swear. I thought Jackson wuz gone. I thought he wuz gone."

"That why you come to me, Jewel? You been trying to lull me to sleep so Jackson could take what's mine? You helping him, Jewel?"

"No, Crown. No. It ain't true. I ain't seen Jackson. I thought he wuz gone."

Crown released her. He looked at her, but he had lost the ability to tell between the truth and a lie. All he knew was he wasn't waiting two weeks to let Jackson have what he'd built.

"I'm going to town. You best be packed when I get back. And don't you even think about taking Sela. She's mine. You ain't go'n' lie with my brother and raise my child."

"Crown, I ain't been with Jackson."

"You saying you ain't wanted him? Can you tell me that, Jewel?"

"Crown, please."

"You get packed, Jewel. I'll be back before day tomorrow. You be packed and ready 'cause you ain't go'n' lie in my bed another day while you wanting my brother. While you plotting with him against me."

"You crazy, Crown. I ain't been with no Jackson."

"Yea, I'm crazy all right and dumber than you, thinking all this time it was me you wanted. Thinking Jackson was gone and we go'n' be happy for once. And all the while Jackson was taking what's mine with you helping him."

"That ain't true, Crown. That ain't true."

"Hush your lying, Jewel."

He crowded her and would have slapped her, as hard as he wanted to hit Jackson. So hard he'd see the imprint of his hand red and raw against her honey skin. So hard she'd lay there against the door and cower for fear he'd hit her again. Something stopped him and he stepped around her instead.

"You wanted to hit me," Jewel accused and Crown couldn't deny it. "I 've taken a lot off a you, Crown, but that's the one thing Mama said I wusn't to abide. I seen it in yo' eyes and I won't abide it."

"Ain't I already told you to go? But don't you even think about taking Sela. 'Cause I'll hunt you down, Jewel. I'll hunt you down and kill you if you take what's mine."

"Hrrumph," Jewel called after him. "I'd any sense, I'd go, but I guess I'm just as onery as you, Crown McGee. You might as well know, me and Sela ain't goin' nowhere. Hrrumph," she growled again. Her anger matching his, she wiped away the last of her tears, shouting after him as he slammed the door behind him.

CHAPTER 37

▼

Crown pulled into town too late to call on anyone, but he went to Cooper's anyway, rousing the dog, the neighbors and Nettie before Cooper stumbled groggily to the door. Cooper hesitated when he saw Crown, shotgun in hand. Crown let the gun drop to his side, since he hadn't sighted his intended target.

"What you want this time a night, Crown? Ain't you got no common sense?"

"I reckon I ain't got much sense at all when my brother can use my friend and my wife against me. You know where I can find Jackson?"

"What makes you think I know where Jackson is?"

Crown raised the gun like a hunter who had decided the doe would do just as good as the buck.

"I ain't playing with you, Cooper. You best give up Jackson unless maybe you want to join him."

"He's been staying with the widow Martin. You likely to find him there most nights when he's done drinking and whoring."

"Where's he do his drinking and whoring?"

"Over at Sadie's. Where else?"

"Thanks, Cooper. Ma'am."

Crown tipped his head toward Nettie and headed toward the widow Martin's; though, it was early yet for the likes of Jackson, and Crown didn't expect him to be there. The widow Martin was less likely though to go calling at Sadie's to warn Jackson, so Crown decided to try her house first. He gloated that he'd figured Jackson right. With the depression, Jackson's pickings had gotten slim. The widow Martin was sixty if she was a day. She had the third largest bank account in Colwin County though and that made her just shy of comfortable. She lived in a two story framed house at the edge of town with a picket fence and gazebo, none of which had seen paint in the fifteen years since her husband had died. She was childless and manless and just ripe to be picked by Jackson.

Crown approached the house carefully, but it was quiet. The lights were dim. The shades were drawn. He knocked politely, then knocked again harder. The widow herself came to the door. She looked Crown up and down over wire-rimmed glasses.

"You Jebediah McGee's other boy?"

"You seen Jackson?"

"Why would I know where Jackson McGee is?"

"Word is he's been keeping you warm at night."

The widow colored a gruesome red against her gray skin, all powdered and wrinkled under a dusty pink nightcap. She gasped and slammed the door firmly.

Crown sneered, satisfied Jackson wasn't with the widow. He headed toward Sadie's and Jackson.

At Sadie's the windows were dimly lit. The building, painted red and green, cast an orange glow in the moonlit night. As anxious as he was to get Jackson, Crown knew better than to walk in Sadie's armed. He set his gun beside the porch, and with no need to knock, he stepped inside. The parlor reeked of moonshine, stale cigarettes and sex.

There was a bouncer up front, a burley man with massive arms and sleepy eyes. Crown still had a scar on his brow from the only other time he'd been at Sadie's. While he looked and listened for signs of Jackson, Crown asked politely if Sadie were available. The man said she had a customer for the night and would Crown like one of the other girls. Crown nodded yes. The man signaled for Crown to wait then proceeded upstairs. Crown waited till the bouncer was out of sight. Then Crown walked through the parlor into a back room where he was sure he'd heard the sweet talking Jackson.

The room was dark and anything but quiet. Crown didn't wait for his eyes to adjust. He didn't wait to see Jackson making love to some woman so he could imagine how Jackson had done the same things to Jewel. He coughed. There was a rustling of sheets, a flurry of feet and cursing.

"Who's there?"

Crown stood motionless.

"I said who's there?"

"Crown."

"Shhiiitt! What you want, Crown?"

"I want to talk to you, Jackson. I'll be waiting outside."

Crown turned his back on Jackson. He should have known better. He should have known his brother was anything but honorable. He should have carried his gun in with him. He should have thought, but he didn't. Not until it was too late and the bullet was ripping through his back and out his chest. He raised his hands to stop the blood. He tried to turn back to Jackson and laugh and say he'd won after all, but he couldn't. He stumbled outside and fell forward slowly into a dark nothing.

Crown's eyes fluttered open. He was still in darkness, and he wondered if he were dead. He was prone, yet he seemed to be moving. His head unprotected bumped against wood. There was pressure on his chest. He looked up to see Cooper hovering over him. Cooper said something, and Crown nodded like he'd understood and then slipped back to sleep. It was dark and cold deep inside and empty like his life had been, and he didn't see much difference, and he didn't much care. He was wondering why he didn't feel any pain, just ice cold like he'd fallen in a river covered with ice and he couldn't get out even if he wanted, even if he tried.

But he didn't try. Crown just let that river of ice cover him up. He let his body slide down deep as he could go, but something kept holding him up so he couldn't quite reach bottom. Too tired to fight, Crown slept.

He woke to Jewel's blubbering and Lenetta's fussing at her to just be done with it and Sela screaming because her mother was, and he went back into that deep cold river because it was a lot more comfortable in there.

Crown slept off and on for eight days while Jewel washed his wound and changed his bandages and turned him so the sores wouldn't come. He'd wake to find her crying and praying like she wanted him to live instead of die. He couldn't understand so he kept trying to return to that river, but he kept rising higher and higher till he saw the sun and it was shining through his window and he couldn't close his eyes anymore.

Crown lay there trying to blink back that sunlight, but it wasn't going anywhere. Suddenly he was hot and too worn to throw off the covers. He tried to call Jewel, but his voice wouldn't work, and besides the house was quiet, and he thought maybe Jewel had finally listened to Lenetta and just been done with it.

He lay there for an hour getting accustomed to heat and light again and trying to feel his own body, his hands and feet and legs, his fingers and even his toes. He wiggled and bent what he could just so he could know it was there.

Then the back door slammed, and Jewel came in with a basket of laundry on one hip and Sela on the other. She walked into the room across the hall, dipped down and put Sela on the floor, piled the linen and clothes at the foot of the bed and started folding and talking like she didn't expect Crown to answer.

"You play nice now, Sela. Let Mama get these clothes done, and we'll go sing to your papa. You'd like that wouldn't you, Crown?"

Crown tried his voice again, but it wouldn't work, and all he could manage was a hoarse cackle that sounded like chickens disturbed from their roosts.

Jewel turned slowly. "Crown, you say somethin'?"

He tried again, nodding at her. Her eyes filled with tears when she saw him staring back at her. She stood for a minute just looking at him. Then she was at his side, stroking his arm and wiping his brow and stuffing the covers tight around him when he really wanted her to take them off.

"Ho … Hot."

She finally understood and pulled back the warm covers leaving only a light sheet against his parched skin. He looked at her for answers, but he couldn't see any that made sense. He was alive when he should have been dead. She was caring for him when he'd told her to go away. When he told her he'd kill her before he'd let her take Sela. When she was free to leave with Sela and Jackson. Why was she there?

Two days later, Crown was lying in bed propped on pillows and dawdling over a bowl of soup that had long ago grown cold. Sela was sleeping peacefully beside him, full of the soup Crown had no appetite for. Jewel was in the kitchen. She came out quickly, standing outside Crown's bedroom and looking at Crown as they both listened to the car sputter into the yard.

Crown watched Jewel. Only when she relaxed did he turn to the window to see Thomas Coleman coming across the yard, nursing his nose with a well-used handkerchief. The lawyer walked up the steps and across the porch until he disappeared under the doorway. He knocked politely even though Jewel was in the hallway staring at him on the other side of the screen door.

Jewel glanced at Crown for support. He nodded yes. She walked down the hallway and opened the door cautiously. Coleman nodded and asked for Crown. Jewel led him to the bedroom. She gathered Sela and left Crown and Coleman alone to talk.

"That was a dumb thing you did, Crown."

"You mean turning my back on Jackson."

Coleman smiled wanly. "They couldn't hold him, with half the town saying you went gunning for him. He said you'd called him out and it was dark and he fired blindly. I suspect that's a lie, but I can't prove it. And the sheriff did find your shotgun outside Sadie's, so Judge Bishop had to call it self defense and let Jackson go."

"Where's he now?"

"Could be anywhere. On his way here though I suspect. I asked the sheriff to give me some time so I could come out and warn you."

"I ain't afraid of Jackson."

"Well you should be. What can you do in your condition? What if he tries to hurt Jewel or Sela?"

"Why would he? It's me he wants."

"No, Crown, it's the land he wants, and they're as much in his way as you are. If you die, they inherit what's yours. That's the law."

Crown said nothing, but inside he was hollow, like his guts had been sucked down to his soles. He knew then that Coleman was right, that Jackson had no more fondness for Jewel and Sela than he had for Crown. He had just used Jewel to bait Crown, and Crown had fallen for it, leaving Jewel and Sela as alone and defenseless as if he were dead.

Crown leaned into the pillow, letting the sunlight bathe him in warmth, but it did nothing for the cold fear he felt.

"How long?"

"Don't know for sure, Crown. The sheriff promised to keep Jackson till I could get out of town. Even that's a stretch outside the law. But I did what I could. Can you move?"

"I will if I have to."

"I could take you and Jewel away if you want?"

"Where we go'n' go? This is our home. I don't intend to let Jackson just sidle in here and take it."

"What's that about Jackson?"

Crown and Coleman turned sheepishly toward the door. Jewel stood there frowning, one hip perched with Sela on it.

"What about Jackson, I say?"

"Nothing to worry you about, Jewel. This here's my lawyer, Mr. Coleman."

Though the look Jewel gave said she was anything but satisfied, Crown turned back to Coleman.

"You staying for supper?"

"Can't. I got a trial over in Silsbee tomorrow. I best head that way. By the way, Judge Bishop granted a postponement till you get better. At least you don't have that to worry about. You folks take care now."

Jewel stepped aside, allowing Coleman to pass. Outside, Coleman climbed into his car without looking back and drove off. From his bedroom window, Crown watched the road even after Coleman had gone.

"You s'pectin' company, Crown?"

Crown turned to face Jewel. She stood with one hand on the door, as if she couldn't quite decide whether to come or go. He saw only fear in her eyes. He wondered why he thought he'd seen something else before.

"Coleman said Jackson might be heading this way."

"You afraid, Crown?"

"I can't do much good if he comes, Jewel. I barely have the strength to raise my head off this pillow. I can't protect you or Sela."

"I heard whut that lawyer said. I reckon he's right. With you gone, me and Sela would just be in Jackson's way."

Jewel had that way of looking like a child, but now she looked all grown up, like a mother trying to figure how she was going to protect her child. Like a woman trying to figure how to save her man.

"I can handle the gun, Crown. If he's within a stone's throw of that barrel he's as good as dead."

"It won't be that easy, Jewel. He can't just come in here and gun us down like dogs. He'd never get away with that. It would have to be something else. Something folks could suspect but never prove. A fire maybe, or poison in the well, or kill us and bury us out there somewhere."

"Well I ain't aimin' to do his thinkin' for him, and I ain't aimin' to wait for him to figure the how and the when. If he comes, he's dead. I ain't go'n' let him hurt what's mine."

"Jewel, you stay away from Jackson. Maybe Coleman is wrong. Jackson was mighty pleasant with you. Maybe he won't hurt you."

"Crown if you fell for that sweet talkin' Jackson you dumber than I eva wuz. If you think I fell for him you're dumber than mud."

Jewel's eyes locked fierce and dark. Crown shuddered. He had seen that look before. He knew how cold and determined she could be. He had known since that night he'd almost buried Sela.

"Jewel, you stay away from Jackson, you hear. You hear me, Jewel?" He cried out to her, but she was gone, sweeping up that bowl of cold soup with exactness.

CHAPTER 38

▼

Jackson came in daylight. A day of worrying had passed with Crown plying Jewel to leave and Jewel assuring him she was going nowhere and neither was he. A night of wondering had dripped by. A morning shrouded in fog hung heavy, lifting slowly beneath a rising sun, and in the middle of it, they heard the telltale drone of the engine and the grind of wheels against the clay and gravel road.

Sela was napping. Jewel had just finished giving Crown a sponge bath, fresh bandages, clean linens and a change of clothes. She had tossed the water out the back door and emptied the bed pan and was returning the chamber pot to its place on the dresser when they heard Jackson's car. She sat down on the bed next to Crown, and he swore he felt her heart race through the palms she placed over his lips to shush him.

"I'm go'n' see to Jackson now," she said. "I want you to lie still and quiet no matter whut you hear, no matter whut you see."

Though both worried and suspicious, Crown said nothing. Resigned, he lay there and massaged the last bit of doubt, wondering if she was for him or against him.

Jackson pulled up in front of the house, blaring his horn as he vaulted out of the car without bothering to open the door. He took the steps in two giant strides bearing a grin and a bouquet of flowers and feigned regret for the near fatal injury to Crown. Jewel sidled up to Jackson, holding him at bay on the porch while assuring him Crown was too far gone to do anything but sleep.

She left to don the blue dress and the lilac perfume, brush her hair and make a pitcher of lemonade. When she returned, Jackson accepted her invitation to lunch, stretching languidly on the wicker settee on the front porch and sipping on the lemonade she'd offered.

Convinced Jewel had been lying all along, Crown seethed.

Jewel sashayed back and forth from the kitchen to the porch, topping the glass of lemonade and slapping Jackson's roving hands while Crown heated up nicely confined as he was to a sick bed as the sights and sounds of seduction drifted into his open window.

"Jewel, what's taking you so long? Forget about that lunch. I got something else in mind," Jackson urged impatiently.

With her hands behind her back and her hips swaying, Jewel stepped out on the porch teasing sweetly. "I s'pect I know whut you got in mind, Jackson, and it ain't meant for daylight. Anyway lunch is almost done."

"There ain't no certain time for what's hungering me."

Jackson stood up rolling the glass of lemonade between his hands. Despite the fall air, his shirt hung loose baring a toned, hairless chest. His pants rested just below his navel, where his abdomen pinched then swelled hinting at what lay below.

"You spike this lemonade, Jewel? You trying to lull me senseless?" Jackson grabbed her by the hair, tilted her head back, and put the glass to her lips. The lemonade dripped down her chin. Jackson put his mouth over her chin, drinking the wasted lemonade and Jewel.

"Jewel." Agony spilled from Crown's lips. "Jewel."

The glass dropped shattering and spraying lemonade and glass shards across the porch. Jackson looked down at Jewel lecherously, let one arm come to rest on her hip and the other in the small of her back and drew her into him. Bracing herself with her left arm on his chest, she arched and let the other arm drop, keeping it free from his prying hands. He laughed wickedly wetting her neck with his tongue. As the radio played inside, he started to grind against her.

They swept the porch in circles till they dropped dizzily side by side on the settee. With her right hand tucked behind her back, her left hand on Jackson's broad, bare chest, Jewel pushed, but Jackson didn't budge. He cupped her breasts in his hands and massaged them through the thin cotton. Jewel lay flat, her breath short and shallow.

Crown wondered how long before they'd be done and would come for him. He wondered how many times Jackson had held her just that way, explored her with his hands, moistened her with his tongue, plied her with his groin.

Jackson rolled on top of her, his hands slipping down to pull the dress above her waist, his knees prying her legs apart. She turned her head as his mouth sought hers.

With eyes glazed, Crown stared back at her through the bedroom window. Jackson raised up off of her just a minute, looked through that window at Crown and sneered. In that moment Jewel turned back to Jackson and raised her hand. Crown thought she meant to pull Jackson to her.

"Jewel." Crown cried out, his voice strained with heartache. Jackson laughed. He didn't see the glint of the blade as Jewel slashed the knife across his throat.

For a moment Jackson froze still sneering. Then his eyes rolled; his head jerked. His hands reached up to stanch the course flow of blood and close the gaping wound. Flopping like a fish out of water, he collapsed on top of Jewel. Blood splattered her face and soaked her dress. She screamed hysterically, punching him, flailing at him with the knife, kicking at him with her feet till finally he rolled off of her and onto the porch, still gurgling and clutching his throat. She kept screaming and flailing at the air and struggling to breathe like she didn't know Jackson was off of her.

"Jewel. Jewel."

Unable to move, unable to pierce through her hysteria, Crown called to her. After a while it grew quiet, and Crown couldn't hear Jackson or Jewel anymore. Minutes passed before Jewel rose off the couch. For a moment she stood shaking and looking down at Jackson. She prodded him three times with her foot before her shoulders relaxed.

"Jewel."

With empty eyes, she turned to Crown's voice and mouthed the words in slow motion. "Sleep now."

He wanted to lie awake, to hold her and stroke her, but the strain had made him tired. Crown drifted in and out of a disquiet sleep.

It was the sound of her scrubbing vigorously that wrenched him awake. Jackson's body was gone. The settee was gone too, leaving the porch bare and uninviting. The scents of ammonia and smoke drifted through the open window stinging Crown's nostrils. He called out to Jewel. She raised her head and swept the hair out of her face. "I'll be there in a minute."

She entered the bedroom with a bucket in one hand and a rag stained pink in the other. The dress clung to her in wrinkled clumps of brown. She reeked of blood.

"You hungry?"

"No. I just wanted to know if you were alright."

"Right as I can be. I got me a heap a mess to clean, though. I best git back to it." She paused a minute considering. "Can a car burn?"

"No," Crown answered staring at her and trying to make sense of her matter-of-fact mood. "You couldn't get a fire hot enough."

"Well, what am I go'n' do?" Jewel furrowed her brow as though she expected to answer the question herself.

Crown looked out at Jackson's car, sitting in the middle of the yard, pointed accusingly at the house and Jewel. If caught, Jewel could go to prison or worse get the chair. Fighting panic, Crown tried to reason.

Unsure just how far he could push her, Crown eyed Jewel. Staring out the window, she looked fiercely determined. Crown hoped she was as strong as she appeared. "Didn't Jackson teach you to drive," Crown asked, trying to sound more confident than he felt.

"A mite. I can start and stop and turn."

"I reckon that's all you'll need. Can you swim?"

"Better than most."

He hated to ask her, but he couldn't think of any other way. "You think you can drive to the river? You'll have to do it tonight, so no one will see you."

"All alone? In the dark?"

"Take the lantern with you. You'll be alright." Crown hoped he sounded more sure than he felt. "You got to go to the deep part, Jewel. Drive it in and swim back to shore. You think you can do that?"

"I reckon if I can git there, I can do the rest." She looked resigned. "Den Jackson won't be no bother, no more."

They were blessed that night with a full moon. Still Crown worried if Jewel would be able to find her way. He worried that she'd be able to keep to the road, that the car wouldn't stall in the shallow banks or trap her in the murky depths of the river. He worried that she couldn't make the fifteen mile trip there and back before day. He would have prayed, but he couldn't imagine God would listen considering the things Crown had done and forced Jewel to do.

He awoke in the night to the sound of the screen door creaking on its hinges, and hoped he had been dreaming.

"Jewel?"

"It's me."

She stood in the doorway shivering and dripping mud. She looked as tired as she sounded. "It's done."

"Where's Jackson?"

"He ain't go'n' bother us no more." Jewel answered, tired and small.

"Where is he, Jewel? Where did you put him?"

"I reckon you know already, don't you, Crown? I put him where he ain't go'n' worry us no more. I put him where he belongs. I ain't go'n' let nobody hurt what's mine."

"I'm go'n' clean myself up and go to bed now. You best git some sleep."

"Jewel, you gonna be all right."

"You askin' me or tellin' me, 'cause I don't rightly know. All I know is me and you and Sela is safe now. We ain't got to worry 'bout no Jackson. I'm too tired to talk about it now. Just know it's taken care of and we ain't got to worry no more."

"I'm sorry, Jewel."

Jewel stepped into the kitchen. Crown's words drowned in the innocence and sorrow Jewel left behind. When she came back, she was stripped naked. Water glistened in pearl-like drops on her honey skin. In the bedroom across the hall, she slid into her gown and scooped up a sleeping Sela. Sela protested and wriggled against Jewel's bosom. Jewel bounced Sela on her hip, cooing and clinging to the one pure and untouched thing. Jewel returned to Crown's bedside looking down at him with dead eyes. She tucked the covers around him.

"G'night, Crown." Cradling Sela, Jewel swept out of the room, leaving Crown alone. He listened to the sounds of Jewel rustling. He listened to her muttering and mumbling about the deed she'd done. He listened to her cooing Sela back to sleep while the unspeakable hung thick and heavy in the house. He listened and knew it was gone. That childlike innocence that made him want her all the more was buried with Jackson and the unspoken thing she'd done to get him there.

CHAPTER 39

▼

The moon gave way to sunrise, and Crown peered out into the fog-shrouded yard. He turned as Jewel opened her bedroom door and stepped out into the hall. The white gown was a bit too snug, pinching at her curves and the soft folds around her belly. Crown wished he could turn back the clock and see her sweet and pure again.

She caught Crown looking at her and turned away. He wanted to call her back to him. To hold her and tell her it would be all right. But he wasn't sure it ever would be. After a while he smelled coffee and oats. She came in and helped him sit up, rolled him so he could use the bedpan then left to empty his waste. When she returned, she brought his breakfast on a tray and sat down to feed him. He didn't feel like eating, but he felt she needed him to so he did. He reached out and held her hand and she let him. It felt good just being close to her, and he wished he could do more because her eyes were sad and her lips were trembling, but she wouldn't or couldn't cry. When the oats were gone, she wiped his chin and blew the hot coffee and pressed it to his lips. He sipped it, and she let the cup down absently.

Crown was tired, and though he wanted to lie awake and see her face, he drifted back to sleep instead. He didn't know how long he had lain there, drifting in and out of sleep. When he saw her again she was wearing his old shirt and a pair of his overalls. Her hair was wet and pulled behind her head. A few limp tendrils framed her face, dripping water down the front of her bib.

Crown wanted to comfort Jewel, but he didn't really know how and the thing was gnawing at him again, looking at her sad and forlorn draped in the baggy overalls with her hair in braids. He kept seeing her smiling and teasing with Jackson and wondering if she didn't enjoy it. If some part of her had wanted Jackson more than she'd ever wanted Crown. Crown knew better than to ask her, but he couldn't help himself.

"You lay with him, Jewel?"

It wasn't what he meant to say, wasn't exactly what he wanted to know, and he wanted to take it back as soon as he'd said it, but he couldn't.

"Ain't it enough that I'm here with you? That you're here and he ain't. Ain't that enough?"

Crown hung his head. What could he say? It should have been enough. He shouldn't have needed to ask, but then why did he feel so low and worthless. Like there had to be something else to it, that she couldn't really want him because nobody ever had before.

Jewel stood up taking the tray and turning her back to him. "There was a time, Crown, when I thought we had a real chance. I thought we had a chance, but I was wrong, wasn't I?"

She was asking him, still reaching for something he didn't yet know how to give much as he wanted the same from her.

He answered her with silence.

CHAPTER 40

▼

Jewel fussed over Crown night and day even while something in her had died, even while there was little hope for the two of them. Crown longed to have the days back to undo what he'd done, the day he'd almost killed sweet Sela, the day he'd called Jewel dumb to her face, the day he'd accused her of lying with Jackson, the day he'd made it so she had to do what she did. He wondered how she could care for him after all he'd done, but care for him she did, till he could sit for a spell under the shade of the porch, till he could take short, quiet walks with Sela, till he was strong enough to make it on his own and he knew he'd have to release her.

Crown took one last walk with Sela, surveying all that had been Jebediah's, all that was now his. The day he'd come to Colwin County nothing had been more important. Now even he was pressed to remember the unmarked soil where he'd laid Jebediah's bones. Now even he found little satisfaction in the land or the farm or Jebediah's wealth without Sela and Jewel. He cried out, and Sela stirred where she lay with her head nestled between his neck and shoulder. Her breath was sweet and warm, filling him with regret. But he couldn't hold them any longer, not with Jewel so sad and the house still heavy with the deeds they'd done.

Crown had not spoken to Jewel much or she him since that day. Their words had been sparse and necessary. Only their touches, brief, tremulous, had hinted how they felt. Now he had to find the words to let her go. He walked slowly back to the house, laid Sela down to finish her nap and sought Jewel where she busied herself dusting and inspecting the bound books in his study. He regarded her for a moment as she inspected a book, fingering the spine with longing. She sighed deeply and turned to find him staring back at her.

"I'm 'bout done here if you need to work, Crown."

Crown swallowed but a lump pressed his throat. He stumbled over the words so they didn't even seem like his.

"I ... That's not why. I mean to say ..." He paused and breathed deep for courage. "If you want to go home, I'll take you."

"Home?"

"To see Mae and Carrie, your pap and the boys."

"Oh."

She turned back to her dusting, putting the book that had dangled in her hands back on the shelf and without turning back or stopping the sweeping motion of the rag, she asked, "You want me to?"

He sensed she needed his approval so he answered, "Yes."

She sighed again, low and long. Her head hung slightly on her chest. Her back heaved as she took a deep breath.

"When?"

"A week from Monday. We'll ride the train. You'll like that."

She didn't answer, just picked up the rag and started dusting feverishly. Crown walked up behind her and took the rag from her hand.

"You don't need to do that anymore."

"I want to. I'll give everythin' a good cleanin' so you won't have to worry for a while."

The finality of her offer hit them both hard. He released her hand, and she continued dusting, rubbing the oak finish on the one shelf long after the dust was gone.

Crown retreated to his room, shut the door and lay on the bed Jewel had been absent from far too long. He pressed his face to the pillow and sobbed.

CHAPTER 41

▼

A week came and went too slow, too fast. On Sunday Lenetta came to pick up Jewel and Sela for church, but Jewel declined saying she was headed to Marlin to visit the folks and she had packing and cleaning to do. Crown knew Jewel had packed the very night he told her she could go and the house couldn't get any cleaner.

Evening came. Crown filled the wagon with Jewel's and Sela's things. He tried to give Jewel the radio, but she wouldn't take it. He didn't know what he would do with it blaring her back at him all the time.

She offered to come to his bed, but he said no. There were better ways to say their goodbyes, ways that wouldn't have him longing for her after she was gone.

Monday morning came. Jewel looked like she'd sat up half the night. She made breakfast, eggs, toast and bacon burned black. Teary-eyed, she apologized, but Crown ate without comment, chasing the meal down with a bitter cup of her coffee.

Afterwards, they headed down Cemetery Road toward town with nary a word between them, just Sela's soft cooing and Jewel's gentle nagging for her to sit still. They came to town, and Jewel went around to say her goodbyes. Crown bought the tickets then hurried to join Jewel and Sela at the siding. Jewel rocked Sela on her knee in a futile attempt to amuse her. Spying Crown, a disconcerted Sela reached for him. He hefted her clumsily, lifting her to his shoulders where she straddled his neck and rested a fat jaw on his head. Jewel looked away, shading her eyes to peer into the distance. Crown had prodded Jewel until she allowed him one last indulgence. The parcel of gifts leaned protectively between her suitcase and Crown's small duffel, just large enough for a change of clothes.

Crown tensed as the rails rumbled and the earth shook beneath his feet. Jewel rose, and Crown balanced Sela with one hand as he stretched out another to help Jewel to her feet. Then he handed Sela to Jewel and reached down for the bags as the train came into view. The flag was up and the conductor leaned out and waved at them. He blew his horn again and again as he pulled to a halt. Crown steadied Jewel then ushered her to the last passenger car where they boarded. The car was nearly empty and they had their pick of seats. Crown chose a private corner giving Jewel the seat nearest the window so she'd have something to remember, something to keep her entertained.

The wooden bench was hard and uncomfortable, but neither of them complained. Sela was soon rocked to sleep by the motion of the train and the passing landscape. Soon Jewel and Crown were nodding too.

It was dark when they reached Marlin. Crown had wired ahead that they were coming. He hoped that Sam and Mae had gotten the wire. That he could deposit Jewel and Sela to their care and catch the next train back to Colwin County. He didn't relish saying goodbye and the quicker the parting, the better.

Jewel's head had fallen to his shoulder. By now they had grown accustomed to the wail of the whistle and the rumble of the tracks and neither Jewel nor Sela stirred. Crown shook Jewel gently. Unconsciously she wiped the drool from her cheek. Crown shook her again, and she looked up at him doe-eyed.

"We're here, Jewel."

She nodded and tried to gather her senses. He gave her a moment then helped her to her feet.

They stepped off the train into a black, moonless night. The station was closed, the town buttoned down for the night. Crown stood wondering silently what he should do. Jewel edged as close to him as she could, and he draped his arm around her shoulder protectively. The train sped away leaving them alone in the night in a town asleep with not a soul in sight.

Crown drew Jewel close and walked her over to a bench outside the station. He eased her down and walked to the edge of the railing peering left, then right, but the night was silent. The air was chill and he took off his coat and laid it over her, then laid down his duffel for a pillow.

"You lie down and rest Jewel. If they haven't come for you by morning, then, we'll go to them."

Jewel lay down as he asked, cradling Sela in her arms. Crown sat down on the platform, bracing his back against the bench to keep Sela from falling should she wake while they slept. Soon Jewel was snoring softly, and Crown's head grew heavy and fell to his chest.

CHAPTER 42

▼

Crown sensed Carrie even before he heard her. He lifted his head as she drew near. She came alone, leading a mule behind her. He had not expected her though he realized he should have, for she had always been responsible when Sam and Mae could not.

Crown rose stiffly, remembering his fondness for Carrie with guilt. He bent over Jewel possessively, then backed away as Carrie approached. Carrie knelt down and nudged Jewel without so much as a nod to Crown.

Crown watched the surprise in Jewel's eyes, watched the sisters hug hungrily, squeezing Sela between them until she awakened and cried out in distress. They laughed then, and Carrie held Sela in her arms and carried on and on as though she couldn't see that Sela bore Crown's mark.

"Jewel, I never thought I'd see you again. I missed you so."

"We missed you too, Carrie. We did, didn't we, Crown?"

Crown shuffled uncomfortably as Jewel reminded him again how he'd been smitten with Carrie.

"Where's Mama? Where's Pap?"

"They're home, waitin' for you. They sent me to fetch you. Mama's down with the rheumatiz so she doesn't stray far from home, and well, you know Pap. The boys took the grain up to Waco. They'll be back in a day or two."

She paused then and looked at Jewel with admiration. "I can't believe you're all grown up and with a youngun of your own. From the looks of her, you've made a fine mama."

Jewel beamed. "You married, Carrie?"

Carrie looked down at her feet, then back up at Jewel. "Charlie, he went up around Dallas way to look for work about three months ago. He sends us money when he can. Pap said I ought to git a divorce, but I reckon as long as he's sendin' money he's aimin' to come back."

Carrie turned then and raised an eyebrow to Crown. "How's this one treatin' you?"

Crown averted his eyes, while Jewel seemed lost for words.

"Never mind, you can tell me when he's not breathin' every word we say."

Carrie reached for Jewel's suitcase, but Crown beat her to it. He tied the bags down on the mule's sagging back and grabbed the lead rope as Carrie and Jewel tried to catch up on the fringes of each other's lives.

They followed the rails about three miles out of town, then turned down a narrow dusty road that led to the farm. The fields were bare. Carrie called out as they approached, and the house emptied. The women and children piled out of the ramshackle house they all called home. Sam and Mae's brood had grown by two daughters-in-law and four crying infants. Crown surveyed the farm near busting with so many mouths to feed, but they seemed happy. Crown understood their contentment with so little, while he had yet to find happiness with much. The Giddings had the one thing Crown had sought with Carrie, had touched with Jewel and lost.

A little snot-nosed boy crawled to Carrie and clambered at her ankles. She bent down and hefted him to her hip. Wiping his nose with the hem of her dress, she smiled.

"This here's my boy, John. Say hello, to your Aunt Jewel."

Jewel leaned close and introduced herself, as John clung to Carrie. Carrie pressed John's small hand to Jewel's face. Jewel smiled and the boy smiled back shyly.

"And this is your cousin, Sela"

"What's wrong with her mouth?" a wiry boy about six interrupted, pointing a crusty finger at Sela.

"Ain't nothin' wrong with it. It is what it is, just like her pa's." Jewel explained kindly. "This here is my husband, Crown."

Crown stepped back as the other children surveyed him suspiciously. The children seemed satisfied enough and suddenly bored with their company, traipsed back to resume their play. Carrie turned to Crown, pointed at the boy who'd asked about Sela and whispered.

"That's your namesake you know. Only we call him June Bug on account of Pap."

Carrie caught one of them short, a tall thin boy who looked a lot like Troy. "David Lee you set Molly out to pasture and bring in Jewel's things."

"Ah, Carrie."

"Don't you ah me, David Lee. You hush up and do as I say now."

Crown handed over the mule and stuffed his hands in his pockets. David Lee shuffled off kicking the dirt and rubbing his ear where Carrie had cuffed him.

Sam Giddings eyed them from the doorway. Even from that distance, Crown could tell that Sam had been drinking. Crown hesitated, but Jewel turned to him again.

"Come on, Crown."

Crown shuffled behind them till he was face to face with Sam. Jewel hugged Sam, but he didn't hug her back, just stood there using her for support while he glared at Crown. Crown grunted and nodded, noting not much had changed, Carrie was feisty as ever, and Sam was still drunk.

Crown followed Carrie and Jewel inside, softening a little when he saw Mae. She was sitting up in bed with a pillow propped under swollen knees.

Mae tried to smile through the pain of her rheumatism. Determined, she stretched out two crooked hands, one for Jewel and one for Crown.

"Come here you two. I never thought I'd see this day. My Jewel all growed up, married to Crown and mother to a sweet baby girl of her own."

Mae greeted Crown affectionately as she would a son, catching Crown off-guard. He looked down at his feet, while Mae squeezed his hand and offered comfort with her words.

"Lawdy, you two look fine. Don't they look fine, Sam?"

But Sam had stumbled outside with a look toward Crown that said he still couldn't abide Crown in his house.

"Don't you worry, Crown. He'll come 'round."

Crown knew Sam wouldn't, but then that had never mattered in Mae's house. The memories flowed back warm and welcomed, the way Mae and Carrie had always made him feel. Crown stole a look at Carrie, then swallowed when he turned back to see Jewel watching him. Jewel turned away but not before he saw the pain and acceptance in her eyes. Jewel placed Sela in Mae's arms so they could get acquainted.

"Crown ain't stayin', Mama. He'll be headin' back tomorrie."

"That right, Crown? Well we'll see 'bout that, won't we, Miss Sela. We'll just see 'bout that."

Crown looked at the back of Jewel's head, willing her to turn around when she wouldn't. He slipped his hand from Mae's, turned quickly and walked outside. Sam was lazing on the porch nursing a bottle of corn liquor. He frowned up at Crown.

"So you brung her back, hey. Well don't think you're go'n' git her all fat and pregnant and bring her back here. You wanted what was mine and now you got it."

"Sam!"

"You hush up in there, Mae. He go'n' take care of Jewel and that there abomination of his one way or 'nother."

Without thinking, Crown grabbed Sam by the bib of his overalls. Crown raised Sam till he was breathing Sam's putrid breath, balled his hand to a fist, and punched Sam square in his obscene mouth. He let Sam go then, and Sam crumpled, his head reeling, his nose welled with blood.

Carrie ran out then leaning protectively over Sam, while Mae apologized to Jewel.

"He don't mean that, Jewel. You know he don't mean that. He just full of that liquor, and you know how he gits when he's full."

"I know, Mama," Jewel answered acquiescing.

"When ya'll go'n' stop making excuses for Sam. He ain't no damn good and ya'll know it. He ain't done none of ya'll no damn good."

"You hush up, Crown." Carrie stood up while Sam braced against her legs, bled into her skirt. "You best stay in town tonight. There's a roomin' house for Colored folks. You can spend the night there. I'll bring Jewel over first thing to say her goodbyes. Go on now, Crown 'fore Pap gits his senses and comes after you."

"I won't be here come morning. Jewel …"

It came out sounding like goodbye when Crown really wanted to ask Jewel to come back with him. But he couldn't find the words. He didn't have the courage to admit he still needed her and wanted her. So he turned his back instead on Jewel and Sela and the only chance he had for the one thing he'd wanted all his miserable life, a family, his family.

CHAPTER 43

▼

Crown walked through the barren fields, down that dusty road and along the rails without looking back. He headed for the siding and that bench where he'd spent the night with Sela and Jewel.

It was early yet and the depot was just coming to life. There were few passengers though, mostly porters moving freight and bosses barking orders. The clerk told Crown there was a passenger train headed for Beaumont about five that evening. The look on Crown's face must have said he preferred not to wait, because the clerk offered that there was a freighter headed that way in an hour or so. Though the freighter didn't normally take passengers, for ten dollars, the clerk would flag the freighter and they'd slow just enough to let Crown hop on. Crown paced up and down the rails till he heard the freighter coming in. The clerk nodded at Crown then signaled the freighter.

Sure enough the freighter slowed, and Crown hopped aboard, standing on the platform between cars looking in the direction of the Giddings' farm for some sense of Jewel. He couldn't feel her, only a void where she should have been so he settled into an empty car and tried to sleep.

When Crown reached Beaumont, he hitched a ride to Boone. He walked the rest of the way to town, picked up his wagon at Cooper's and headed home. He took his time, stopping at his own farm to see the grain piled high as both threshers hummed. Crown should have been happy for he'd raised a good crop and the prices were fair again and the machines would likely last the season. He tried to think of the business, but Jewel kept seeping into his thoughts, and though he dreaded going home without her, he finally did.

The house was dark and cold and damp, so Crown lit a fire. He turned on the radio to Jewel's favorite station, letting the bawdy music keep him company. He fixed a light supper and wanting for something to do went to his study to read. Soon the lifeless words coaxed his eyes to rest, and he fell asleep with his arms dangling over his chair.

"Jewel?"

Crown shook his head, trying to waken because it didn't make sense that she was there with him.

"What you doing here? Where's Sela?"

"I put her down. She's plum tuckered. Come on to bed, Crown."

Jewel offered him her hand. He stood and followed her, not even minding when the book thudded to the floor.

Crown woke startled, but it was only a dream he couldn't return to, now that he couldn't sleep. He could only sit in that chair hoping the dull words of the almanac would lull him senseless again.

He was there when morning broke through the window, bathing his face in sunlight. He turned his neck stiffly. Unaccustomed to the quiet, he listened for Jewel banging in the kitchen or Sela's soft cry, but there was no one but him in the house.

He wasn't hungry so he made a pot of coffee then headed for the farm. The machines were still humming. The hands toiled mindless that they would soon work themselves out of a job. Crown had nothing but good help and no trouble that couldn't get fixed on its own. So by noon he found himself back at the house, doing odds and ends to keep busy, anything so he wouldn't think of Jewel. The trouble was it wasn't working and as soon as the sun lay down, he lay down with it, crawling in the bed with only his loneliness to keep him warm. He cried softly, hugging the place Jewel should have been, until his eyes swelled shut and he slept fitfully.

Sometime in the night, a wagon rattled into the yard. The front door opened and shut. The sounds called Crown to wake, but he resisted. Then something touched his cheek, and he flinched. The bed sank, and he felt the heaviness of her, too real for the dream, too good to be real.

"Crown, Crown, you wake?"

"Jewel?"

He let his eyes open, and she was still there looking back at him misty-eyed and content.

"Jewel."

Crown sat up straight and looked at Jewel looking at him. He touched her face so soft and warm. Beneath the glow of the moonlight, her eyes danced with specks of gold. He stroked her hair soft as cotton, with a thin coat of oil that made it shine. He breathed in the scent of her, all lilacs and babies.

"Why'd you come back, Jewel? I thought that was what you wanted, to go home."

"Ain't this my home?"

He nodded and reached for her. She leaned into him, fitting into his curves like they'd been made just for her.

"I got to cryin' somethin' awful when you left. Mama said it's 'cause I don't belong to her and Pap no more. Said I'm Crown's Jewel now." Jewel laughed.

"Then Carrie, well she got to cryin' for Charlie, and Mama packed her off to Dallas and told her to go git her man. Said she and Pap had the boys and their wives and younguns, and they didn't need us moping around after our men. So I caught the first train home I could."

She took a breath and looked Crown dead on. "Don't you want me and Sela?"

"I want you, Jewel. I—"

"Don't say no more, Crown. You don't need to say no more."

She sat up in the bed, pulled her knees under her chin and giggled like she had been holding some secret and was glad to finally get it out.

"I got somethin' to tell you, Crown. We got another one on the way. I think this'ns a boy. Feels all heavy inside, not like Sela at all."

Jewel rested Crown's hand on her belly. He tensed and tried to pull away but Jewel wouldn't let him.

"Don't be afraid, Crown. It's go'n' be all right this time. If he looks like you or thinks like me, it's go'n' be all right long as we stick together. We got to stick together. You promise me."

Jewel was lying down and drawing Crown down with her, and he'd never wanted her more. "You promise me 'cause I want a passel of kids just like Mama, and I want you to give 'em to me."

Crown lay down beside her, exploring her with his hands in a way he hadn't before. Jewel's breasts were full and swollen and tender to touch. She winced so he touched them more gently, then went down to her rounded belly and below as she opened up for him. He looked at her lying in the moonlight and kissed her. She kissed him back that way she had of sucking his breath and he moaned pulling her to him till he couldn't get any closer.

"I promise, Jewel."

978-0-595-48335-8
0-595-48335-6

CPSIA information can be obtained
at www.ICGtesting.com
Printed in the USA
FSOW01n1446090715
8685FS

9 780595 483358